THE LITTLE SHOP OF MURDERS

DIANE KELLY   MILLIE RAVENSWORTH
VICTORIA TAIT   NIKKI KNIGHT   ERYN SCOTT
LISE MCCLENDON   CARLENE O'CONNOR
LONDON LOVETT   J NEW   FLORA MCGOWAN
GERALDINE MOORKENS BYRNE   KATHRYN MYKEL
ACF BOOKENS   DEBBIE YOUNG   RACHEL MCLEAN

'Don't Toy with Me' is copyrighted (c) 2023 by Diane Kelly

'A Man with no Imagination' is copyrighted (c) 2023 by Heide Goody and Iain Grant

'The Forget-Me-Not Antiques Mystery' is copyrighted (c) 2023 by Victoria Tait

'It was our Song' is copyrighted (c) 2023 by Kathleen Marple Kalb

'Always and Furever' is copyrighted (c) 2022 by Eryn Scott

'Wild Irish Dreams' is copyrighted (c) 2012 by Lise McClendon

'Architect of a Murder' is copyrighted (c) 2023 by Carlene O'Connor

'Blooms and Blackmail' is copyrighted (c) 2022 by London Lovett

'Second-Hand Murder' is copyrighted (c) 2022 by J. New

'The Lady of the House' is copyrighted (c) 2023 by Flora McGowan

'Requiem for a Violin' is copyrighted (c) 2023 by Geraldine Moorkens Byrne

'Nightly Nuisance' is copyrighted (c) 2022 by Kathryn Mykel

'The Gift of Dragons' is copyrighted (c) 2022 by Andrea Cumbo

'Nowhere to Hide' is copyrighted (c) 2023 by Debbie Young

'Murder in the Bookshop' is copyrighted (c) 2023 by Rachel McLean

No part of this book may be reproduced in any form or by any electronic or mechanical means, including information storage and retrieval systems, without written permission from the authors, except for the use of brief quotations in a book review.

1

DON'T TOY WITH ME

DIANE KELLY

Resumes in hand, I exited the charming wood-frame rental house. My lungs filled with fresh autumn air and my eyes took in the beautiful oranges, golds, and reds of the foliage. In no time, I reached the old-fashioned Main Street. The North Carolina town boasted only 3,000 residents, but untold numbers of tourists ventured up to the town on weekends or holidays. Until recently, I'd been one of those venturers. But when the gift shop I'd managed in Charlotte closed, I'd decided to move to the mountains to regroup.

The scent of blueberry scones and fresh-brewed coffee lured me to my first stop, Peak Perk. After ordering at the counter, I inquired whether they might be hiring.

"Sorry." The woman handed me a scone and a mug of coffee. "We're fully staffed. But I saw a 'help wanted' sign at the toy shop."

I thanked her, took a seat, and quickly polished off my

breakfast. Caffeinated now, I headed down the block, ready to land that job. I passed a bustling diner and an art gallery filled with paintings of wildlife. At the corner, I glanced across the street to see a real estate office. A sign at the curb read Reserved Parking For Dale Dickson. A shiny Mercedes sedan sat in the spot. My gaze moved to the next block. *There it is.*

I crossed the street and made my way to the shop. The sign over the window featured the shop's name, Timeless Toys, as well as its logo, the face of a clock with no hands. Judging from the classic playthings in the window, Timeless Toys was the perfect moniker. There were rag dolls and teddy bears, wooden train sets and stick horses, along with basic wood blocks painted with alphabet letters. I saw kid-sized musical instruments, too, including xylophones, drums, and easy-to-master wooden recorders. The sign on the door was turned to Closed, but movement inside caught my eye. Someone was working in the storeroom at the back. I rapped on the glass.

A moment later, a man in his thirties appeared, his broad shoulders filling the doorway. He had hair the color of maple syrup and sported a nicely trimmed beard. He wore a red and black buffalo plaid flannel shirt, blue jeans, and black boots, like a modern, sexy Santa. *Ho, ho, ho and hubba hubba!*

I pointed to the Help Wanted sign. "I'm here about the job!"

He opened the door and held out his hand. "I'm Nick Klaus."

He's got to be kidding, right? His name sounded like Saint Nicholas and he worked in toys. If he hired me, would that make me an elf? I shook his hand then gestured around. "You made these toys?"

"Not the dolls or stuffed animals or board games," he said. "I order those wholesale. But I make the wooden train sets, the blocks, the toy chests, and the dollhouses." He hiked a thumb over his shoulder to indicate the rear room from which he'd emerged. "My workshop's back there." He told me he'd worked as a carpenter for years, building toys on the side for extra income. "I realized my heart was in toymaking, not cabinetry. I like the creative aspects. Making toys is easier on my back, too."

I stepped over to admire a dollhouse. The attention to detail was amazing, each shingle perfectly placed. "You're very talented."

"Thanks. And you are …?"

"I'm talented, too. Just with business, not crafts."

"No. I mean, *your name*?"

Sheesh! I'd forgotten to introduce myself. "Ciara Doubrava. I have fifteen years retail experience. I managed a gift shop in Charlotte until it went out of business."

He cringed. "That fact doesn't recommend you."

"We didn't go down without a fight. The shopping malls of yesteryear simply don't get the foot traffic they used to." I circled a finger in the air. "But quaint tourist towns like this? You've got lots of profit potential."

He pulled two stools from behind the counter. He took a seat on one and held out a hand, inviting me to take the other. "Tell me some of your ideas."

I perched on the stool. "You should throw a grand-opening party for locals and offer a discount to everyone who comes. Put a decorative snowman out front. It'll grab people's attention. You could use the alphabet blocks to spell out jokes in the window."

He cocked his head. "Such as?"

"Such as— What do you call a train with a mouthful of bubble gum? A *chew-chew* train."

"That's a horrible joke."

"I've got a worse one. Did you hear about the horror movie in which a man smashes toys? It's a real *block buster*."

He groaned, but afterward we shared a laugh.

I acquiesced. "Maybe the blocks could just spell 'Come in and play.' You could have one train set and dollhouse that you allow children to play with. Their parents will see how much fun they're having and buy them their own toys." I offered other suggestions, such as customizing toy chests with a child's name for an extra fee and offering gift wrap for a small additional charge. "You should hire me now, before someone else snaps me up."

"I'll need to check your references first."

I handed him a copy of my resume, pointing to the reference at the bottom.

He pulled out his cell phone and dialed my former boss. After identifying himself, he asked, "Would you recommend I hire her?" He listened for a bit, then he thanked her and returned the phone to his pocket. "Sorry. She says you were a lousy employee. Rude. Always late. Lazy."

"What?!"

A grin played about his lips. "Just kidding. She sang your praises. Problem is, I can't pay you what you're worth. I'd only planned to hire a salesclerk, not an assistant manager."

"What wage are you offering?"

When he told me, I scoffed. "You're right. I'm worth much more. Tell you what. Pay me a five-percent commission on top of the hourly rate. That way, you only have to pay me if the shop profits, and you know I'll work hard because I'll have skin in the game."

"It's a deal. When can you start?"

I slid out of my coat. "How about now?"

Nick led me to the storeroom. There was a door and windows along the rear wall that looked out onto an alley and provided natural light. Shelves along the front wall held inventory of small manufactured items, such as slide whistles, kazoos, and kaleidoscopes. Farther back, three long tables stood in a row. Each held toys in various stages of production. Freshly sanded blocks awaiting paint. Framed dollhouses in need of walls and roofs. Wooden trains waiting for wheels. In the front corner of the storeroom was an office. It was windowless, yet brightly lit with an overhead fixture, as well as a floor lamp featuring a colorful tiffany shade. He gestured to the safe that stood in the corner.

"You can store your purse in the safe. The code is nineteen forty-three, the year the Slinky was invented."

After stashing my purse, I gestured to the outlet on the wall perpendicular to the safe. "May I plug in my cell phone?" I'd thought it was charging overnight, but I'd found it unplugged on the rug this morning. My cats must have knocked it off the bedside table while I slept. *Furry troublemakers.*

"Be my guest."

I inserted the plug into the outlet and stuck the

connecting end into my phone, but I heard no *ping* to indicate the device was receiving electricity. "Is something wrong with the outlet?"

"The bottom one works or the lamp wouldn't light up." He bent down and unplugged my charger, then moved the lamp's plug to the top socket. The lamp didn't light up now. "Looks like the top outlet is broken." He moved the desk over a few inches so I could access another outlet in the wall beside it.

I tried again and my phone lit up, receiving juice. "Should my first task be to submit a repair request to your landlord?"

"No need for a repair," Nick said. "There's enough other outlets. But it's a good idea to let the landlord know. Send an e-mail so there's a written record." He opened the desk drawer, retrieved a business card, and handed it to me.

The card read CHARLES "CHIP" DICKSON, MAINTENANCE & REPAIRS – DICKSON BROTHERS PROPERTIES, LTD. Below were the man's phone number and e-mail address. I plopped down in the desk chair and sent a message that noted our discovery. *No need to fix the outlet,* I wrote. *Just wanted to make you aware of it.*

Nick showed me how to ring up purchases and run a daily total on the register. The rest of my first day was spent helping customers, rearranging the toys to better use the display space, and setting up a designated play area near the window. I also made plans for a grand-opening celebration. It was a great first day on the job and, even though none of the toys used batteries or electrical plugs, I sensed electricity flowing between my new boss and me.

Over the next couple of weeks I settled into my role. The grand opening party was a huge success. I assisted in production and became proficient in painting wood blocks and dollhouses, and attaching wheels and connectors to train cars.

When I arrived for work on the final day of October, I came across Nick in the office, counting out twenty-dollar bills. I knelt down to stash my purse in the safe. "What are you doing?"

"Preparing the rent payment. My landlord insists on cash. He doesn't want to risk a check bouncing." He slid the stack of bills into a manila envelope, fastened the brad, and wrote *Timeless Toys* across the front.

Cash transactions were a bad idea. They left no paper trail. Though I could understand the landlord's concern, there were better solutions.

"Why doesn't he accept payments via PayPal or Venmo, instead? Or bank-to-bank transfer? He'd be assured the funds were good, and the tenants would have proof of payment."

Nick shrugged. "He issues handwritten receipts when he collects the rent. I keep them in my records."

Nick was smart to cover his bases in case of a tax audit.

In the early afternoon, Nick had stepped out to grab a quick sandwich, and I was replenishing the stock of card games when the door opened. In walked a sixtyish man in gray pants and a white button-down shirt under a black sport coat. His pewter-colored hair was shorn short, and his face was clean shaven. He offered me his hand. "I'm Dale Dickson. I don't believe we've met."

"I just started here." I introduced myself. "Nick said you'd be coming by."

While Mr Dickson waited at the counter, I scurried back to the office and retrieved the rent envelope from the safe. I carried it back to the counter. Mr Dickson reached into his sport coat and pulled out an old-fashioned receipt book and pen. He lay them on the counter, counted the money in the envelope, then wrote out a receipt. He separated the duplicate slips and handed the top slip to me. "My brother Chip will be by soon. I handle the financial matters for our business, and he handles the maintenance and repair work. I'm utterly useless with tools." He issued a self-deprecating chuckle. "Chip will be installing Christmas lights out front. Time to get Main Street ready for the holidays." With that, he raised a hand in goodbye and left.

Nick returned with his lunch. He'd bought a sandwich for me, too. We took our food to the back room and chatted over our meal. I learned that Nick had grown up in Winston-Salem, and had fallen in love with the mountains when his parents had brought him and his siblings up to the high country one winter to play in the snow. "We had so much fun they made it an annual event."

I shared that my first memory of the mountains was also a family vacation. "We rode a train through the Nantahala Gorge. The scenery was beautiful. We even saw a bear!"

We'd just finished eating when noises came from outside the store. The *clunk* of a toolbox being set down on the sidewalk. The scrape of a metal ladder on concrete. The *clink-clink* of a string of icicle lights against the front window as Chip carried them up the ladder. While Nick went back to work on a custom dollhouse, I stepped outside to introduce myself. Chip was a portly, slightly unkempt version of Dale, with hair in need of a trim and stubble on his cheeks. He wore a jacket over his coveralls, and a hat with flaps to keep his ears warm.

His breath formed fog in the cold air. "Got anything needs fixing while I'm here?"

"No," I said. "Other than the outlet in the office, everything's in working order."

"You've got a broken outlet? I'd be happy to replace it." He pointed his hammer at a white van parked at the curb. "Got parts in my van."

He must've forgotten or overlooked the e-mail I'd sent. "No need. It's not a problem."

He proceeded to hang the lights while I followed a customer into the store. I sold her three dollhouses, one for each of her granddaughters, plus full sets of furniture for each house. I'd earned quite a commission.

I went to the back room to inform Nick of the big sale I'd made.

He pumped a happy fist, then put his hands to his head. "At the rate we're moving inventory, I can't keep up with production."

"I could work overtime."

"You're a lifesaver!" He grabbed me in a hug, but just as quickly released me, a blush coloring his cheeks. "Sorry. I didn't mean to cross a line. Boss and employee, and all that. I just ... appreciate you."

"No worries. We both know who's really in charge here." I shot him a wink. His expression shifted, relieved and intrigued. I should have been ashamed of myself, but it was darn fun to toy with him.

THANKSGIVING WEEKEND BROUGHT SO many customers they could barely squeeze past each other. Nick and I repeatedly rushed to the stockroom to replenish inventory. The shop brought in thousands of dollars. The money was great, but the joy we'd bring the children was equally inspiring.

When we closed each night, I left two-hundred dollars in start-up cash in the till for the following day, and put the rest in the zippered bank bag. The cash intake normally didn't amount to much, a few hundred dollars at most. Other than children who brought in cash they'd saved in piggy banks – which we also sold – most people paid with debit or credit cards. Every few days, Nick took the cash to the bank for deposit. However, as the end of the month approached, he'd been retaining the cash to pay next month's rent when Dale Dickson came to collect on the first.

Knowing the weekends before Christmas would bring even more tourists, Nick and I stayed late every night for several days. On the last day of November, just after we'd closed the shop for the night, Nick counted out cash for the December rent, slid it into an envelope, and secured the envelope inside the zippered bag in the safe. We worked on into the late hours, singing Christmas carols. It was nearing midnight when I sprinkled silver glitter over miniature pine trees to resemble snowflakes. When I went to screw the lid back on, the jar slipped from my hands and fell to the floor, sending up a spray of silvery flakes.

Nick looked down at the mess, then up at my tired face. "Let's call it a day and clean the mess in the morning."

He drove me home and walked me to my door to ensure I got safely inside, a sweet, though unnecessary, gesture. There was virtually no crime in town, especially not violent crime.

I ARRIVED at the shop before Nick the following morning, December first. To my surprise, silver glitter littered the office floor. Although I'd gone into the office to retrieve my purse last night before Nick took me home, we'd both been careful to avoid the spill.

After stashing my purse in the safe atop the bank bag, I exited the office and grabbed a broom and dustpan. Silver glitter was all about, as if someone had tramped through it. *Could the shop have rats?* I dismissed the idea. We kept nothing edible on site, nor had I seen droppings. I chalked it up to the heating system. Glitter was lightweight and the warm air flowing from the vents could have blown the mess around.

I swept up as much glitter as I could, following up with the vacuum. Each time I thought I'd finished, the lights would reflect off yet another errant silver flake. I finally threw up my hands. *A few flakes of glitter never killed anyone.*

I arranged alphabet blocks in the window display,

spelling out funny holiday messages: Toys To The World And Toys Without Batteries Give You A Silent Night.

Nick arrived a few minutes later. After greeting me, he went into the office. I heard him opening the safe followed by a *zzzip* as he opened the bank bag. After a beat of silence, he called, "Ciara? Where's the rent money? And yesterday's cash?"

I returned to the office. "It's not in the bag?"

He shook his head, his eyes flashing in alarm. "I'm calling the police."

In minutes, a stocky officer arrived. His name badge read Gibbs.

Nick filled Officer Gibbs in. "Four grand in cash for the shop's rent is missing, plus around three-hundred dollars in cash receipts. It was in the safe when we left last night."

The cop glanced around. "Got security cameras?"

"I didn't see the need," Nick said. "I wouldn't expect a classic toy shop to be targeted and, other than when the rent is due, we keep little cash on hand."

I chimed in. "When I arrived this morning, I noticed the glitter I'd spilled by the worktable last night was tracked all over the floor. I assumed the heating system had blown it around." I showed them the contents of the vacuum cleaner bag. The glitter flashed from among the dirt and sawdust. The broom likewise contained pieces of glitter among the straw. Three or four shiny flakes were stuck to the dustpan, too.

The officer examined the windows and doors. "No signs of forced entry. Who has keys to the shop?"

Nick said, "Just me, Ciara, and my landlord."

The cop cocked his head. "That's the Dickson brothers, right? They own most of Main Street."

Nick nodded. "Dale comes by to pick up the rent on the first of each month. That's why I had it in the safe."

"Who else knows you pay rent in cash?"

"Chip Dickson, I suppose." Nick gestured to me. "Ciara. The Dickson Brothers' other tenants would know since they pay their rent in cash, too."

Gibbs pondered a moment. "Was the safe already installed when you leased the space?"

"It was," Nick replied.

"Did you reprogram it with a new passcode?"

"Immediately."

"Does your landlord have an override code?"

"No," Nick said. "I verified that with Dale Dickson when I leased the shop. I even contacted the manufacturer of the safe to double check. No one can circumvent my code. The only person I've shared my code with is Ciara."

"If only you two know the code..." He turned my way, brows arched. "Judges go easier on thieves who confess and return stolen funds."

I was insulted, but could understand why he'd consider me a suspect. "I didn't take the money."

Nick's gaze locked on mine, just as the officer's had a moment before. But while the officer's look had been accusatory, Nick's was reassuring. "I know you didn't, Ciara."

Gibbs spoke as if I wasn't there. "She's only worked for you a few weeks, right?" The implication being that Nick might not know me as well as he thought he did.

Nick didn't back down. "It wasn't her."

The policeman tried a different tack. "You're sure you put the money in the safe? You didn't accidentally take it home or stick it in a drawer somewhere?"

Nick shook his head. "I'm certain I put it in the safe."

"I saw him do it." I was tempted to tell Gibbs that if I'd been guilty, I would have jumped on the maybe-Nick-accidentally-misplaced-the-money bandwagon to deflect suspicion from myself. I thought better of it, though. The officer was only doing his job and I'd be asking the same questions if I were in his shoes.

Gibbs didn't argue further. "I'll dust for prints." He retrieved a fingerprinting kit from his patrol car and dusted graphite over the safe's keypad and handle. He used clear tape to lift the prints. "I'll let you know if anything turns up. I'll also check with the officers who worked the night shift, see if they noticed anyone about."

Nick thanked him, and the man left the shop. The deep lines between Nick's brows told me he was extremely upset.

"Maybe we'll get lucky and the lab will identify the burglar's fingerprints." Even as I said it, I knew the probability was slim. A burglar with a record would have probably worn gloves to avoid leaving prints. Heck, we hadn't even been able to figure out how anyone had gotten into the shop without busting a lock or window. *Could they have come through an HVAC vent?* A glance at the unfinished ceiling in the storeroom told me that nobody could fit inside the ducts. They were only six inches in circumference, and made of flimsy, flexible material insufficient to support much weight.

Who had taken the money and how had they gotten inside?

WHILE NICK HEADED to the bank for cash to replace the stolen rent, I headed to the coffee shop. A cup of spiced apple cider might cheer him up. I placed the order with the barista, and stepped aside to wait.

The manager, whom I knew from my many visits, greeted me. When I told her about the burglary, she frowned. "We had a similar burglary in August. The rent payment disappeared from our safe. Only three of us knew the code, me and my two assistants. There were no signs of a break-in, so it looked like an inside job. Neither confessed, so I let them both go. What choice did I have? Rent money disappeared from the art gallery's safe last spring, too. The owner told me about it. She thought she might have failed to close the safe, and they'd had a lot of people in for a showing, so she gave her employees the benefit of the doubt. She changed her code. It hasn't happened again."

The barista slid the cider onto the counter. "Here you go."

I thanked him and picked up the drink. As the spices mulled in the cup, I mulled things over in my mind. "Whoever stole your rent might have also stolen ours," I said to the manager. "May I see your safe? Maybe there's some clue we're missing."

"Sure." She led me back to her office.

I eyed the safe. It was the same model we had in the toy store. "Was the safe already installed when you leased the shop?"

"It was," she said, "but I changed the code."

I glanced around, wishing the walls could talk. Nothing

was plugged into the top outlet of the electrical socket on the wall perpendicular to her safe. Between lamps, a computer, a printer, an internet router, a paper shredder, and a phone charger, all the other outlets were in use. In fact, an adapter had been plugged into an outlet to accommodate the devices. I pointed to the empty socket. "Why isn't that outlet being used?"

"It's never worked. We make do with the adapter."

It seemed coincidental that the toy store and coffee shop had broken sockets, but what could it have to do with the burglaries?

I returned to the toy store and handed Nick his cider. "Thought a warm drink might lift your spirits." He thanked me, and I told him what I'd learned. "Doesn't it seem odd that someone stole rent money from their safe, and they have a broken outlet too?"

"Let's take a look."

We walked into the office and knelt on the floor. Neither of us noticed anything unusual about the socket.

Nick stood. "I'll get a screwdriver and take the cover off."

As Nick went to the workroom to round up the tool, I unplugged the floor lamp. A few seconds later, Nick was back beside me on the floor. He unscrewed the outlet cover. We leaned in to take a closer look.

He activated the flashlight on his phone and shined the beam into the holes on the upper socket. "Is that glass inside?"

I squinted into the hole. The flashlight's beam reflected off a tiny circle of glass the size of a pencil eraser. It resembled the camera lens on a cell phone. A lightbulb switched on in my mind. I'd seen enough spy movies to know gadgets could be something other than what they seemed. "Is it a camera lens?"

Nick glanced from the outlet to the safe, a few feet away. "A camera would explain things. It could have transmitted video of us entering the code on the safe."

"But who—?"

We simultaneously cried, "Chip Dickson!" It made perfect sense that Chip had burglarized the shop. The guy handled repairs and could have easily installed the spy device. He also had keys to the shops.

"Let's see what he has to say for himself." Nick pulled out his cell phone and placed a call to Chip. He frowned. "It's going to voicemail." Once the outgoing message concluded, he left a message of his own. "It's Nick from Timeless Toys. Call me back A.S.A.P." He returned the phone to his pocket and drummed his fingers on the checkout counter. "He could be avoiding me. Let's see if he's at the real estate office."

We marched down to Dickson Brothers Properties. Chip's van was nowhere in sight. The reserved parking spot for Dale's Mercedes sat empty, too.

Nick and I stepped into a lavish foyer decorated with poinsettias. A sixtyish woman with a sleek blond bob and stylish attire sat at the reception desk. The nameplate on her desk identified her as Dawna Dickson, Office Manager. *She must be married to Dale.*

A nameplate on the door behind her read *CEO DALE DICKSON*. The door was ajar. Through the crack I saw an enormous oak desk. An oversized computer monitor sat atop the desk, and a cushy rolling chair sat empty behind it.

The woman looked up from her computer. "Hi, folks."

Nick said, "We need to speak to Chip right away."

"Maintenance emergency?"

"No," Nick said. "But it's important."

She gazed at Nick, waiting for clarification. When he offered none, she didn't push. Instead, she lifted her receiver and dialed Chip's number. She listened for a few seconds, then left a voicemail. "The tenants from Timeless Toys came by looking for you. Call them. It's urgent." With that, she hung up the phone. "I'm sure we'll hear back soon."

Nick and I returned to the toy shop. As we stepped inside, I recalled Chip's reaction when I'd mentioned the socket was out of order. "He seemed surprised."

"How could he be?" Nick replied. "You sent him an email about it weeks ago."

Hmm. "Chip offered to fix the outlet right then. He said he had parts in his van."

"Maybe he already had the code and wanted to remove the evidence that he'd been spying on us."

"Could be."

Nick called Officer Gibbs to give him an update. In minutes Gibbs was back at the shop, staring into the socket. "You might be on to something." He looked up. "I spoke with the officers who worked the night shift. They saw your car here and a couple of the diner staff stayed late cleaning up, but that's routine. They didn't notice anyone on foot, but someone could have gotten in and out fast while they were patrolling elsewhere. I'll check the outlets at the coffee shop and art gallery. I'll also notify officers to look out for Chip's van. If he's around town working on a property, one of us will spot him eventually."

If... I wondered if Chip had seen Nick and me through the hidden camera. He might have realized we were on to his spy device and left town, either permanently or until he could come up with a viable explanation.

Gibbs used his radio to put out an alert, then departed the store.

THREE HOURS LATER, Dale Dickson came into the shop to collect the rent. After Nick handed the replacement rent envelope over the counter, he said, "Chip's not returning our calls."

Dale's expression turned grave. "I haven't heard from Chip myself since this morning. Maybe his phone battery's dead."

Or maybe he's running away with Nick's money...

Having collected the rent, Dale left the shop. With firm answers—and Chip—eluding us, the best thing Nick and I could do for the time being was get back to the business of building and selling toys.

Before we knew it, dinnertime arrived. My stomach growled. "Why don't I pick up supper at the diner?"

"My treat." Nick handed me his debit card.

My heart warmed at the thought he trusted me. "I'll be back in a flash." *Little did I know how true my words would be...*

I donned my coat and headed out into the dark, frigid evening. The icicle lights Chip Dickson had installed lighted my way. I only wished they could illuminate me as to whether he was, in fact, the guilty party.

The diner was decorated in holiday décor. An artificial tree stood near the door, flashing lights strung around it. Paper snowflakes adorned the walls. I placed my order at the counter, which was outlined with a long, festive garland, and sat down on a stool to wait. I swiveled on the stool, noting Dale and Dawna Dickson sitting in a nearby booth. Dawna faced me. A woman sat next to her, face pinched with worry. *She must be Chip's wife.* Dale had his back to me. All I could see was the back of his head, his shoulders above the top of the booth, and the side of his left leg, his foot cocked up at the heel. The lights on the Christmas tree flashed and something else flashed, on the bottom of Dale's shoe. *Oh, holy night! It's silver glitter!* Dale had stolen our rent money, not his brother. I'd earlier thought the glitter was a nuisance, but the stubborn stuff had just identified the thief.

I leapt from my stool. "It was you!"

Dale rose from the booth, glancing my way. "I have no idea what you're talking about." His actions belied his words. He edged toward the door.

I yanked the garland from the counter and dashed his way, lassoing him with the greenery. Before he could gather his wits, I wrapped the strand tight around his body, immobilizing his arms in a Christmas cocoon.

Officer Gibbs walked in the door. I expected the lawman to demand an explanation, but he'd already pulled his handcuffs from his belt. "Good job, Ciara. I'll take it from here."

I sprinted back to Timeless Toys. "We caught the thief!"

Nick and I ran back to the diner. All heads were turned toward Dale Dickson, who stood next to the booth where his wife and sister-in-law still sat, slack jawed. His wrists were shackled. The garland lay puddled at his feet.

Gibbs read Dale his rights. "We found your brother."

Chip's wife attempted to rise to her feet, but was impeded by the table. "Where is he? Is he okay?"

"He's being checked out in the emergency room." Gibbs filled us in. "I searched the county property records for real estate owned by Dickson Brothers. One was a vacation cabin in the woods. I figured a remote location like that would be a good place for a criminal to hide out, or at least to stash stolen money. I drove out to look around. The place appeared empty but, when I peeked through a window in the shed out back, I saw Chip's van hidden inside. I heard groaning so I forced a window open and climbed through. Chip was lying in a pool of blood. He had several goose eggs on his head and had just regained consciousness. He said Dale attacked him with his hammer. He had no idea why."

On hearing these details, Chip's wife shoved Dawna out of the booth. The bewildered woman landed on the floor with an indecorous *thud*. Chip's wife got in Dale's face. "How could you?" She delivered his cheek a solid *slap*.

Realizing she was in no state to drive, Nick offered to transport her to the hospital.

I said, "I'll cover the store."

Nick reached out, took my hand in his, and gave it an appreciative – and dare I hope affectionate? – squeeze. My heart lit up like a Christmas tree.

Details came to light over the next few days as Dale sat in jail, awaiting arraignment on burglary and attempted murder charges. Dale had purchased the spy outlets online and learned how to install them by watching YouTube videos. The secret cameras contained motion sensors that alerted Dale to movement in the offices. He'd receive a text message on his cell phone, and could log in to watch the feed live or review the footage later on his large computer monitor, where he could better see the details. He'd watched the owners and employees of the art gallery and coffee shop opening their safes, as well as Nick and me accessing the safe in the toy shop, thus obtaining the combinations. As landlord, he had keys to each of the properties and could easily get inside. He knew which properties had alarm systems, and avoided those spaces. He figured the tenants and police would assume the thefts were inside jobs and he'd get away with it. As CEO, he had Chip's e-mail password, and had deleted my e-mail about the non-working outlet so Chip wouldn't come across it. He'd neglected to empty the e-mail system's trash folder, however. The police found the message there.

Chip recovered, though he'd have permanent scars from the hammer. Dawna had no idea her husband had been ripping off tenants. She filed for divorce and took over as the firm's financial manager. Dawna and Chip renamed their business Charles Dickson & Associates. They no longer required that rent be paid in cash.

As we closed the shop on Christmas Eve, Nick handed me the cash to put into the safe. I bent down, retrieved the bank bag, and unzipped it to find a sprig of mistletoe. He took it from me, held it over his head, and grinned.

"Don't toy with me, toymaker," I teased. I stood, stepped forward, and pressed my lips to his for a warm and wonderful kiss.

ABOUT DIANE KELLY

Diane Kelly writes funny stories that feature feisty female lead characters and their furry, four-footed friends. Diane is the author of over three dozen novels and novellas, including the Death & Taxes white-collar crime series, the Paw Enforcement K-9 series, the House Flipper cozy mystery series, the Busted female motorcycle cop series, the Southern Homebrew moonshine series, and the Mountain Lodge Mysteries series. Find Diane online at DianeKelly.com

2

A MAN WITH NO IMAGINATION

MILLIE RAVENSWORTH

Izzy King's primary mode of transport was her bicycle, even in chilly autumn. It was fast enough to get her around the small rural town of Framlingham, but slow enough to see what was going on as she passed. And what was currently going on was the emptying of a bungalow into a large skip on the driveway. Izzy slowed down, because she hated waste, and it looked as though the person doing the clearing was not being all that selective.

"Morning," she said, as a middle-aged man wheeled a barrow from the front door, past a car with a *B.M.W. Motors* advert on the side door, and to the skip where he started emptying the contents.

"No, you can't just pop your own junk in the skip. I paid for it and I plan to use all of the space."

"Sorry?"

"That was what you were about to ask, wasn't it?"

"No, not at all." Izzy was taken aback by his aggressive

tone. "If anything, I might take some stuff out if you're throwing all of this away."

He shrugged. "Sure. Just don't make a mess."

The barrow contained a pile of bedlinen and he started to pull it out and hurl it over the lip of the skip.

"You know, the charity shop would love that stuff," said Izzy. "It looks in good condition."

"Who's got time for that, eh? You want it? Here." He waved a hand over the wheelbarrow. Izzy only had a small amount of space in her bicycle's basket, but she could save a couple of things. She saw an old blanket, so she pulled that out, and then she spotted something even more special.

"Oh hey, this is a handmade quilt. Who do you think made it?"

"Probably my aunt, she liked that sort of thing. Go on, clear off now, you're slowing me down."

"Your aunt is—?" Izzy wasn't sure what she was asking. She waved a hand at the house.

"What? She's dead, yes."

Izzy carefully folded the quilt and tucked it inside the blanket. She put the bundle into her basket and rode off.

When she arrived at the Cozy Craft sewing shop she took them inside to show her cousin Penny.

Cozy Craft stood in one corner of Framlingham marketplace. The town was not large but served as a hub for the farms and villages for miles around in this corner of rural Suffolk. Perhaps the market itself was not as big and as bustling as it had been in centuries past, but its stalls of fresh produce and artisan foodstuffs brought in locals and tourists alike several days a week.

Izzy and Penny shared the running of the shop and shared the same love of sewing and fabrics, inherited from their grandma, Nanna Lem, who had wisely passed the reins to them while she still had a retirement to enjoy. Alike in many ways, Izzy and Penny nonetheless often approached things from a very different point of view. Izzy liked to embrace the chaos of creativity, revelling in an unusual challenge, while Penny was the one who made sure the shop actually made a profit, by insisting on things like records, spreadsheets, and charging people money for the unusual challenges.

"Look what I just found!" said Izzy, unfurling her bundle onto the fabric cutting table.

"Found?" asked Penny as dust drifted down from the quilt. She walked over to see. Monty the corgi raised his head but didn't move from his basket. He was probably waiting to see if Izzy had brought something edible that might see a few crumbs go his way.

"There's a grumpy man emptying his dead aunt's bungalow on Love Lane. He was about to toss this into a skip. It's heart-breaking to imagine what else he's thrown out."

Penny smoothed the blanket and picked up the edge of the quilt. "Both of these are lovely. This blanket looks quite old."

"It's got a Witney label, and the style of it looks vintage," said Izzy.

"Witney?"

"It's a town in Oxfordshire, famous for woollen blankets."

Penny kept a hand on the blanket, but turned her

attention to the quilt. "This is all handmade, quite lovely. I wonder when it was made?"

"Nineteen seventy six," said Izzy.

"How on earth did you know that? Secret maker's marks?"

Izzy held up the edge and showed Penny the embroidery bordering the design. *Made by Sue Harewood September 1976*

"Oh nice. So lovely to know who made it and when. Who would throw a thing like this away?"

"I'm guessing that Sue Harewood was the aunt of the man I met today. He didn't seem interested in it at all."

"But has he looked at it? I mean *really* looked at it?" asked Penny.

They laid it out flat so that they could see the entire design. It was a mélange of colours, with deep blues and purples at its heart. Some of the fabric between the blocks was velvet, which gave it a very luxurious feel. It was around six feet square and comprised nine large blocks, like a noughts and crosses grid, with a slightly different design inside each block.

"The colours are gorgeous, no fading at all," said Izzy. "It's been carefully designed too, with each of the panels using the same colour scheme, even though the patterns are quite different."

Penny peered in close to look at the stitching. "Beautiful work, and not a mark on it."

"I wonder if she left any other family," said Izzy. "We could look up her obituary and see what it says."

"Doesn't Glenmore Wilson write those?" Penny said. "I bet he would know. Why don't we shut the shop for half an hour. We could show the quilt to Nanna Lem, she would enjoy seeing this."

Glenmore Wilson wrote the obituary column in the *Frambeat Gazette*, the tiny local paper that Izzy helped to run in her spare time. Glenmore was the oldest member of the editorial team, and according to the logic in Izzy's head (although she would never say it out loud) the most likely to know the people who had died.

Nanna Lem and Glenmore both lived in Millers Field sheltered accommodation on Fore Street. They all sat in the community lounge at Millers Field. Nanna Lem examined the quilt while Glenmore opened a packet of chocolate Hobnobs. For a one-armed elderly man, Glenmore was surprisingly adept at opening a packet of biscuits with one hand. He had served in the military in his youth and Izzy sometimes wondered if he'd picked up such skills in the army.

"This visit makes a pleasant break from Thursday Whist Club," said Nanna Lem. "We've had to call a halt to it after someone had an improbable winning streak and unseemly accusations of cheating were made."

"Your grandmother was the one who made the accusations," said Glenmore.

"And Mr Wilson here was the man with the uncanny good fortune," said Nanna Lem.

The two older people gave one another stern looks, although Izzy was strongly of the opinion that the relationship between the two of them was deeper than either might be willing to admit. Perhaps even containing seeds of a secret senior citizen romance.

Penny and Izzy explained what they knew about the quilt.

"Hmmm, I do remember writing about Sue Harewood passing earlier in the year. It will be in my folder," said Glenmore. He went to fetch his records, leaving Penny and Izzy sitting with Nanna Lem.

"This is beautiful work. I might have sold her some of the fabrics, back in the day," said Nanna Lem. "See here? This is a Laura Ashley print; I remember it being really popular. Harewood. Harewood. Oh, I do remember her. Younger than me and not a Fram girl originally. Came down from Norwich in the eighties with her sister's family, I think."

"Oh, an outsider then," said Penny smile.

Izzy knew exactly what that smile meant. Penny had been born in the town but had moved north with her parents as her child. She'd been back in her home town for well over a year now but knew she would be forever regarded as an outsider, not a local. In a rural market town like this, it could sometimes take generations to be properly assimilated.

"Do you think she had a theme?" asked Nanna Lem, tapping the quilt. "People quite often do with a big project like this."

"Huh," said Penny. "Something that ties these designs together you mean?"

Nanna Lem nodded.

"Well this one looks like a lion," said Izzy. "I love his face." It was a stylised seventies lion with a spiky mane surrounding a cheerful face.

"Some of these other ones are a little bit odd," said Penny. "It's like they are deliberately imperfect. See this one, it's a gorgeous wheel with seven spokes, but this one here stands out as it's a different colour."

There were several of the blocks in that style, different designs, but with a piece that was oddly coloured.

Glenmore returned with his folder. "Here we are. Susan Elizabeth Harewood, died in April aged seventy."

"That's no age," said Nanna Lem.

"Carbon monoxide poisoning. The chimney flue was blocked by an old heron's nest. She leaves a nephew only by the looks of it. Bradley Willingham." There was some mild teeth-sucking accompanying the uttering of the name.

"Know him?" said Penny.

"He owns that hideous car sales place on the edge of town. The one with the massive advertising hoardings," said Glenmore. "Stupidly calls itself B.M.W. Motors."

"Because it sells BMWs?" suggested Izzy.

"Don't believe it does. Says he named it after himself. Bradley Something Willingham Motors. BMW indeed! That's a clear sign of a man with no imagination. Wouldn't be surprised if a lawyer in Munich hasn't already sent him cease and desist letters."

"Glenmore dear," said Nanna Lem, "we're trying to understand this quilt. See how some of the blocks have these different coloured segments?"

"Ah, well..." he said.

Izzy was perplexed to see his expression change into that of a schoolboy who'd been caught drawing rude pictures on the blackboard.

"Glenmore?" said Nanna Lem. "Is there something you want to tell us?"

"I don't know if I should say," he said.

"Yes. It appears you jolly well should," said Nanna Lem sternly.

Glenmore cleared his throat. "It's an old card marking trick. You know when you want to know what a card is by looking at the back? You can put a tiny mark that corresponds with the number and the suit. If the pattern on the back was a wheel then you might end up with something like—"

He started to point but Nanna Lem slammed her arm down on her chair. "I knew it! What did I say? I *knew* you were cheating somehow; I just didn't know how. Penny, pass me those playing cards from that side table!"

Penny hesitated.

"Now!"

Nanna Lem started to examine the playing cards, making small noises of outrage.

"I think I see what you mean, Glenmore," said Izzy. "So this one here, is four of seven. It's a code for something where there's seven things."

"Like days of the week," said Penny. "The fourth day of the week."

"So this one here could be months of the year!" Izzy jigged with excitement.

Glenmore and Nanna Lem briefly forgot their card cheating feud and joined in.

"It's a record of a date then," said Nanna Lem. She pulled a notepad out of the craft bag at her feet. "We have Wednesday."

"Or Thursday," said Penny. "It depends whether you have Sunday or Monday as being the first day."

"An older person will most likely have Sunday as the first day of the week," said Nanna Lem firmly. "Now, the month is what?"

"It's the seventh of twelve, so it would be July," said Izzy. "What's this one in between though? It would make sense if it was a number. A date in July."

They all stared at the panel. It wasn't a geometric design, but a picture showing stylised birds in a tree.

"Well at the risk of stating the obvious, there are seven birds in that tree," said Nanna Lem. She made a further note on her pad.

"Wednesday the seventh of July," said Penny. "Oh wow. The next one along is less cryptic."

Izzy grinned. It actually had tiny numbers in each corner of a beach scene. "Nineteen seventy-six again."

Nanna Lem sat tall in her chair. "Now at this point, we could perhaps check to see whether the seventh of July in that year was a Wednesday."

"On it!" said Penny, busy on her phone. "Yes! Yes, it was."

"Oh!" said Izzy. "The lion. It's a Leo. The zodiac sign for that birthday."

"So this quilt was made for someone who was born on that day in seventy six," said Penny.

They all stared at each other for a long moment.

Penny spoke first. "The nephew is not that old. He's in his thirties at most."

"Let's look at the other panels. perhaps we can work out a name?" said Izzy.

"Well, the last two give us Harewood," said Nanna Lem. "A hare and a wood. Beautiful applique. I wish I could pass on my admiration to Sue in person, this is very fine work."

It was so obvious, Izzy thought. Pictures that looked random, and yet they were anything but.

"It's just these two then. It could be the first names of a person."

The first picture was of a field, some hedgerow and sky, with a single standing stone.

"Of course, a standing stone is sometimes known as a menhir," said Glenmore. "Although that would be a most unusual name."

Everyone gave Glenmore a polite smile.

"A more straightforward answer would be that the person's name is Peter," said Nanna Lem. "Peter the rock."

They all made an appreciative groaning sound, as if Nanna Lem had told a bad joke, or exposed a pun. All except Penny. "What? I don't get it."

"It's a Bible thing," said Izzy. "Saint Peter was known as the rock. It's like in French the name Pierre is their version of Peter and it's the same as the word for a stone."

"Huh. A word nerd thing," said Penny.

Izzy took a small bow. She wrote the word nerd column in the *Gazette* and often pulled interesting word facts out of the air.

"His middle name is Ray then," said Nanna Lem.

She was right. the picture depicted a sunset with exaggerated rays shown in different colours.

"Peter Ray Harewood," said Izzy. "We know his birthday. We should give him his quilt back."

"But who is?" said Penny. "Another nephew? If the nephew you met—"

"Bradley Willingham," said Izzy.

"He's a Willingham. Presumably, Susan's sister married a Mr Willingham. So, if this quilt belonged to a Harewood... Did Susan have a brother?"

Glenmore was shaking his head before Penny finished the question.

"So, is it Susan's son?" said Izzy.

"Susan Harewood was never married," said Glenmore.

"It is still biologically possible to have children without getting married," Penny pointed out.

"An unmarried mother? In the seventies?" said Nanna Lem. "That would have been scandalous."

A thought popped into Izzy's head and, by the looks of things, it had popped into everyone else's head too.

"Oh."

"Oh."

"Oh, indeed," said Nanna Lem darkly.

~

THE QUILT SPENT the rest of the week draped over the cutting bench in Cozy Craft.

While shoppers came in looking for that ideal dress pattern or the perfect fabric for their latest sewing project, the quilt sat there, a taunting mystery.

"But isn't there more at stake here than a quilt?" asked Penny, while they were enjoying a mid-morning cup of tea and a digestive biscuit. "If Susan had a secret son in the seventies, maybe even given up for adoption—"

"Taken even. The authorities were forcefully persuading unwed mothers to give up their children even as late as seventy-six."

"You're kidding," said Penny, shaking her head.

"Hard to comprehend," agreed Izzy.

"But if this son exists then he might want to know about his mum. He might even be entitled to some of her belongings. Even the house."

"If the nephew is steaming in and throwing everything out then we need to act quickly," said Izzy. "I've actually been doing some searches."

"Any luck?"

"Facebook is a surprisingly useful tool at times," said Izzy, waggling her phone.

"Oh?"

"Gambling on the possibility that his adoptive parents kept his first name, I've been looking for any Peter Rays born in seventy-six and focussed on Norwich, in case he was still in that area."

"And?"

"A dozen possibles. Some Peter Rays who live further away. A few Peters in Norwich. Some where they've not given their age on their profile but they look like they're maybe nearly fifty. I messaged them all."

"I'm curious to know what kind of a message you would send in a situation like this," said Penny.

"I said that I had found something that might belong to him and asked them if they knew someone called Susan

Harewood. I got a reply. I gave him my number but he said he was coming down here."

"When?"

Izzy looked at the pendulum clock on the wall. "In forty-five minutes."

"And now you choose to tell me?" said Penny.

"Do we need to tidy the shop especially for guests?"

Penny looked around the place critically, but of course everything was in order. She had made it so.

"I thought I told you to stop sneaking Monty digestive biscuits," said Penny.

"I haven't," said Izzy.

Penny pointed at the crumbs scattered around the dog basket.

"I have no idea how they got there," said Izzy unconvincingly.

For the next forty-five minutes they continued to sip tea and munch biscuits. Izzy snapped further pictures of the quilt with her phone because she wanted to document some of the detail. The neat piecing of the corners, the tiny embroidery stitches forming the eye of the hare, she even noticed that the pile of the velvet on the joining strips all faced the same way.

The shop door jangled and a man stepped in. "Hello. I'm looking for Izzy King."

"Peter Ray?" said Izzy.

"Well, just Peter mostly," he said.

He had a lined face and there was more than a little grey in his salt and pepper beard, but he had sharp bright eyes and a ready smile.

Izzy strode forward and shook his hand. "We messaged earlier. I'm Izzy."

"Is this the quilt?" Peter said, walking towards the cutting table.

He spent some time studying the panels and ran his fingers over the embroidered signature.

There was a momentary hesitation. "You asked about Susan Harewood," said Peter. "She's my birth mother."

Izzy looked across at Penny. She wasn't sure if she was ready for this conversation. "I see. If it's not a crazy question, when were you born?"

"Seventh of July seventy-six. Can I ask what this is about?" Peter sounded confused and who could blame him?

"Susan, your mother – did you not know her then?" asked Izzy.

"I met her for the first time this year. My own parents – my adoptive parents, my mum and dad – they've been dead a few years, and so I thought it was way past the time when I should try to find my birth mum. I found her. We spoke. We had a coffee in Norwich and she seemed so nice. I tried to phone her afterwards but I guess she— I don't know."

"Peter, I am so sorry to tell you this, but the reason she wasn't in touch was because she passed away."

He nodded slowly. "I looked her up after your messages and I found her obituary in a local paper. And here was me thinking she'd decided not to contact me again."

"No, she wasn't ignoring you," said Izzy.

"I've taken the liberty of asking a solicitor, a friend of a friend, to speak with you while you're here," said Penny. "He can help you to establish whether you have a claim on your late mother's estate."

"Estate?" said Peter. "No, I didn't come over here because I want her money. I got in touch with her to make a connection and understand where I came from. I've got a family of my own. And I—" He ran his hands over the quilt. "My daughter is studying textiles at university. She'd ... she'd love this. Far more creative than me, though I do my best. I'm a thatcher." He held his hands out as though his craft was written on them. "Not much call for proper straw thatching these days. Fill the rest of the year as a chimney sweep." He chuckled. "Not much call for that either,"

Izzy was struck by his words. "Did you mention this to your mum?"

Peter frowned. "Mentioned what? The thatching work?"

"And the sweeping."

"Well, yes. We had a lot of catching up to do and—" his lined cheeks blushed a little "—I guess I wanted my mum to be proud of me."

"Because you do know how she died."

His face suddenly became serious. "I had questions about that. I had mentioned my work, she mentioned she had a real fire at home and assured me she had the flue swept out in June."

"Oh, some time ago then?" said Penny.

"But don't you see?" said Peter. "Herons build their nests very early. February, March. And they do like a nice big chimney. More sturdy than a tree."

Penny frowned, her hands touching the air as though to grasp at meaning. "But that doesn't work. Heron nest building in Spring; the flue cleaned in Summer. How could it have possibly happened?"

"Indeed," said Izzy.

Twenty minutes later, Izzy, Penny and Peter were outside the bungalow on Love Lane. There were noises from within the house and the skip looked mighty full.

"This was her house," said Peter, to himself as much as anything.

"She lived alone, but she had a happy life, I think," said Izzy.

Penny saw something in the edge of the skip and pulled it free in a cloud of plaster dust. It was a thick heavy book, a photo album.

"No, you can't put things in the skip," said Bradley Willingham, coming out of the house with a rolled-up carpet over his arm. "It's full as it is."

"We're not putting anything in the skip," said Izzy.

Willingham blew a piece of sweaty fringe away from his face. "Oh, it's you. Come to find more treasures?"

"We found one," said Penny, tilting her head towards Peter.

"This is Susan Harewood's son," said Izzy. "Peter Ray."

"Just Peter really," said Peter. "Hi. Cousins, I guess."

He held his hand out to shake but Willingham just looked at it. "Cousin?" He forced a laugh. "Where'd you dig this one up?" he said to Izzy.

"Norwich," said Peter.

"Did Susan Harewood leave a will?" asked Izzy.

Willingham said nothing.

"She told you about finding her long lost son though, didn't she?"

Willingham frowned. He was not a convincing actor. "She didn't ... she didn't tell me anything."

"Oh," said Penny. "Then it might just be a coincidence."

"What coincidence?"

"That Peter here happened to mention herons' nests blocking chimneys to Susan and within a couple of months she dies from carbon monoxide."

There was a pause sufficient to see the cogs whirring in Bradley's mind. He pointed at Peter. "You mean he...?"

"Not he," said Penny. "*You* own that B.M.W. Motors place – you know, the one with trademark infringing name. Have lawyers from Munich been in touch yet?"

"Or maybe you just wanted Aunty Susan's money for general purposes," suggested Izzy.

"Are you accusing me...?" he said.

Izzy shrugged. "It has been pointed out that you are a man entirely without imagination. Who could say if you heard what your aunt had to say about a heron's nest while recounting her discovery of her long lost son? Who could say if you panicked at the thought of someone laying their hands on a house that was central to your future financial plans and put that exact plan into action? That you blocked her flue with a homemade heron's nest, suspecting, *hoping* it might lead to deadly carbon monoxide poisoning in the house."

Bradley Willingham threw down the rug on the drive. "Scandalous! I'm going to call my solicitor!"

"Probably a good idea!" Penny called after him.

Izzy felt a cold wind blow across the back of her neck as

she watched him storm back to the house and then, when he had slammed the door behind him, it was gone.

Next to her, Peter had pulled a worn picture out of his wallet, and held it next to an identical one in the dusty album from the skip. It was a black and white picture of a small baby, wrapped in a lacy shawl, being held by a smiling if sad-looking woman.

"Only picture I ever had of the two of us," he said. "I never knew there were all these other ones."

He closed the photograph album slowly. "You figured out who I was based on that quilt. That is so incredible; and my mum was an incredible lady for making such an amazing thing. I wish I could have spent more time with her."

"She made that quilt with a lot of love," said Penny. "And no one is ever truly gone when there is still love."

ABOUT MILLIE RAVENSWORTH

Millie Ravensworth has been writing (and sewing!) for years, and it seemed like a natural step to combine the two things in a series of cozy mysteries. She lives in England and has an adorable dog who likes to be at her side when she is sewing / writing, but he'd much rather she played fetch with his favourite toy!

Izzy King and Penny Slipper who appear in the story in this collection can also be found in the Cozy Craft Mystery books that are available to read now.

3

THE FORGET-ME-NOT ANTIQUES MYSTERY

VICTORIA TAIT

Twenty-nine-year-old Dotty Sayers drove her green Skoda Fabia into the attractive Cotswold town of Chipping Norton. She passed the Palladian-style town hall which she'd always thought imposing and out of place with its stone-columned portico entrance. Finding a space next to The Blue Boar pub, she parked and crossed the road, pausing outside the narrow frontage of the Forget-Me-Not Antiques shop.

Taking a breath, she nervously pushed open the pale blue door and entered, carrying her wicker basket. The butler-style bell swung above her, the clanger creating a tinkling sound as it repeatedly struck brass.

The familiar scent of cloth-bound books and silver polish hung in the air, instantly reminding her of the antiques auction house where she usually worked.

"Good morning, dear. Are you Dotty?" asked an old-fashioned looking lady who wore her hair scrapped back into a bun. She had long gold earrings and wore a vintage green tartan dress with a high, frilly black neckline and long black puff sleeves.

Dotty was pleased she'd chosen to wear her navy, green and grey gypsy-style skirt with a plain blue top and cardigan rather than trousers this morning, as she'd have felt underdressed.

"It's so kind of Gilly to let you help me out, and good of you to spend three days looking after my shop," continued the woman, who Dotty presumed was Mrs Marriot, the owner of Forget-Me-Not Antiques. "My father is completely hopeless looking after himself, and my mother would be worried sick in hospital if he was left on his own in the house."

Mrs Marriot paused for breath.

Dotty waited, unsure what was expected of her.

Mrs Marriot smoothed her hair and, blushing slightly, said, "Let me show you around." She soon overcame her awkwardness as she explained, "The shop is quiet at the moment, so you shouldn't have any problems. Everything should be labelled and priced." She picked up a silver-backed hairbrush from a silver tray displayed in the front window and checked a white luggage label. "Each label has a short description, price, and a number which corresponds with an entry in my ledger."

Still holding the brush, she walked across to her desk beside the wall, next to the entrance door. Two tall, circular glass display cabinets were positioned either side of it. From a drawer, Mrs Marriot produced three black hardback A4 notebooks. "I've never got the hang of computers. Everything I need to know about an item is in these."

She turned the label of the brush over and read. "Seventy-eight. I start afresh each January when I go through all my stock and rewrite everything in these books. Here we are. A silver-backed antique hairbrush inscribed with 'Marjorie' and 'First September Nineteen fifteen. Bought at Cirencester Auction House with a box of other items for twenty-five pounds on the sixth of June Twenty nineteen. And it's currently priced at twenty-five pounds." Mrs Marriot looked up at Dotty and asked, "Does that make sense?"

Dotty nodded and replied, "Yes, and you're very organised."

"Thank you," replied Mrs Marriot, blushing again and closing the ledger. She continued to show Dotty around her shop.

The narrow shop, with only a door and a small, mullioned bay window facing the street, was long. Steps led down from the first room to a second larger one, where shelves lined each side wall and several small tables were crammed with items. Against the very back wall, a dresser held a display of jugs, bowls, and other porcelain items. Beside it was a door leading to a small kitchenette, toilet, and storeroom.

"And that's it," declared Mrs Marriot as she finished her tour. "What do you think?"

"You have a lovely shop," replied Dotty politely.

"Thank you." Mrs Marriot smiled proudly as she checked her watch. "My taxi will be here in a few minutes. Let me quickly show you how to record a sale and how the card reader works. I have a small amount of change in a cash box if you need it, but most people pay by card."

Two minutes later, a car horn sounded and Mrs Marriot locked the cash box, returned it to the bottom drawer and handed Dotty a keyring with several different sized keys.

"That's me," said Mrs Marriot, picking up a worn leather Gladstone bag, which reminded Dotty of something doctors carried on old TV shows. Mrs Marriot also wheeled a small black suitcase out from behind her desk.

"My parent's number is in on a piece of paper in the front of one of the ledgers should you need me. I don't have a mobile," were her parting words.

Dotty sighed with relief as the butler's bell tinkled and Mrs Marriot closed the front door behind her.

What I need now is a cup of tea, thought Dotty.

∼

THE REST of the morning was quiet and uneventful.

At quarter past twelve, a small plump woman bustled purposefully into the shop and asked, "Would you like anything from the pub for lunch? I run The Blue Boar, and Mrs Marriot asked me to keep an eye on you."

"Oh, thank you," replied Dotty, "but I brought some sandwiches with me. Perhaps tomorrow?"

The plump lady smiled pleasantly and handed her a laminated menu. "This is our sandwich and snack menu. The soup tomorrow will be lentil and bacon. Chef's making it now, and it smells delicious."

Dotty smiled back. "That sounds good. Thank you."

"If you change your mind today, or you feel like a cup of coffee later, just call the number at the top of the menu and ask for Lindsay. And if I don't hear from you, I'll pop back tomorrow, same time, to check you're OK and see if you want to order anything." With a motherly smile, Lindsay left.

～

Dotty opened Forget-Me-Not Antiques at half-past nine the next day, her wicker basket tucked under her arm. Instead of her usual sandwich tin – she'd decided to treat herself to soup and a sandwich from The Blue Boar pub – she carried several books on antiques to read if the shop was as quiet.

During the morning, she did have several customers.

"I'm looking for a present for my wife," explained an elderly, grey-haired gentleman. "She recently broke a photograph frame and was very upset. I thought a replacement might cheer her up."

Dotty led the man into the back of the shop, where several silver and silver-plated photograph frames were displayed on the central tables and outer shelves.

"This is perfect," said the man picking up an ornately decorated silver frame.

He didn't quibble at the price tag of one hundred and twenty pounds and Dotty was satisfied with her first sale of the day.

Rather than reading a book, she found a duster, some furniture spray, and some cloths under the sink in the kitchenette and decided to do some cleaning.

The circular display cabinet to the left of the reception desk contained only a few items, but they were exquisite and very different from everything else in the shop. They included a gold necklace with matching bracelet and earrings, and what looked like deep-pink rubies, a tiara which sparkled so delightfully Dotty wondered if the stones were real diamonds, and a golden Fabergé-style egg displayed on a delicate gold stand. She tried to open the case with one of the keys on the keyring Mrs Marriot had given her, but none of them worked. She hoped nobody asked to look at the contents.

Dotty was busy dusting a small collection of first edition books when the bell tinkled and a lady dressed in a bright red trouser suit entered.

"Good morning," greeted Dotty politely. "Are you looking for anything in particular?"

"Not really," the woman replied airily.

Dotty left the woman to browse, wondering if she was only killing time in the shop before an appointment as she kept checking her watch.

The doorbell tinkled again and two more women entered. One wore a bright floral printed dress and green cardigan, and the other wore jeans, a white blouse and navy jacket.

"What can you tell me about this?" asked the first woman from the back of the shop. Dotty turned, as the bell stopped tinkling, and descended the steps. She glanced round to check the newcomers – examining a painting on the wall opposite the desk – before directing her attention to the woman in the red trouser suit who was holding up a silver candlestick.

Dotty checked the label. "It's Georgian, and solid silver. I might be able to tell you more by checking the ledger." She started moving towards the front of the shop, but the woman said hastily, "And the price?"

Dotty stepped forward and, checking the label, said, "Three hundred and fifty pounds."

The woman paused, before putting it back down. "Too much."

Dotty twisted her head towards the front of the shop, where she could only see the woman wearing the floral dress. Just as she started to move, the red trouser-suited woman said, "This is cute. How much?"

Couldn't she read the label?

Frustrated, Dotty once again turned her attention to the red-suited woman who held up a porcelain figure of a tabby cat.

Dotty took the ornament and read the label. "It's part of a pair. That's the second one." She pointed at another porcelain cat, which was lying down. "They're both Royal Crown Derby and priced as a pair at a hundred and seventy-five pounds."

Dotty thought she heard a noise at the front of the shop and tried to hand the cat figurine back to the lady who glanced over Dotty's shoulder and said, "They are rather attractive. Do you know when they were made?"

"I'm afraid not. Please excuse me." Dotty took a step back but the lady, who once again glanced over Dotty's shoulder, said quickly, "I'll take them."

Dotty was relieved the red trouser-suited woman had made her mind up and agreed to buy the cats. As she picked up the second cat, from the table display, the woman asked, "Have you had this shop long? It's rather quaint."

Dotty had the feeling her interest was feigned but she answered as courteously as she could, "It's not mine. I'm just looking after it for a few days while the owner is away."

This time, the woman allowed Dotty to walk to the front of the shop where the other two ladies were examining the first edition books.

Dotty carefully wrapped the porcelain cats. "That's one hundred and seventy-five pounds," she said as the doorbell tinkled and Lindsey from The Blue Boar entered.

As the red trouser-suited lady paid with her card, Lindsey looked at the other two women and scratched her head. She stepped towards the window as they passed her and left the shop, followed by the trouser-suited woman carrying her purchases.

"I swear I saw a woman leaving your shop just now wearing jeans and a navy jacket," declared Lindsey, "But I must have been mistaken. How has your morning been?"

Dotty looked up from the desk where she'd been making a note of the sale and replied, "Not bad. I've only sold two items, but they were both reasonably high value ones."

"Good, good. And can I fetch you anything for lunch?"

Dotty smiled. "You tempted me with the soup yesterday, so can I have that and a hot meat roll?"

"Certainly. It's beef today. Do you like it rare, medium or well done?"

"Medium please."

As Lindsey turned to leave, she said, "I see our local film props expert, Jackie, has removed most of her items. Is she bringing any more? They were fun, and so detailed."

"What?" asked Dotty, perplexed.

"The jewellery and ornaments in the front display case."

Dotty looked up at the circular display case nearest the door and gasped.

It was empty.

～

"I don't understand," cried Dotty. "The case was locked. I don't even have the key to open it."

Lindsey stepped forward. "Before you start panicking, let me call Jackie, as it's her items which have been stolen. I have her number on my phone at the pub." She moved towards the front door. "And I'll bring you a brandy with your lunch."

Dotty slumped down on the stool behind the desk and covered her face with her hands. How could she have been so stupid? To let the shop be robbed on only her second day.

She cast her mind back through the morning's customers. She doubted the man who'd bought the silver photo frame for his wife was involved, or the customers after him who were two mums with toddlers who'd kept trying to grab things. None of them had left her sight.

No, it must have been the two women who had entered after the woman wearing the red trouser suit. Dotty remembered glancing back and seeing only one of them, but how had the other opened the display cabinet? She must have picked the lock. And known exactly what she was doing, as she'd been so quick. When Dotty had returned to the desk with the porcelain cats, both women were examining the first edition books.

The front doorbell tinkled again.

At least she could rule out any other suspects. If they'd entered the shop when she'd been in the kitchenette or at the end of the shop, the doorbell would have given them away.

"Here you are, pet." Lindsey placed a black rectangular tray on the desk. "Drink the brandy first, and settle your nerves. No doubt you've been going over the morning's events in your mind. Any idea what happened?"

Dotty nodded and picked up the bulbous brandy glass. "I think the items were stolen not long before you came in. I was distracted by another customer at the bottom end of the shop." She sipped the brandy, feeling it burn the back of her throat, and returned the glass to the tray.

"Now, I've just spoken to Jackie," announced Lindsey in a bright but firm voice, "and she said not to worry. She removed the actual props from the case on Monday, for the filming of the period drama, and the items in the shop were her earlier prototypes. She was going to bring some more for the display, but decided to wait until Mrs Marriot got back."

Dotty bowed her head in relief. That was probably for the best.

"So, you don't need to bother yourself with the police. And no harm has been done. You just eat your lunch before it gets cold, and I'll be back for the tray after the lunchtime rush."

The bell tinkled again as Lindsey left the shop. Dotty

removed the aluminium foil covering the bowl of soup and a spicy aroma filled the room. It was delicious and did for more for her nerves than the brandy.

As she bit into her hot beef roll, she thought about Lindsey's comments. What if the thief struck again and stole from another antiques shop? Even though nothing valuable had been taken, she should still report the crime. But she didn't want to go against the owner of the item's wishes. Perhaps she should call her friend Keya – Sergeant Varma of Gloucestershire Police – and see what she thought. She dialled Keya's number.

When Keya answered her phone, Dotty came straight to the point. "Hi, I'm in a spot of bother."

"Found a fake painting in the auction?" asked Keya.

Dotty usually worked at Akemans Auction House and Antiques Centre and Keya presumably thought she was calling from there.

"I'm not at Akemans today. I'm in Chipping Norton, minding an antiques shop for a lady who's gone away for a few days, and we've just been robbed."

"Oh no! Shall I call the local constable and ask him to come over?"

Dotty hesitated before replying, "It's a little delicate. Apparently, the owner of the stolen items doesn't want to bother the police. Could you possibly come over in an informal capacity?"

"I'll have to come in uniform. I've just finished giving a talk at the primary school in Stow-on-the-Wold."

Stow was not far from Chipping Norton. "OK, but be as discreet as you can," requested Dotty.

∽

Twenty minutes later, Keya pushed open the door of Forget-Me-Not Antiques and looked up at the tinkling bell. "That's a good early warning system," she commented.

"Exactly, which means one of this morning's customers must be the culprit."

"And you think know who, don't you?"

As best she could Dotty described the woman with the floral dress and her friend, who'd worn jeans and a navy jacket.

"But you didn't see either of them by the glass cabinet?" probed Keya.

Dotty shook her head. "I was at the other end of the shop with another customer and the half wall blocked my view of the cabinet. But it was definitely locked."

"And you said there had been some valuable film props in the cabinet until recently."

"That's what Lindsey told me. The lady from The Blue Boar pub."

The bell tinkled again and Lindsey bustled in but froze when she saw Keya. "Jackie said no police. And Mrs Marriot won't be happy when this gets out."

Dotty stepped towards Lindsey and said, "This is my friend, Keya. She does work for Gloucestershire Police, and I felt I had to let her know in case the thief steals from other shops."

Lindsey pursed her lips.

"I'll just file a report so if there is another robbery, at least it can be checked against this one," confirmed Keya.

"I suppose that's OK," conceded Lindsey. "Personally, I hope you find whoever did this, and lock them away."

∼

DOTTY HAD no further incidents at Forget-Me-Not Antiques and even sold a set of Golden Jubilee gold proof coins for four thousand pounds. Mrs Marriot was delighted, admitting she thought she'd paid too much for them at a house sale.

But the theft of the prototype film props still played on Dotty's mind. It was an unsolved mystery which frustrated her, even two weeks later.

Gilly Wimsey, who ran Akemans Antique Centre, had asked Dotty if she'd mind working one Saturday so she could take her children, Thomas and Olivia, to London for the day. Dotty was happy to help out as she knew how excited the children were about going on the London Eye, a huge wheel soaring above the Thames with observation pods for passengers.

One of the students, who worked the checkout at the antiques centre on Saturdays and during the holidays, called Dotty over to check the price of an item.

Dotty confirmed, "Yes, we cleared out Mr Noakes' stall last weekend after he passed away. His wife didn't want any of the stock, so we're selling it at a discount and donating the proceeds to Dementia UK."

Out of the corner of her eye, Dotty saw a streak of red. She looked up and watched the same red trouser-suited women who'd been in Forget-Me-Not-Antiques stride across the floor of the antiques centre.

Akemans Antiques was housed in a three-storey converted stone flour mill. The ground floor was a large open-plan space with a myriad of stalls and booths. Gilly Wimsey managed a few stalls, but most were rented out to individual dealers who sold a huge variety of items, from household furnishings, to vintage clothes, to old camera equipment.

The lady in the red trouser suited disappeared between two rows of stalls.

"Thank you," said the student to Dotty.

Dotty stepped sideways behind a large clay urn as she watched two more women push open the heavy wooden door and enter the antiques centre. One wore a bright floral print dress with a green cardigan, and the other wore jeans and a navy jacket. Surely three women, wearing the same outfits as her mysterious customers in Forget-Me-Not Antiques, was not a coincidence.

Dotty removed her phone from her pocket and quietly called Keya.

"Hiya. Are you calling about lunch?" asked Keya. "I'm tidying up my spare room, but I'd love an excuse not to."

"I'm working at the antiques centre today," replied Dotty. "And I think we're about to be robbed. The same women who were in the Chipping Norton antiques shop the day those items were stolen have just appeared, and I have a nasty feeling they're up to no good."

"I'll come over," offered Keya. "But I'll also call the station and ask them to send someone. We need to make this official."

"I'll keep an eye on them," suggested Dotty.

"Don't spook them. If they recognise you, they may leave and we'll lose this chance to catch them."

Dotty agreed that Keya was right and her main priority was to prevent the women leaving until the police arrived.

The woman wearing jeans and a blue jacket walked along the front line of stalls, on her own. Where was her partner with the floral print dress? The woman turned and walked down a line of antique stalls.

Dotty was pleased the women was no longer in sight when the tall figure of PC Ryan Jenkins, wearing his black and white police uniform, entered the antiques centre.

He spotted Dotty and strode across, his round, guileless face screwed up in concern. When he reached her, he said, "Keya told me you have some potential thieves."

Dotty quickly told him about the three women.

"We need to catch them in the act," Ryan said. "With the stolen goods or find a witness who's seen them take things. From what you've told me, the latter is unlikely. They clearly know what they're doing. How long have they been here?"

"About twenty minutes," replied Dotty.

"Let's give them another ten. I doubt they'll want to be here longer than half an hour, as they'll know people will start to get suspicious."

Dotty and Ryan waited. Dotty discretely pointed out the woman wearing jeans and a navy jacket who was back with her friend in the floral dress.

They watched as the two converged with the woman in the red trouser suit.

"Now!" said Ryan and he strode towards the three women. Dotty followed him, at a slower pace.

"Excuse me, ladies," said Ryan in a polite, friendly manner. "May we have a word?"

"What's this about?" asked the woman in the red trouser suit.

Dotty stepped forward, and for a moment the woman stiffened before relaxing and looking back at Ryan.

"As I said, we'd just like to speak to you." Ryan turned to Dotty and asked, "Where can we go?"

"The auction house reception," replied Dotty.

"Lead the way." Ryan ushered the three women after Dotty. They entered the adjoining single-storey auction house through a door connecting it with the antiques centre.

Dotty turned on the lights and pointed towards a grey sofa and tub chairs, positioned around a reclaimed elm coffee table. The three women sat down.

Ryan stood beside the spare chair as Dotty hovered behind him. He said, "I'd like to check the contents of your bags."

"Certainly," replied the women wearing the red trouser suit, tipping her black bag up so everything inside fell onto the coffee table. A gold encased lipstick tried to roll off and the women wearing the floral dress caught it.

Dotty noted there was nothing unusual in the handbag. Just the normal collection of wallet, phone, hair brush, makeup and a small book entitled A*ntique* S*hops* *of* S*outhwest* E*ngland*. There was no sign of anything stolen from the antiques centre.

The contents of the bag belonging to the woman in the floral dress were similar and only the women wearing jeans had some unusual items. Inside her bag were a pair of white baby socks, but she didn't have a child with her, and what looked like a multi-function Swiss Army knife. Ryan picked it up and pulled out a long thin piece of metal which reminded Dotty of a dentist's tool.

Ryan turned to Dotty. "Nothing here's been stolen from the antiques centre."

Dotty's shoulders slumped. "I'm sorry to waste your time. But I was so certain..."

Ryan turned back to the ladies and apologised. "Sorry for the inconvenience and your time. You're free to go."

The woman in the red trouser suit smiled in a superior manner at Dotty as she pushed past her.

Surely the three women should be protesting loudly about their treatment and having their bags searched. Yet none of them had uttered a word of complaint. Something wasn't right.

After everyone had left, Dotty turned the auction house lights off and she was just locking the door when a bell jangled and a woman's nasty voice said hastily, "Henry, stop that."

Dotty turned and watched a young boy clamp his hand around the clanger of a handbell to silence it.

The doorbell.

Dotty glanced across at the three women who were still in the building and noted the one with the red trouser suit giving a slight nod. It wasn't for the benefit of her companions. So who was she signalling to?

Dotty scanned the room and caught sight of yet another woman wearing jeans and navy jacket disappearing into a stall on the front row. But the first women in jeans and a navy jacket was walking away from Dotty, between two different rows of stalls.

Dotty turned to Ryan, who looked at her regretfully and said, "There's something troubling me about the contents of that third woman's bag, but as nothing in it appeared to be stolen, I'm afraid there's really no more I can do."

"There's a fourth woman!" exclaimed Dotty.

"What?"

"Yes. I thought the woman wearing the red trouser suit was a distraction, and she was, but so were the other two. There's yet another woman in jeans and a jacket."

Ryan glanced towards the antique centre entrance and queried, "Like her?"

Dotty spun around as a woman clad in jeans, carrying a bulky leather shoulder bag, made a dash towards the entrance. As she reached for the handle of the heavy wooden door, she looked round at Dotty and Ryan and smirked.

The next moment she was lying flat on her back – thrown completely off balance by the force of the door opening as Keya crashed through it. Her bag clattered to the floor and from it, antiques and collectibles scattered everywhere.

"Oh *toda*!" exclaimed Keya, standing in the open doorway, taking in the scene. "I'm so sorry."

She leaned down to help the woman to her feet, but Ryan had already bounded across the room and happily told the prostrate woman, "You're under arrest."

THE FOLLOWING WEDNESDAY LUNCHTIME, Dotty, Keya and Ryan were sitting in the bay window of The Axeman pub in the village of Coln Akeman, half a mile from the antiques centre.

"We're all in Inspector Evan's good books. Even you, Dotty," grinned Keya.

The Welsh police inspector did not always appreciate Dotty's help with official police cases.

"And for once, other police forces are praising us," Keya added. "Thanks to Ryan's computer skills."

"It was nothing really," said Ryan, trying to act dismissive.

"Nothing," cried Keya. "You managed to link up twenty-five other cases, spread across five regional police forces. That's quite a clear-up rate. And Worcestershire in particular owe us big time. The same gang stole some expensive jewellery from an antiques shop in Malvern, and most of it was discovered in one of the suspect's houses."

"And we found the film props, which I returned them to Forget-Me-Not-Antiques," admitted Ryan. "The lady owner was delighted to see them and gave me this, for you." He handed Dotty an envelope.

"But how did they rob Forget-Me-Not Antiques?" asked Keya.

Dotty looked across at Ryan, who she suspected had drawn the same conclusion she had. He nodded his head for Dotty to continue.

"I thought our suspects were restricted to those in the shop that morning," said Dotty. "That nobody else could have entered without the doorbell alerting me. But I was wrong."

"One of the women inside the shop muffled the doorbell, by putting a pair of baby's socks over the brass clanger, I think," added Ryan.

"What?" Keya drew her eyebrows together.

Dotty nodded. "When Ryan asked the three women to empty their bags in the auction house reception, one of them had some strange things, including a pair of baby socks. I suspect she also had a lock pick set."

"She did," agreed Ryan.

"I believe she was the one who silenced the bell and unlocked the glass cabinet," said Dotty. "This allowed the fourth woman to enter the shop without me knowing, and quickly remove items from the cabinet before leaving again. Lindsey, who works in the pub opposite, was confused as she'd thought she'd already seen the woman wearing jeans and navy jacket leave the shop. The two women were dressed exactly the same."

"They're sisters, and look very similar," added Ryan.

Dotty looked at the envelope in her hand and opened it, removing a vintage Victorian-style card depicting an elegant lady wearing a large hat decorated with flowers. Several notes and some coins fell onto the table.

Ryan picked them up while Dotty read, "Thank you for your help in the shop. By the way, the porcelain cats you sold were priced at seventeen pounds fifty, not a hundred and seventy-five. I've been waiting to see if the buyer would return them, but as they haven't, I enclose the difference. I hope you treat yourself with it."

Dotty smiled. The purchaser of the porcelain cats was

presently awaiting trial for theft, so Dotty doubted she'd be returning to demand her money back.

"There's a hundred and fifty-seven pounds fifty here," said Ryan.

Dotty looked up, grinning. "It looks like lunch is on me."

ABOUT VICTORIA TAIT

Victoria Tait was born and raised in Yorkshire, UK, and never expected to travel the world. She's drawn on her experiences following her military husband to write cozy murder mystery books with vivid and evocative settings. Her determined female sleuths are joined by colourful but realistic teams of helpers, and you'll experience surprises, humour and sometimes, a tug on your heart strings.

4

IT WAS OUR SONG

NIKKI KNIGHT

I play *You're the Inspiration* once a night. No more. Except on the night of the murder.

Not that I knew about the murder then. All I knew at the time was that one of my regulars really needed a song. When you run a tiny radio station in a small Vermont town, you try to give listeners what they need. It's the whole reason we're here.

A lot of small towns don't have their own radio stations anymore, because of consolidation in the industry and the simple fact that it's incredibly hard work. WSV had given up and turned over to angry syndicated talk until I showed up and took it local again.

Not that it was my big life plan. I'd figured I'd seen the last of the place when I left Simpson for my first major-market job almost twenty years ago. Until my big New York City career hit a wall when the station went all-sports and replaced *Jaye Jordan's Light Rock at Work* with *The Bully Ballers Show.*

Right about the same time, my husband decided he wanted different things after surviving cancer. Blonde things, mostly.

So I took my severance, bought what was left of WSV, and moved in over the store with my tween daughter. We're managing. The listeners keep me going.

They start calling in for my all-request show an hour or so before air and keep right on going until I wrap up after midnight. Sometimes they call during the recorded morning show, and the satellite music that bridges the rest of the day, too.

Mostly, they just ask for a song they like or which means something to them. I get a lot of milestone anniversaries, birthday favorites, and breakup ballads. Sometimes a little appreciation. Listeners see me – well, hear me – as a friend.

They're the main reason we do this. We sure don't do it for the money. My first boss told me that, back when I was a big fat kid with a bigger, fatter voice. I'm stress-skinny now, but my voice, and my love for the work haven't changed. I do it because I'm giving people what they need.

What a woman with a trace of Boston and more than a few tears in her voice needed just before midnight that Monday night was *You're the Inspiration.*

I'd already played the Chicago classic for a wedding anniversary couple in the first hour of the show, and I've learned the hard way that if I don't keep to my rule, I'll end up playing it every damn hour. Maybe more.

But there was something in her voice. It hadn't been there

the other times she called, asking for get-up-and-go Kelly Clarkson or Katy Perry girl-power stuff.

Something was different tonight. None of my business what. It was the last hour of the show.

"I don't usually play it more than once a night," I said. "But for you I will."

"Thanks, Jaye."

As she said my name, I heard it: the little note of appreciation and relief that makes it all worthwhile.

One more satisfied listener.

I thought that was the end of it.

∽

"Being a local business owner means going out in the community, Jaye." Sadie Blacklaw, Town Clerk, yoga buddy, and generally wonderful human, glared at me over her rhinestoned reading glasses.

It was midday on Thursday, three busy days after I'd broken my rule and I was trying to get the commercial affidavits for the previous day finished and filed in time to tape some narration for my voice-work side hustle before school pickup. Sadie, as several of my friends often do, had stopped by for a cup of the very good coffee that is my one luxury.

"Going out to what?" I asked.

Sadie, who was perfectly turned-out in a red boiled-wool jacket and long black skirt, her short blonde hair perfect despite the winter wind outside, sighed. "A wake. Everyone will be there."

"A *wake*?"

"I hate them and I'm not going alone." She gave me a definitive nod. "We'll go after school pickup and before the show, and Ryan can do her homework with Xavi next door at Rob and Tim's."

Typical Sadie. When she wants something, she sets it up so her mark can't escape. I was sure she'd already called my neighbor, her nephew, to set up the homework date with my daughter and his son.

I know when I'm trapped.

I took a sip of my own coffee. "All right."

"And Jaye, honey?" She held my gaze. "Put on a blazer and lipstick, will you? A little dignity and style ... and you never know who might be there."

Well, that much turned out to be true, anyhow.

∽

SLATER'S FUNERAL Home was an old Victorian house at the far end of Main Street, where it had been since sometime in the late eighteen hundreds when the first Slaters started laying out their neighbors. It took Sadie and me maybe five minutes to walk there from the station, actually a nice break on a March day, since the wind had eased a bit.

Not so nice when we got inside. A suitably grim male Slater took our sensible down stadium coats and motioned us to a "repose room."

I tensed a little. I grew up in rural Western Pennsylvania, where a wake is called – and literally is – a viewing. Took me years to get that last sight of my grandfather out of my mind.

Sadie elbowed me. "Relax. It's closed casket."

"Oh. Okay."

A faint smile. "We're not *that* old fashioned."

Whew.

As we walked in, I realized I'd forgotten a very important question.

"Um, Sadie, who are we here for?"

"Bran Foster. Owned the little appliance shop in the plaza."

"Really? That's too bad." I shook my head. "I bought the washer/dryer there. He didn't let me buy the fancy one that was recalled a few weeks later."

I remembered Bran Foster's carefully explaining I *could* get the spiffy new model for our little apartment above the station, but he wasn't sure if the bugs had been worked out, and he'd hate to see me stuck with a lemon. The kind of thing businesspeople do in a small town because they care about the long-term relationship, not just today's sale.

"That was Bran. Good man." She sighed. "Jeanine's a poll worker. Teaches at the High School. Son's at college out of state."

"What happened?"

"Apparently just dropped dead in the kitchen Monday night. You know how most men are. Don't go to the doc unless their wife or something makes them. And then…"

I did know. The only reason Ryan still had a father was because David was deliberately and consciously determined to take care of himself, so he kept asking questions when he had a cold that wouldn't go away. The first doc thought it was nothing. The second one found the lymphoma.

If David had been the usual guy—

Poor Jeanine Foster.

I heard a few soft voices as we walked in, but none I recognized, so I was reasonably sure no one else I knew was here. After a lifetime in radio, I'm very good with voices, and I only need a word or two.

The "repose room" probably hadn't changed since the first Slater hosted a wake at the turn of the twentieth century. Maybe they'd re-upholstered the dark velvet hobnail couches. I sure hoped they had. There was a big stained-glass window on one wall, which gave the room some warm light, amplified by a couple of porcelain lamps and what was probably a Tiffany knockoff.

Probably. The thing about Northern New England is that everyone is so low-key that you can never be sure who's got what.

Every funeral scene I've ever read refers to the overpowering smell of flowers, but hothouse blooms don't really have much scent. Instead, the room was pleasantly redolent of expensive candles. Probably an innovation from one of the current Slaters.

Jeanine Foster was sitting in a big deep-red velvet chair near the (thankfully) closed casket, in a dark-green matched skirt and sweater that gave her skin a sickly cast. She had that tight, resolute expression people have before the big ugly cry.

A couple of people who looked vaguely familiar from school events surrounded her, and pulled back when they saw us.

"Jeanine."

"Sadie. Thank you so much for coming." Jeanine stood

and took Sadie's offered hands. New Englanders aren't huggy. "And – I'm not sure we've met…"

I froze.

Even though it's a small town, most people don't know what I look like, especially not in a navy blouse and blazer from my New York work wardrobe instead of the moto jacket and snarky tees I usually wear.

But I knew her. By her voice. She was the extra *You're the Inspiration* request. On Monday night.

"Hi," I said, holding out both hands as Sadie had done. "I'm Jaye Jordan."

Her eyes widened. "Oh, dear God." She crumpled into the chair, exploding in tears.

First Sadie, and then everyone else in the room, stared at me. They clearly wondered what horrible thing I'd done to the poor widow.

But I wasn't the one who'd done something horrible.

Jeanine took a breath and looked up. "I didn't plan it, you know," she said. "There was an opportunity, and I took it."

"Opportunity?" Sadie asked. I'd caught Jeanine's odd phrasing, too.

"He was going to sell the business out from under us and take off for Florida," Jeanine said, her voice wobbling but not breaking. "Why should he take everything and leave after all the work I'd put in? I did the books and chose the models and backed him up – even though I was holding down a full-time job."

"You sure did," I said, keeping my tone soothing.

"Yeah, you should know about this, huh?" Jeanine asked.

"I heard about your husband. You got him through cancer and the rat ran off to chase chicks."

I shrugged. "Something like that." Not the time to point out that there was a lot more to it. There always is.

"See, I wasn't going to make that mistake," she continued. "Not when I got the chance to stop him."

The room was suddenly terribly still.

"He came home Monday night talking about his arm and shoulder bothering him. Radiating pain into the neck, he said." Jeanine's face hardened.

"And...?" Sadie prompted.

"I told him it must have been from putting in a dishwasher that afternoon. No big deal."

"Stop talking," I said. "If you don't—" A decent lawyer could still help her. Extreme emotional distress, diminished capacity, something. Mercy, if she wanted it.

"I know what I did." Jeanine shook her head. "I heard him collapse in the kitchen. And I waited. I knew what I'd do if I saw him. I'd remember when it was good and forget what he'd decided to do to me."

The air, full of the soft, warm scent of expensive candles, was tense and quiet, as all eyes focused on Jeanine.

"I read a book and I waited. Listened to your show, Jaye."

An endorsement I didn't need, for sure.

"And after midnight, when it was quiet, I went in and found him."

"And called in a request," I said.

"Once I was sure it was over. Then I could remember the good."

I nodded. Sadie stepped away and pulled her phone out of her purse. Time to bring in the cops.

"And I played it for you." It didn't make me an accomplice, but…

She took my hands then, looked into my eyes with a faint dreamy smile. "First dance at our wedding, back when we were together, and hopeful, and everything was ahead of us."

My throat tightened. I remembered swaying to a different song, with flowers in my hair and a man who'd just promised to love me until death did us part, neither of us realizing that some things are harder than death.

I wasn't capable of what she'd done. I hoped. But I understood why. I nodded.

Jeanine's eyes overflowed. "It was our song."

ABOUT NIKKI KNIGHT

Nikki Knight describes herself as an Author/Anchor/Mom… not in that order. An award-winning weekend anchor at New York City's top all-news radio station, 1010 WINS, she writes mysteries including LIVE, LOCAL, AND DEAD, a Vermont Radio Mystery from Crooked Lane, and as Kathleen Marple Kalb, the Ella Shane and Old Stuff series. Her short stories appear online and in anthologies, and have been short-listed for Black Orchid Novella and Derringer Awards. She, her husband and son live in a Connecticut house owned by their cat.

5

ALWAYS AND FUREVER

ERYN SCOTT

Louisa Henry jogged down the staircase leading from her apartment into her bookshop. The sound of her footsteps was joined by the patter of many tiny, padded feet. As she stopped in front of the door at the bottom of the staircase, Lou glanced down and counted to make sure all her cats were present and accounted for.

"Everyone's here," she said with a smile.

In addition to her personal cat, Sapphire, Lou's bookshop was home to a handful of rescue felines. They had literary names like Anne Mice, Purrt Vonnegut, and Catnip Everdeen, and it was her mission to give them a loving, safe place to live until they were adopted into their forever homes.

She opened the door, and the group of them spilled into the bookshop, sticking close by as she started her morning chores. The cats were used to the routine, and they knew they would get their morning meal downstairs in the bookshop.

After setting a bowl of food in front of each of them, Lou started up her shop computer, made coffee, turned on the various small lamps she had littered around the place to brighten up some of the darker corners, and went to open the front door.

She didn't usually have a line waiting at the front door when she unlocked it each morning and flipped the sign from CLOSED to OPEN. Lou's regulars would trickle in during the first hour, lured in with the promise of time spent with the cats but kept there by the newest additions to Lou's inventory. And trickle in, they did.

Forrest, a local psychologist, was already there. While his presence was guaranteed daily, his timing usually depended on when he had clients scheduled. If he was there first thing, he must have just finished up with an early morning session.

"Beautiful morning out there," he said. His deep voice had such a calming effect on Lou that she was sure his patients felt just as at ease during their sessions. Forrest settled into his normal chair in the small reading lounge Lou had set up in the middle of the bookshop.

Not only did Lou love a cozy place to sit while she was deliberating about books, but she wanted to encourage customers to spend time getting to know the foster cats in hopes that they might make a connection. Her regulars weren't able to have their own cats, for one reason or another, but helped Lou so much in making sure the cats were brushed and given attention every day.

Next, George wafted in with a wave. George was a tech-savvy young woman who'd grown up in town and had become the official expert on all things techie. Not only did she have an immense amount of knowledge, but she also had a patient and straightforward way of explaining how to use different technological items to the older residents in town. Named after the author George Elliot, the young woman and Lou had become fast friends. She plopped onto the floor of the bookshop, instantly surrounded by cats, her fingers ready to scritch backs and ruffle ears.

Lou's last regular tottered in a few minutes later. Silas was a mostly grumpy septuagenarian. Coming from New York City, Lou wasn't bothered by his blunt nature. It didn't hurt that he was the one true love of the usually shy Catnip Everdeen.

Lou had only lived in the small Pacific Northwest town of Button for a handful of months. But in a town that truly was as cute as a button, the residents had proven to be as sweet as pie. Well, most of them. Silas had a little crustier exterior than the rest. But Lou was getting to know him better as the months went by, and she could say with confidence that, just like a pie, he had a soft, gooey center too.

"Where's Catnip?" Silas grumbled a few minutes later.

He'd taken his usual seat on the tweed love seat and was almost through the first page of his daily paper when he'd scowled, set it down, and scanned the bookshop.

Lou and the other regulars adopted similar frowns as their gazes roamed around the space.

"I just saw her this morning." Lou wrinkled her nose, remembering seeing her eating breakfast with the others.

"Well, she's not here," Silas said, getting to his feet with a concerted effort and a few grunts. "If she was, she'd be in my lap by now."

The man wasn't wrong. Whereas the orange-and-white cat hid from almost everyone else, preferring to watch from under a chair or in between a bookshelf and the wall, when Silas was around, she turned into a full lap cat. The moment she heard his voice each morning, she came running, sometimes accompanied by a sweet, meowed greeting.

Together, the four of them searched the bookshop – a few of the other cats following on their heels on the off-chance they were looking for something treat related.

"That's so weird," Lou said half an hour later, after they'd exhausted all of Catnip's regular hiding places.

George's face pulled into a grimace. "Do you think it's possible that she snuck out the front door?"

Lou blinked. All the cats naturally gave the shop door a wide berth, scared of the bell. "I suppose it's not out of the question." Worry that the poor thing was wandering out on the streets gnawed at Lou.

The group moved the search party outside, Lou staying with the shop while they swept Thread Lane and down the surrounding alleyways, looking for a hint of orange and white. Inside, Lou kept the search going, trying to convince the other cats to show her where their foster sister might be hiding.

But an hour later, there was still no sign of Catnip Everdeen.

At first, Lou had brushed off Silas's worry. The shy cat was a master of hiding, precisely how she'd earned her name. She was an observer, always on alert, just like the literary heroine of Suzanne Collins's *Hunger Games* series.

The terrible possibility that she wasn't merely hiding sank in the longer they went without a sighting. During the second hour, Noah, the local veterinarian, showed up to help, having heard the news from those searching up and down the street. He brought backup too. His nine-year-old daughter, Marigold, helped brush the cats on a weekly basis and often surprised Lou with the things she noticed about the cats that Lou didn't. Given that it was only Marigold's second day of summer break, Lou valued their help.

She especially appreciated Noah when he stopped near the register and tilted his head. "Have you moved this? It looks like Catnip could've squeezed into this space between the wall and the counter."

Lou approached the area, peering into the gap. It looked large enough for the cat to access.

"I don't see any signs of her in the opening," Noah said, kneeling next to Lou. "But pieces of furniture like this sometimes have compartments underneath or along the back that cats can hide inside." He chuckled. "We once lost a hamster at the clinic for two days because he crawled into the unused space at the back of Kathleen's desk," he said, mentioning his office manager.

Lou gestured to the desk, excited about something new to try. "I didn't even know this moved."

"It used to be over there when this was a comic book shop in the nineties, when I was a kid, so I think it does." Noah looked at it, gripping a few different points before he got enough leverage to scoot the desk away from the wall.

George, Forrest, and Silas scurried over, excited to see if there would be a cat hiding behind the register counter.

But there were no small compartments for her to hide inside. In fact, there were only a few stray papers and a lot of dust in the space where the piece of furniture had been.

Silas coughed, pretending to be inundated with dust. "Didn't you clean when you moved in here?" he asked Lou.

"Of course I did." Lou fixed him with a glare. "I didn't think this moved." She bent down to pick up the papers while George went to the back room to grab a broom.

In her hands, Lou held a few old order slips. She flipped through them, noticing one of them was different. Instead of a printed page, this one was handwritten.

"Silas," Lou said, her voice shaking. "Why is there a letter addressed to you behind my register?"

The old man reached over and plucked the letter from her grasp. "Let me see that." His eyes pored over the text.

Sure, it could've been a different Silas. It wasn't a super-common name, but it also wasn't out of the question there could've been more than one Silas who'd ever lived in Button. But from the way his expression dropped, Lou knew immediately he was the desired recipient of the letter. Before Lou could ask him anything more, Silas rushed out of the bookshop, the letter flapping in his clenched fist.

"Did you see who it was from?" George asked, following Silas with her gaze as he stormed down the street and out of view.

Lou shook her head.

"No need to guess," Forrest said, keeping his voice low even though Silas was gone.

"Yeah, it's pretty clear, given where we are," Noah added. When George and Lou gave him a confused look, he said, "When he was in his twenties, Silas was left at the altar by a woman named Frannie." Noah's face crumpled with discomfort.

Lou inhaled to cover the worst of her shock. Even George took a step back in surprise.

"George, I'm surprised you haven't heard any of this." Forrest's forehead creased as he took in the young woman. George had spent all her twenty-two years in the small town.

She blinked. "No. I never – I mean, it makes his grumpy attitude make a little more sense, but—" She cut off, simply shaking her head once more.

"From what I've heard, Silas and Frannie were crazy about each other from the moment they met. I think they must've been about your age, George," Forrest explained. "Their wedding was going to be the talk of the town that summer."

"But?" Lou asked, a dread building inside her.

Noah took over the story, knowing it just as well as Forrest. "But, the day of the wedding, Frannie never showed. She left a note behind for her parents, saying she'd met someone else and was going off to start a life with him."

"Silas must've been devastated," Lou whispered.

"And that's why he never married," George said, her eyes widening with understanding.

Lou frowned. "But why did you say it was clearly from Frannie because of where we were?" she asked Noah.

"Frannie's family owned the bookshop in the seventies,

before Kimberly or Nina," he said, mentioning the two previous owners that Lou knew about.

Lou's lips parted. Not only was it a surprise that the building had housed a bookshop for the better part of fifty years, but it was also shocking to learn that Silas came there just about every day even when he had every right to hold negative feelings toward the place.

"So that must've been *the* letter, then?" George guessed. "The one Frannie left her parents to let them know she was running off with another man."

Forrest puffed out his cheeks.

"Must've been," Noah said.

Lou shook her head, but it was at that moment that her best friend, Willow, entered the bookshop, ready to help search.

"I'm guessing by the sad look on all your faces that you haven't found Catnip yet?" Willow asked.

"No – but our sad expressions are because of something else." Lou filled in her friend about what they'd found behind the register while Noah, Forrest, and George pushed it back into place. Willow and Lou were about to get back to searching for the cat when Easton, Willow's neighbor and a local detective, walked into the bookshop.

"Oh, I texted Easton too," Willow said, jabbing a thumb toward the man as he approached.

"You really think we need to involve the law?" Lou asked under her breath, so only Willow could hear.

Willow shrugged. "He's a detective. Finding stuff is his job."

Lou didn't argue any further. She wasn't going to turn

away any help, even if she thought calling in a detective for a missing cat might be a bit overkill.

"Thanks for coming. We're just taking a moment to reset after our latest discovery," she explained to Easton. "Which was not the cat, but I learned something interesting about the former owners of this building." Lou let out a sardonic laugh, showing it was something she would've rather not learned.

Easton's face wrinkled into a grimace. "Oh, you found out about the murder?"

Noah cleared his throat loudly from behind Lou. They all turned to see him shaking his head at Easton.

"No." Lou crossed her arms. "I learned about Silas's ex-fiancée. What murder?" She turned toward Noah as she asked the question.

He glanced over toward where his daughter was in the used-book section to make sure she couldn't hear before saying, "The man who owned the place in the nineties, between the Doyle family and Nina, was murdered."

"Here?" Lou frantically tried to meet everyone's gaze, but she stopped at Willow. "You didn't tell me this was a crime scene when I bought it."

Willow held up her hands. "I didn't know about this. I have no idea what he's talking about. When I moved to town, Nina was the owner. That's all I know."

Lou turned back toward Easton and Noah.

Forrest glanced at his watch. "I'm sorry, but I have a client." He placed a reassuring hand on Lou's shoulder as he walked by.

Easton watched him leave like he was jealous. He

turned back toward Lou. "It's nothing terrible. The man who bought the place from the Doyles – Weston – turned it into a comic book shop. He was really into collecting, and he was cutthroat about how he acquired his collections."

Noah ran a hand through his dark hair. "He made a lot of enemies over the decade he owned this place."

"One of whom decided to get revenge when Weston bought a really expensive item off him, convincing the guy it was only worth five dollars, when in actuality, it was worth thousands," Easton added.

Lou wrinkled her nose. "That's awful, but not worth killing over. Right?"

The group nodded in consensus.

"True, but when the guy – Trace was his name – found out he'd been duped, he came to demand the item back. He and Weston got in a heated argument, and he ended up grabbing his neck and—" Noah let the rest of the sentence speak for itself.

Lou shivered. "Okay, I think I've learned enough history of my *home* for today," she said, emphasizing the word so they knew she had to live there. "Let's keep looking for Catnip."

The news of the murder stayed with Lou as they searched, and she couldn't tell if it was that news or the fact they still hadn't found the cat that had her feeling down. She was losing hope when Easton froze and let out a stern "*Shhhh!*"

Everyone stopped, turning their attention to where the detective stood, near the back wall of the bookshop.

"I heard a meow." Easton's eyes roamed the ceiling as he waited.

Lou looked at the other cats in the shop, in various states of agitation at all the worry and movement going on in the shop. They were used to people coming and going, but they could feel the anxious energy hanging in the air.

"It could've been one of them." Lou gestured to the other felines.

"They've been meowing all morning," George confirmed.

Easton shook his head, resolute. "This was distant, muffled somehow."

Lou rushed to join him, hope pushing her forward. "Maybe she got stuck somewhere," she said, excitement palpable in her words.

Everyone in the shop stayed silent for the next minute and a half, barely daring to breathe lest they might miss the next meow.

Lou was about to suggest that it was a fluke, when a faint meow broke through the silence. "It came from over here."

Lou moved to stand next to the long shelf which spanned the back wall of the bookshop. On the other side of the wall, a staircase led up to Lou's apartment. But they'd checked the staircase, as well as Lou's entire apartment, many times just to make sure Catnip wasn't there.

Crowding around the bookshelf, the search party waited and listened.

"Catnip, you back there?" Lou called.

She meowed again. Lou followed the sound, kneeling and peering at the bottom shelf of books. They were in the cookbooks section, and unlike the smaller paperbacks and hardbacks in the fiction shelves, the large food-centric tomes could often stand on their own without being sandwiched in or propped up like other books. Because of that, Lou hadn't filled the bottom shelf to the max, leaving a space to the far left.

A space just large enough for a svelte cat to slip through.

But through to where? Lou crouched even lower, practically placing her ear to the floor as she peered into the space between the cookbooks on the bottom shelf. Even in the darkness, she could tell there was an opening in the wall in the spot directly behind the books.

She reached her hand forward into the darkness. A coarse, hairlike substance poked at her fingers. Lou yelped, wrenching her hand out of there.

"Does anyone have a flashlight on them?" she asked the group.

Everyone there patted their pockets and purses, then produced their cell phones. Lou's was sitting over on the register counter, so she took the first phone passed her way and pointed the light into the space.

There was a triangular hole in the wall, about as big as one of the cookbooks, cut diagonally. In the opening, the stiff bristles of a broom were visible.

"There's a broom blocking the opening," she told the group.

Hearing her voice, and possibly seeing some of the light filter into the space through the broom bristles, Catnip meowed again, sounding louder than ever.

"We're coming to get you, girl. Don't worry," Lou told her as she got to her feet. "This seems to be a false wall. I can't tell how big the space is behind it, but I think it'll be easier to get to her if we move this bookcase."

Everyone got to work on stacking the books on the shop table before hauling the bookcase away from the wall. The place had been a working bookstore when Lou had purchased it earlier that year, so even though she'd cleaned and reorganized the area, she'd never had cause to move the large bookcases lined up to create aisles through the shop. If she had, she would've noticed the small opening in the wood-paneled wall.

Easton leaned down to inspect the triangular-shaped hole. Being that it was basically the bottom left-hand corner of the panel missing, it seemed like a handle, a way to open it. Easton fit his hand in the hole and pulled.

The wood groaned, and Easton let off on the pressure, but then the wall moved toward him, the top half moving away like an old garage door, swiveling on a point in the middle. Catnip Everdeen meowed and raced out to meet George, rubbing against her leg. She bent to pick her up.

"I'm going to get her some water," George said, taking her over to the bowl.

As Easton lifted, a small room became visible, no bigger than a closet, but hidden away underneath the staircase. Based on the assortment of brooms, dusters, and the timeworn vacuum cleaner sitting in one corner, the place had been used as a cleaning closet of sorts.

But that wasn't the only thing inside. About ten plastic bins were stacked in the space. Lou couldn't quite tell at first what they held.

Easton let out a thin laugh.

"Weston's collection," Noah said, as if he were looking at a myth come to life.

Easton's eyes were wide. He found a latch on the wall that held the door in place. "When the police arrested Trace for Weston's murder, he said he'd searched for the collection and hadn't ever found it, but no one believed him. They all thought he'd sold it by the time they caught up with him. But he really hadn't ever found it."

Lou and Willow regarded each other, stunned, as the identity of the items in the bins became clear to them.

"Wait," Willow said, incredulity lacing her tone. "Weston's *super valuable* collection was—"

"Beanie Babies?" Lou finished.

Noah and Easton nodded. Lou felt like laughing for a moment as everything settled over her.

"I mean, I guess I remember them being popular back in the nineties," Willow said.

Lou almost scoffed at her friend's cavalier phrasing, knowing the two of them had been crazy about the things when they were younger. They'd spent time, money, and energy tracking down the trendy stuffed animals, always searching for the most elusive, rare varieties.

"What was the one Weston convinced Trace was only worth five dollars?" Lou asked, stepping forward until her fingers brushed along the bins.

Noah squinted, unable to remember.

But Easton proved he had the detail-oriented memory of a detective, because he narrowed his eyes and said, "It was a super-rare bear. Weston convinced Trace it was a different one, missing a rose, and wasn't even worth the original price."

"He convinced him that Curly bear was Always bear without its rose?" Willow blurted. Her chin jutted back, and embarrassment crept into her cheeks in patterns of pink and red as she revealed how obsessed about the stuffed animals she'd been. "Er ... or something like that."

Trying to change the subject to save her friend from any more embarrassment, Lou said, "I can't believe this has been here the whole time." Lou blinked as she took in the hidden room.

"This is what blocked her from getting out." Willow picked up a broom that had fallen sideways, its bristles blocking the small opening Catnip had squeezed through. "She must've knocked it over as she crawled through and then couldn't get back out."

It all made sense.

"Well, thank you for all your help, everybody." Lou was so glad Catnip was safe. Still, a pit sat at the bottom of her stomach. She wished Silas hadn't been hurt in the process.

"What are you going to do with these?" Noah asked, eyeing the stuffed animals.

Lou raised her hands, palms up.

"She's going to see if any of them are still valuable so we can sell them," Willow answered for her.

∼

It took three days to go through the bins of Beanie Babies. They'd found most of them weren't worth more than a few dollars now, not having lasted through the hype of the nineties. But they also found not only the Curly bear, but the rose-holding Always bear Weston had tricked Trace into thinking he was selling.

After dropping off most of the bears at the local hospital to be given to kid patients who needed cheering up, Lou and Willow returned to the bookshop.

The five Beanie Babies they'd kept were on the register counter, lined up. Four were in protective plastic cases, and an internet search had confirmed they were worth anywhere from a couple hundred dollars to a couple thousand.

"You selling stuffed animals now?" a gruff voice asked, causing Lou and Willow to glance up.

It was Silas.

"We haven't seen you in days, Silas," Lou said, surprised at his sudden appearance.

Well, actually, she was just plain surprised by his *appearance*. The man was dressed to the nines. Silas normally wore a pair of dark gray or khaki slacks, finely pressed, and either a short-sleeved button-up or a long one, depending upon the season. During the winter, he even put sweaters over the button-ups. And he almost always wore a black bowler cap. His fuzzy wild eyebrows were as much a part of his signature look as was his hat.

But that morning, he looked like a completely different person.

"Sorry." He shifted his weight. "I heard you found Catnip, but I had some things to take care of."

"Silas, did you get a … haircut?" Willow asked.

His gray hair had definitely gotten a trim, but that wasn't

where it ended. His eyebrows had been cleaned up as well, and hair wasn't visibly protruding from the man's ears and nostrils.

"Sharp outfit," Willow said, adding a whistle to the end of the statement.

Silas wore a suit that appeared to have been tailored to fit him just right. It was a dark blue color, accented with a bright pink button-up underneath. And while the man still wore a hat, he'd traded in his trusty bowler hat for a snazzy fedora. The houndstooth hat sat tipped just ever so slightly atop his head.

"Why the change in your look?" Lou asked warily.

Silas stopped in the middle of the bookshop, glancing furtively at the couch and then down at his pressed suit as if he were worried he might wrinkle it if he sat down.

He shrugged. "Decided it was time to put myself out there again. Start dating."

In Lou's mind, that was the best-case scenario. Finding the letter and finally seeing his ex-fiancée's words on the page must've given the man the closure he'd needed to move on. It had obviously helped him let go of whatever feelings he was still holding on to.

"Dating?" Willow asked.

Silas puffed out his chest and nodded.

Lou and Willow shared a quick, knowing look before turning their attention back toward Silas.

"Oh, that's great." Willow's tone was too sweet and too loud.

Lou cleared her throat in warning as Silas glared at them.

"Well, it won't take long to find a date dressed like that," Lou added, trying to salvage the situation.

"Or when I tell them I once had a woman who told me she would rather die than be without me." He beamed.

Lou tilted her head in question. Willow pressed her lips together.

"Oh? What woman was that?" Lou asked, intrigued.

Silas pulled the yellowed letter out of his interior suit jacket pocket he'd folded in thirds, lengthwise, but Lou recognized the timeworn page from earlier that week. He tapped the letter against his knee and smirked. "My fiancée, Frannie."

Confusion swirled around Lou. Willow must've been feeling similarly lost because she let out a long, "Huh?" under her breath, so only Lou could hear.

"Frannie?" Lou asked sweetly, hoping to cover her surprise. "I didn't know you were ever engaged, Silas."

At that statement, Silas snorted and rolled his eyes. "Nice try, sweetheart. I know the whole town's been yammering away about me and Frannie all week. I'm sure you heard all the wrong details too."

"Wrong details?" Willow stepped forward.

Silas's eyes sparkled as he unfolded the letter in his hand. "She didn't run away with another man. I knew she wouldn't have, couldn't have. But that was what her parents told everyone."

"Why would they do that?" Lou asked.

"They didn't want us to be together," Silas explained. "They hid it well around me, so I never knew they disapproved. Frannie shielded me from their disapproval as well, hoping she could change their minds. But apparently she couldn't, so they gave her an ultimatum: lose her family forever, or move away and never speak to me again."

"That's awful." Lou cocked her head to one side.

This had taken place in the seventies, but it sounded more like the eighteen hundreds, given how they were trying to control their daughter's life.

"She wrote me this letter, and asked them to give it to me," Silas said. "They did not, instead writing a fake letter, the one I'm sure you heard about, that explained how Frannie had fallen for someone else and would never see me again. Here, see for yourself."

He handed over the letter.

Lou unfolded it, holding it between herself and Willow so they could read it together.

Dear Silas,

I'm so sorry, but I can't marry you. As much as I would rather die than be without you, my parents have given me an ultimatum. They've never accepted us, but I thought they might come around, so I shielded you from their incorrect and premature judgments.

Today, the day of our wedding, however, they have informed me I have a choice: you or them. I love you so much, but they are my family. So, I'll leave town. My cousin lives in California, and she says I can come work in her restaurant while I start a new life.

But please know that, had things gone differently, you would've been my first choice, and I will love you, always and forever.

Love,

Your Frannie

Lou and Willow finished reading at the same time. Willow sniffled, and Lou felt her eyes watering. She held the precious letter out toward Silas.

"She thought that was the letter they were going to give you. She thought she would get to explain herself?" Willow asked, her voice light with romance.

Silas nodded.

"But they didn't." Lou's tone was decidedly flatter.

Silas shrugged, surprising Lou with his nonchalance about the topic. "They knew if they'd handed me this letter that I would've gone after her; I would never have rested until I'd won her back. Them telling me she'd found another man and was happy with him was the smart thing to do. It made me let her go."

Lou drew in a breath and let it settle. "Well, I'm glad you're feeling okay about it all, but I feel awful for Frannie. Living with a controlling family like that must've led to a miserable life," Lou guessed.

"That's just the thing," Silas explained. "I got on the social medias you young'uns are always talking about, and I found her."

"You did?" Willow teased.

"Don't sound so surprised." Silas wagged a finger at Willow. "She's a widow, and she's living in Olympia." He smiled as he mentioned Washington's capital city, close to where Lou and Willow had grown up. "And I'm going to go see her."

Lou and Willow grinned, happy for their friend as he sauntered out the door.

Looking back at the Beanie Babies sitting on the counter, Lou pushed the Curly bear toward her best friend.

Willow's eyes lit up. "Wait. Are you sure?"

Lou nodded. "I know that was the one you wanted most, growing up."

Willow clutched the case and squealed. "You're the best friend a girl could ask for."

Lou thought of Frannie's letter to Silas. She gestured to the Always bear holding the rose. "Always and *fur*ever," she said with a chuckle.

ABOUT ERYN SCOTT

Eryn Scott is the author of heartwarming cozy mysteries. Her Whiskers and Words cozy mystery series features deep friendships, strong families, a tight-knit small town, twisty mysteries, and a whole lot of adorable cats. She and her husband live in the Pacific Northwest with a handful of beloved animals. She enjoys knitting, hiking, skiing, horseback riding, and reading.

6

WILD IRISH DREAMS

LISE MCCLENDON

Maybe it was a song on the radio. Or the precocious nature of the human mind. Or that cosmic finger dangling with ruby rings. When Quinn Meara showed up at the Second Sun Gallery two days after I dreamed about him, sneaking up and whispering, "Can it be the one and only Alix Thorssen, lass of m' heart," I felt an uneasy shiver. Not that I knock coincidence. Sometimes it feels like it's the only thing that makes sense in this crazy world.

Jackson Hole's summer season was winding down. Autumn was here with her golden aspens and blue skies. I'd given my salesman the afternoon off to hike in Yellowstone National Park before he headed back to Eugene for college. Soon the snow would make the Tetons' sheer granite cliffs treacherous. Labor Day weekend had been our last big hurrah and now, ten days later, most of the customers were the Winnebago set, doing the windshield tour before heading south for the winter.

Quinn had aged well, his Irish pallor suntanned, his black hair shiny but uncombed, nearly to his shoulders. It had been ten years, back when I'd been with my partner Paolo, since I'd seen him. Although his blue eyes tended to heat up around any woman – even me – Quinn had been just a friend, an aspiring artist who didn't quite have the drive, the talent, to make it to the big time. His appearance didn't surprise me. Maybe I expected him to walk through the door of the gallery. All of which seemed pretty weird to me, but, as I say, weird is the stuffing of this rag doll we call life.

I locked up early and took Quinn upstairs to my apartment. A mistake perhaps, but I was into whatever fickle stream of destiny I had going, excited to see an old friend, to catch up on his life.

His baggy khakis and black t-shirts, rundown Converse All-stars, same as always, were reassuring. He brought back memories of the happy days in New York when Paolo had taken me under his wing, when his friends became my friends, when I conquered my fears of the city and learned to laugh again. These thoughts led naturally to Paolo, the link between me and Quinn.

"So you haven't heard," I said, pouring him a beer. He took the glass, flopped onto the sofa. His clear brow was the answer. "Paolo's gone. He's—" Even after a year this wasn't easy. "He's dead, Quinn. He died last year."

Quinn frowned into his beer. I sat beside him. I hoped he didn't ask any questions about Paolo's violent death, but people usually did. I opened my mouth to head them off when he stood up suddenly.

"I can't believe it." He put his hand to his forehead, then over his mouth, gazing at nothing. "He can't be dead. I've come so far." He had a desperate look in his eyes for a moment, then glanced at me and winced. "I mean, I had so hoped to see him."

His voice held anger. I tried to figure it out, decipher his face. Then he closed his eyes, popped them open, and smiled. "I guess I haven't been a very good correspondent."

"You're in New York still?"

"Off and on." He paced with the beer in his hand, finally stopping at the window that had a slice of mountain view. "Can't believe I've never been here, all these years. I was in Nantucket for three summers, painting. It's to hell-and-gone out here in Wyoming. Why the hell did you move out here anyway? It's miles and miles from – well, from anything."

Dealing with this attitude was a daily grind in the gallery, and over the years I've found it best to simply change the subject. First I take the time to clench my molars. Then I think, they've had their say, established the center of the universe (wherever they're from), now can we please move on?

"You're still painting? That's great."

Distracted, he leaned on a stiff arm against the window frame. "Then. Lighthouses, seagulls, cute shit like that. I had to quit that." He turned to me, grave. "Paolo's really gone. That guy was so full of life, I figured he'd live forever."

"He was ready to go back to New York."

Quinn made a deprecating sound. "That would have been smart."

"What do you mean?"

"Nothing. Listen." He looked around the small apartment, with its blue walls, starry ceiling, and open kitchen, then peeked in the door to the solitary bedroom. "Mind if I crash on the couch? Just for a night, I promise. I'll look for a motel room tomorrow."

When I shrugged and said, "Sure," he gave me a bear hug and a hard smack on the lips that was way too exuberant, and inappropriate, to be romantic. This was where my better judgment came back from vacation and sent up the warning flag. But it was too late, he was taking me out for tacos I'd end up putting on my credit card and beers he found some other Irishman to pop for. By the end of the evening I was taking down pillows and comforters and tucking in Quinn on the sofa, and wondering what the hell I'd done. As it turned out, I wasn't the major perpetrator. But you knew that.

In the morning Quinn was dragging ass so I left him coffee and went to work. We had four paintings to ship and I needed my salesman to work the floor while I did that. Before long it was lunchtime and Quinn came bouncing down the back stairs, fresh from the shower. He helped me manhandle the largest frame into the crate, set the blocks, and hammer it in. I appreciated the help, I just had a suspicious nature, I told myself. He was a decent guy who wouldn't take advantage of a friend.

He leaned against the crate and pushed my dirty blonde hair from my eyes. "Could you see clear to letting me crash a couple more nights? I'm a little short. I've got to get to a bank and get things straightened out."

Getting things straightened out at the bank usually meant bad news. But I smiled. We all have troubles. I would hate it if a friend kicked me out when I was broke.

"Let's go to lunch. My treat." That lit up his Irish eyes.

Over bean sprouts and wheat germ I pecked away for information, nosy soul that I am. He took the train out, he said, since he doesn't own a car. Then a bus up from Rock Springs. He was so proud, he said, when he read the gold lettering on the plate glass window, saw the space, the bright, colorful, modern western art.

"I try," I said, always vulnerable to flattery. "It's not as easy as it was. No vacations unless I shut down the store. The help just isn't that reliable, always disappearing at the hint of greener pastures or snowier ski slopes."

Quinn set down his fork. "You need me? You got me."

"No, no. My salesman is great, and it's the slow season from now till Christmas."

He shrugged, a bit too quickly, went back to his salad, and I let out a silent breath of relief.

"Besides, you're on vacation, right?" I said. His smile wasn't one of pleasure. Well, New Yorkers just take longer to relax. "So if you're not painting, what are you doing now?"

"Finance. Stocks, investments."

Quinn with his long hair, ill-fitting clothes, worn-out shoes and empty wallet: Mr Wall Street? Right.

I toyed with the lettuce on my plate. "So, you're heading west from here, to Seattle? San Francisco?"

"South," he said. "Telluride, Santa Fe."

"I have a friend with a gallery in Santa Fe, you might look her up." Share the pain, friend, that's my motto. She was going to kill me.

"Probably won't be there long, but thanks." He flashed his smile again. His eyes jerked left as they followed someone behind me entering the café. "Now there is one beautiful woman."

Luca and I saw each other at the same time. She joined us. "Luca Segundo, this is my friend Quinn Meara from New York. Luca is Paolo's sister."

"From Argentina?" He grinned, appreciating her all over again. "Imagine that. I come to see Paolo and get something beyond my wildest dreams."

Luca smiled. As a gorgeous, exotic female she was too familiar with this sort of talk. She flicked her eyes at me in question. All I could do was raise my eyebrows. "Quinn knew Paolo in New York. Luca moved here after he died."

She put out her delicate hand. "Very nice to meet you, Mr Quinn. A friend of Paolo's is a friend of mine."

Quinn took her at her word. After we left the café, he stuck close to her down the wooden boardwalks and escorted her home rather than return to the gallery. Luca could take care of herself, but sooner or later we were going to have to have a talk about Quinn.

It came sooner than I thought. They arrived with a bottle of Argentinian wine as I was closing up the gallery. The two of them made a beeline for my apartment as if Luca was a little eager to get rid of the Irishman. They were talking about her homeland when I joined them upstairs, Quinn asking all kinds of questions and Luca doing her best to satisfy his curiosity. While he was in the bathroom, she leaned back on the sofa in relief.

"Santa Maria, that man has the gift of gabbing. He ask so many questions I think my head bursts."

"What about?"

"Everything! He want to know about our hometown, the old one up in the mountains, and also about Buenos Aires, the revolution, all the old stuff." She poured herself some more wine. "I bring him back to you. I am finished."

"Maybe he just saw *Evita* too many times." I made excuses to hasten her escape, but Quinn got in a last few questions about her country. As I put pasta on to boil, I wondered why he was so interested. At dinner, I asked.

"I have this travel bug. That's why I'm here." Quinn wrapped spaghetti around his fork and stuffed his mouth.

"You're going to Argentina?"

"Someday. You know. It's on the list."

"Did you get things straightened out down at the bank?"

Quinn slapped his forehead. "That woman was so beautiful, so interesting. Do you know she has sixteen varieties of orchids in that house? Incredible."

"That was Paolo's house," I said.

He sobered, nodding. Then finished off the wine in his glass.

The next morning when I stumbled out to start the coffee, Quinn was gone. A note on the counter explained, he was off to take muffins to Luca. And here I thought he'd left town, for shame. Maybe he was smitten, with Luca, with Argentina, with Evita, with ... muffins?

Just after seven that night he leaned on the emergency

buzzer at the gallery entrance, raising a ruckus. He was sweaty, panic in his sky eyes.

"What's the matter?"

"Nothing." He ran his hand through his hair and squinted into the street. "I just thought you weren't home. I guess I hit the buzzer a little hard." He tried to laugh.

Upstairs I gave him an old t-shirt to wear and noticed for the first time that he had brought no luggage with him. He showered, collected himself, put back on the dirty khakis, and rinsed the black shirt in the sink, draping it over the tub. At least he did laundry.

He didn't want to go out that night. He seemed preoccupied, twisting his hair like a girl. Somehow I liked him better as a blabbermouth. Now my instincts were to draw him out, cheer him up, at least get him drunk. But my efforts, weak as they were, failed.

I had another dream that night. Quinn was there, and Paolo. They were laughing, like the old times. Quinn had a big painting, an abstract, the kind of meaningless but colorful thing he did. Paolo was talking but I couldn't understand him. He had the most beautiful voice; I could hear it in my dream. Then something shifted. He put his foot right through Quinn's painting, ripping the canvas, destroying the piece. Then I was running, Quinn was running beside me, but I didn't want him there.

I woke up pounding the mattress with my legs, drenched in sweat. The moon was full over the square. I lay for a moment, something Paolo once said coming back: that Quinn wanted things, expected things to happen without the hard work. I mulled this, let it slip naturally into my picture of our old friend, and went back to sleep.

In the morning the coffee roused him. He stretched, smiled, and announced he would be leaving today.

"Oh? Where to?"

"South. It's cold up here already." He took the mug. "I never liked snow."

After breakfast he was gone. With nothing to pack it was a snap. I watched him skip across the square in the September sunshine, wished him well and wondered when I'd see that Irish face again.

That wonder lasted all of six hours. In mid-afternoon the policeman came by with a grainy photograph taken from the video recording system at Pioneer Bank's automated teller machine. There was Quinn, working hard with a screwdriver that looked suspiciously like mine.

I looked up at the policeman, a gnawing in my belly. On one hand he was my friend. That meant something. On the other hand, he was apparently a bank robber and I have a pretty solid need for justice. I don't like people who don't work for what they've got, and a molar gnashing started just thinking that he'd done this while he took my hospitality, such as it was, spaghetti and couch and all.

"Do you recognize him?" The policeman had caught the sadness in my face, that first step toward telling the awful truth.

"Yes." I sighed, rubbing my eyebrows. "He was staying with me here, for a few days. He left this morning."

The policeman blinked. "You better come down and make a statement."

By the time I got to the station the FBI had been called, as bank robbers were one of their specialties. I got through telling the sordid tale of Quinn the Houseguest to a lieutenant when the Feds arrived. They seemed pretty hot under the collar for a robbery where the perp made off with all of nine hundred bucks.

"Miss – Thorssen is it?" The man didn't remember me, but I remembered him. He'd once searched my underwear drawers. On duty, of course.

"Yessir. Newburg, is it?"

You had to hand it to him, he hardly batted an eye. "Do you recognize this man?"

He handed me a glossy photo of Quinn, this time taken at a distance, in a ball cap and holding a large caliber handgun in his hand. My heart sunk to new depths.

"That's him."

"Quinn Meara? Is that the name he gave you?"

"He's got other ones? What's he doing here?"

"Robbing the Jersey Atlantic National Bank in Newark."

"Okay." What else is there to say? They had pictures of him in the act. What was he thinking? "I suppose there are others."

"Not as clear. But we think he's been involved in five bank robberies since June."

"Making a career of it."

"So it would seem." Newburg slipped the photo back in his navy blazer. "A woman was killed in Pennsylvania, during a robbery. We have reason to believe Quinn Meara pulled the trigger."

I couldn't think of a damn thing to say. Outside the

golden sun sliced across the dry leaves on the sidewalk. Newburg went on: "Do you know where he was headed, Miss Thorssen?"

"South, he said. Telluride, Santa Fe. But he said he wouldn't be there long."

Newburg told one of his cronies to alert the Border Patrol.

"What kind of vehicle was he driving?"

"He didn't have a car," I said.

He said something about stolen vehicles to the crony. Then, "Do you know of any contacts he might have in Mexico?"

I shook my head. "Haven't seen him for ten years. And we were never close."

Newburg grimaced. "Just as well."

I turned to leave. "He did ask a friend questions about Argentina."

"His friend?"

"No, mine. My ex-partner's sister, she's from Argentina."

"I think you better take us to her, Miss Thorssen."

Paolo's bungalow at the base of Snow King Mountain glowed in the afternoon light over Teton Pass. Frost had zapped Luca's marigolds and pansies and lobelia, but a few hardy chrysanthemums held forth in the flower beds. The rosy door, its color chosen after consultation with thousands of paint chips, looked dusty. No one answered our knock.

Three agents and I waited on the stoop. Newburg gave a tip of his head to an agent who rounded the house. The other agent got his weapon out. I began to twitch. Newburg knocked again, harder, called for Luca. "Ms. Segundo? Please open the door."

I shrugged. "She has a rather active social life."

The agent returned from the backyard, shaking his head. Newburg tried the front door while two agents jumped around the lawn, peeking in windows. I hoped Luca wasn't taking a bath.

"I don't know why you think he's still in town," I said. "Would you hang around?"

Newburg was itching to give the door his shoulder, but my words were calculated to dissuade him. I let them take me home where I fixed a terrible TV dinner and tried to remember what Paolo had told me about Argentina, the mountains, the pampas, the cities. All I could really remember was his yearning, the loss of his mother country. And the way he looked when he did the flamenco.

I called Luca at seven, and again at eight. I was getting concerned. Maybe Quinn had taken her car – and herself – with him. At eight-thirty I couldn't stand it and hightailed it back over to the bungalow.

The place looked the same, windows dark, no porch light. I pounded on both doors then searched for a key Paolo used to hide under a flowerpot. But Luca had rearranged all the pots.

Back on the street, I called the police station on my cellphone. Newburg said they'd had no contact with Luca. They put a description of her vehicle out on an All Points Bulletin.

I knew better than to roam Jackson looking for a certain car. Between car rentals and four-wheel-drives, there were dozens of duplicates. Luca drove Paolo's white Jeep, of which there were legions. But if he wanted a different car? I headed toward the airport.

A flight had just arrived so the rental car booths were all staffed. I asked at Hertz, National, Budget. None of the clerks had been working during the day. I asked to see contracts, and was turned down flat. Then I saw Gina.

Gina Westermiller worked as a porter when she wasn't trying to be a pro snowboarder. Just five-two she was manhandling duffle bags and fishing rod cases and dog crates when I spotted her. Before I could dash down the short length of the terminal, she had loaded her hand truck and headed out the door. She greeted me with a grin, tossing her blonde hair back as she attacked the next set of luggage.

"Going somewhere, Alix?"

"Um, no. Just a question: If you take off on an international flight you have to show your passport, right?"

"Right."

I followed her outside with the luggage for a Crown Vic. She tossed the bags into the trunk like candy.

"So if somebody left here today one of the security guys would probably remember their passport."

"Are you kidding? People come here from all over the world." She rolled her truck back inside. "Besides that federal suit over there's been checking everybody's ID personally since I came on shift."

Somehow I'd missed the clean-cut agent chewing gum by the vending machines. I thanked Gina and made my way over. He straightened defensively but when I introduced myself my name seemed to ring a bell.

"Quinn Meara was staying with me. I think he may have a friend of mine along as – well, have her along."

"Luca Segundo?"

"Right. But coming out here, flying under his own passport, that can't be smart."

"The boy isn't known to be particularly smart. If you know what I mean."

Driving back to town, I figured Quinn had bugged out of that airport first thing in the morning if he was using his own passport. *If.* Then it hit me. The real reason he'd come to Jackson. He knew Paolo was dead. If Quinn cut his hair, put in brown contacts, he could pass for Paolo. The dark hair, the tan. With Luca along they'd look like husband and wife, and she could do all the talking. Where had he gotten hold of Paolo's passport? From Luca's, of course.

I sat in my Saab in the alley behind the gallery, trying to figure out if I could sleep. Luca was out there somewhere with a desperate man on the run. I figured she could handle herself, but not like this, not with a man who probably had a gun, hunted by the cops from here to Timbuktu.

I had set the whole thing up for him. If he hadn't known about Luca from me, he probably would have split. There would be time for recriminations. But now the questions remained: What would he do with her, where would he dump her, what shape would she be in? He'd killed before, or so the FBI believed. I only hoped he wanted Luca's help through Argentinian immigration.

I slapped the Saab's steering wheel. What if they drove somewhere else, then got on an international flight? The FBI would have alerted the airlines. He would be on a no-fly list.

Would they drive to Salt Lake, Denver, Santa Fe? A lot of miles, many chances of discovery. How else does one get long distances without being noticed?

The train. He said he'd come to Rock Springs by train. But there was no passenger service to Wyoming; Amtrak had ditched us years ago. He must have hitched out in a boxcar. Or taken a bus. He wouldn't chance that now. But there was a once-daily freight train traveling up the old Union Pacific spur to Jackson in the summer months. I wasn't sure of the schedule, but I sometimes heard the whistle late at night.

I squealed out of the alley and headed toward the makeshift depot, a dark string of painted wooden buildings on a raised platform in South Park. As I steered down the hill into the grassy pastures now dotted with housing developments and soccer fields, I could see the lights of the depot shining on rust-colored boxcars and fat black oil cars. After midnight now, men still worked, uncoupling, loading, unloading freight. I scanned the gravel parking lot for the white Jeep but didn't see it.

If Quinn and Luca were here they were either already aboard, having jumped on as soon as the train arrived, or were waiting until just before it left. The first man I found was an over-bulked weightlifter without a neck who didn't deign to answer questions. The next fellow, older with close-cropped reddish-gray hair, was just as muscular but obviously from hard work.

"Shoulda left ten minutes ago. Soon as we get these crates on, she's gone."

I occupied myself with the Coke machine while they used a forklift to get the last crates aboard. Then an official-looking dude came out with a clipboard and told them they hadn't uncoupled one of the cars. Grumbling, two men went down to the end of the string of twenty-some cars. Some clanging and cursing later, the job was done.

The night was cool. I pulled my pile jacket tight around me. The cold can of soda didn't help the chill on my hands. The men's breath made foggy clouds around the platform as they gave me sidelong looks. What was I doing here? What was I going to do if Quinn—

Movement in the shadows between the boxcars. I walked down the platform, checking underneath, between. I jumped down to the gravel and dry weeds, leaving the Coke can behind. Dust and chilly air blew up from the ground. Someone hollered at the depot and a hoot went up.

I heard a bump. Not sure where it had come from, I ran along side, trying the doors. Soon the train would be taking off, my window was closing. The third boxcar from the last was empty, its door ajar.

"Luca!"

I called her name again and heard a scuffling. "Quinn, are you there? I came to warn you. The FBI is everywhere." Quiet. "I know you're there, Quinn."

They emerged from the shadowed corner as the train began to roll. I walked along, keeping the door at my shoulder. "Luca! Are you all right?"

"What about the FBI?" Quinn had, as I suspected, cut his hair, badly. He had Luca by the arm. She looked scared, her long hair loose and wild.

"They know you broke into the ATM, Quinn. They know your name."

"Thanks to you, I suppose. Are they with you?" He stepped back, pulling Luca. The train was picking up speed. I began to jog.

"I just came to warn you. And maybe to—" I sucked air. The older freight man was looking at me curiously as I jogged by the platform in the narrow space between it and the cars. It occurred to me, glancing at the crunching steel wheels, that this wasn't so brilliant. "To convince you to let Luca go."

"Please, Quinn. I have helped—" Luca said softly.

"I need you in Buenos Aires."

"You don't need her, Quinn, you've got the passport. Let her go." Then he showed me the gun. "Quinn, don't." My chest was heaving, the words faint.

He pointed the gun at me. "Stay out of it, Alix."

Running hard now in the dark on the slanted gravel bed for the tracks, I tried a last time. "As a favor to Paolo. He was your friend."

My foot hit a large rock. I spun in mid-air, saw the face of the kindly freighter as I went down. Later I felt this was one of those cosmic hand things again. At that moment the brakes were applied, an awful, screeching noise, as I fell into the gravel not a foot from the tracks. I rolled away, felt the thump of a bullet in the dirt behind me, and saw Luca at the door of the boxcar.

"Jump, Luca!"

The crunching footsteps and a zing of another bullet made me lower my face to the dirt, but not before I saw Luca's terrified face as she leapt off the train. I got to my hands and knees, scrambling toward the crumpled form.

Luca was curled up, holding her ankle and moaning. The train stopped. The sound of a heavy door sliding announced my freighter's arrival in the opposite side of the car. It took him a couple seconds to kick Quinn out the door and another second to jump down and knock the gun out of his hand. As the FBI took Quinn away later, I heard the freighter tell Newburg: "I got no truck with freeloaders."

Luca and I both thanked him before I whisked her away to the emergency room. The freighter stood in the small crowd of his coworkers, workingman's hands on his hips, his dirty coveralls on his massive frame, a satisfied grimace on his weathered face.

I went back the next evening to shake his hand, to thank him for saving Luca's life, and mine. The night air was crisp, the stars in their places. The cosmic dust had settled. Quinn's wild dreams of easy fortune had come to a screeching halt. My Irish dreams had been fulfilled by an appropriate savior.

Stitched in red on the freighter's burly chest, his name: *O'Leary.*

ABOUT LISE MCCLENDON

Lise McClendon is the author of numerous novels of crime and suspense. Her bestselling Bennett Sisters Mysteries continue to charm readers worldwide. Her first mystery series was set in Jackson, Wyoming, featuring art dealer, Alix Thorssen. When not writing about foreign lands and dastardly criminals, Lise lives in Montana with her husband and has recently become a fan of sunny winters in the desert. She enjoys fly fishing, hiking, picking raspberries in the summer, and cross-country skiing in the winter. She has served on the national boards of directors of Mystery Writers of America and the International Association of Crime Writers/North America, as well as the faculty of the Jackson Hole Writers Conference.

7

ARCHITECT OF A MURDER

CARLENE O'CONNOR

Tara Meehan's phone alerted her to a voicemail just as she reached Renewals, her architectural salvage shop in Galway, Ireland. According to the time stamp the call had come in an hour ago, but her phone had been in silent mode. She pushed the play button with one hand as she fumbled in her handbag for her keys with the other. And although the wind was indeed at her back, it resulted in her black hair flying into her face, making it difficult to see what she was doing.

When she finally got it all sorted she learned the message was from Andrew Harding, the renowned architect whose sale she was hosting today. And although she'd only spoken to him a handful of times, there was no mistaking his tone. He sounded distressed. She put the message on speaker as she entered her shop and his voice filled up all five-hundred square feet of the shop.

"*Tara, it's Andrew Harding. I was hoping to reach you. I'm afraid* The Lady of the Lough *has been spoken for. Between you and me I had no choice. I've called the interested parties personally and I'm afraid I've ruffled some feathers. I was going to display her anyway, but a very particular client can no longer be trusted. I am going to sneak into your patio a little early to remove her before they arrive. Clients can be horrid!"*

He'd ended the call without saying goodbye. She'd given him the key to the shop, and she had already told him he was welcome to set up the sculptures on her private back patio whenever he liked, but she was taken aback by his message. *The Lady of the Lough*, a gorgeous stone sculpture, was Andrew Harding's latest acquisition. He had heard of Tara's shop through her Uncle Johnny who owned an architectural salvage mill by the Galway Bay, and she'd graciously agreed to host a private sale for him.

Her patio was intimate and cozy, the perfect place to arrange his multiple garden sculptures for sale – the rarest and most coveted being *The Lady of the Lough*. Why on earth had he sold it before the bargaining could even begin? Which of his clients was the horrid one? Hopefully not one of the three coming today. She'd been told there were three buyers all drooling to acquire the stone lady and they would be battling it out this afternoon. Tara was getting a percentage of the sales for hosting and of course she hoped they'd have a nose around her shop while they were here. Andrew Harding had wealthy clients who, like her, had a passion for architectural wares.

What did he mean, he had no choice?

She entered her shop, deposited her handbag on the counter, and turned to survey her domain, imagining everyone's first impression. Located just off the pedestrianized Shop Street just up from the Galway Bay, this was Tara Meehan's happy place. She'd opened it a few years ago after working at her uncle's architectural salvage mill, Revivals. A transplant from New York City and an interior designer, Tara had decorated the shop herself. It was her lifelong dream.

A crystal chandelier sourced from an Irish manor house hung in the center of the shop, illuminating bamboo floors. A series of antique cabinets displayed a rotating selection of hand-picked items, and old Guinness advertising signs hung at varying heights on the walls. White orchids topped surfaces, sculptures stood in every corner, and fireplace accoutrements were set up near the small working fireplace. On the mantel, she displayed antique brass and iron candleholders. She'd personally chosen every single item in the shop. Pottery from the eighteen-hundreds was gathered in one section; vases, tiles, and antique fixtures in another. Stone lions, which she priced high enough that she wouldn't sob if anyone bought them, flanked the fireplace. The cabinet by the register was filled with antique jewelry. A small section of crystal glassware occupied shelves in the middle. Old doorknobs and decorative knockers were laid out on an old wooden barrel with *Jameson* carved on the side. And her favorite bit about the shop was that it had French doors leading out onto a private patio. *Heaven.*

On the patio, larger architectural items, such as old wrought wrought-iron gates, were stacked up against the back of the building along with garden sculptures and fountains. Summer was coming, and despite the rain, (or maybe because of it) the demand for garden statues was peaking. Harding's men had delivered half a dozen statues for the sale, and they were currently set up on the patio draped in white cloth until the big reveal. She had assumed *The Lady of the Lough* was one of them, but now she wasn't so sure. And what about Andrew? Had he snuck in, removed sculpture and left? Or was he still here? If he'd left - was he leaving her on her own to deal with his clients?

Tara had been more than happy to host, but was he really dumping all of this in her lap at the last minute? Given the date to this little affair had already been abruptly changed – apparently one of his clients said today was the only day that could possibly work – she was already on edge. A storm was expected in a few hours, and most of Galway planned on staying home.

Tara glanced at her floors, which had been mopped just last night – and noticed a large set of muddy prints going out to the patio, which someone had done a poor job of attempting to wipe away. There were smears every few feet. She followed the partial footsteps out to the patio. Strung with lights that were now off, and dotted with planters and a bench, the featured garden sculptures were covered in white sheets. To the left of the bench was a sundial on a pillar, and since it did not belong to Tara, she assumed it was a part of the sale, but not so fetching that it deserved a dramatic unveiling.

"Mr Harding?" she called out. The muddy boot prints continued, and she followed them to the very last covered statue near the stone bench. There, they stopped. As if he'd been standing here one minute and had evaporated into thin air the next. She shook her head, a feeling of dread rising in her out of nowhere. She continued around the patio. It came to a dead-end straight ahead. At her feet lay a pool of red. *Blood.* Tara screamed and jumped back.

"Are you alright?" a voice called out.

Tara screamed again and turned to see three figures stepping out onto her patio from inside the shop. Three middle aged persons stood in front of her, a woman flanked by two men. It was the woman who inquired as to her well-being. She had dyed blonde hair and a black trench coat. She was wearing three-inch heels, and Tara made a mental note to warn her not to get them caught in the patio stones. Perhaps she should have warned all of them to wear sensible shoes, but that was the least of her worries at the moment.

Tara shook her head. "There's blood."

"Are you injured?" the man on the left said. He was bald with a red goatee, and was casually dressed. Tara couldn't help but notice his boots. Had he been here earlier?

"I'm not the cause of the blood," Tara said. "I'm trying to find out what's going on."

"That sounds mysterious," said the remaining man as he smoothed down his salt-and-pepper hair. He wore a fitted gray suit and black pointy shoes. The woman took a step forward. Tara held up her hand. They all stopped in their tracks. Tara edged forward past the last covered sculpture, and that's when she saw the body. Andrew Hastings, the architect. His eyes and mouth were wide open and there was a red slit across his throat. The bottom of his boots were muddy. Blood pooled and snaked around him, seeping into the stones.

Tara's hands flew to her mouth. She whirled around. "Go inside."

"What on earth is the matter?" the woman cried out, as she elbowed the men in front of her to have a gawk.

Tara held up her hand once more. "Andrew Hastings is dead," she said.

∽

Dark clouds swirled overhead as they waited on the footpath for the guards. The whipping wind brought the scent of the ocean, mixed with the yeasty tang of last night's ale. A stunned silence hung over the group. Tara formally introduced herself, hoping to get the three talking. The woman stepped forward, confident in her heels. "I'm Victoria Martin."

The burly man tipped his tweed cap. "Kevin O'Leary."

It wasn't until the thin man felt everyone's eyes on him that he spoke up. "Gregory Trust."

"When did Hastings arrive?" Victoria asked.

Tara shook her head. "I received a voicemail from him over an hour ago, but I didn't listen to it until minutes before I discovered him."

"Barely dead an hour," Kevin said. "Who would do such a thing?"

"I knew there was something strange about his message," Victoria said. "To whom did he give *Lady of the Lough*?"

"You mean sell to the highest bidder," Kevin said. "Hastings was all about money."

"How does he know we wouldn't have paid *more*?" Gregory said. "This is quite the betrayal!"

Tara was gobsmacked. Poor Andrew Hastings was dead, and they were all still concerned about the sculpture? Horrid is right.

"I'm sorry," Victoria said as if reading Tara's mind. "No matter what – he didn't deserve to die." She dabbed underneath her eyes as if expecting to find a tear.

"Do you think this was a random attack?" Kevin asked.

Tara thought about that. If the killer was long gone, he or she must have escaped through her shop. There was no way out of the patio unless someone had scaled ten-foot stone walls. Technically it was possible, but there was nothing but a narrow path between buildings on the other side of the patio walls. Definitely not enough room to cart off a sculpture. It was too heavy to carry for long and no vehicles could drive behind the wall. Was the *Lady of the Lough* still on the patio?

Or had Andrew Hastings forgotten to lock the shop door behind him and someone devious had followed him in? Or was his killer one of the three standing in front of her?

"Did you all arrive together?" Tara asked.

They shook their heads. "I stayed at the Galway Inn," Victoria said. "I walked here after enjoying a nice breakfast just down the way."

"I drove," Kevin said. "My lorry is parked a few blocks from here."

"Why did you drive your lorry?" Victoria asked, squinting.

"To bring home my sculptures," Kevin said.

"We weren't going to be allowed to bring them home today," Victoria said. She turned to Tara. "Isn't that right?"

Tara nodded. "I was told I would have the sculptures to display for the entire month. You all agreed to it."

Kevin crossed his arms. "So I drove my lorry. It's my mode of transportation. And I thought maybe there was a chance she wouldn't need all those sculptures hanging around."

"I took the bus," Gregory said. "I intended to have my pieces shipped." He glanced at Tara. "After the month of course."

"This means *The Lady of the Lough* should be here," Kevin said. "No matter what scoundrel stole it from beneath us. Isn't that right?" Anger flashed in him. This was not a calm man.

"I believe that was the plan," Tara said. "Only his voicemail suggested he'd thought better of it." He'd come here early this morning to remove her. Because of a horrid client. Someone *knew* he'd promised the sculpture to someone else. And that someone could not bear it.

"Did he tell you who bought *Lady of the Lough*?" Victoria asked.

"He did not," Tara said.

"What did he mean by he had no choice—?" Kevin looked at the other two.

"That's exactly what he said to me," Tara said. "I think maybe someone was threatening him."

"That doesn't surprise me," Victoria piped in. "I play poker with Andrew Hastings at the beginning of every month. Lately he's been losing. And when he loses, he drinks. And when he drinks – he's unpredictable. Even violent." Her eyes flicked to Gregory Trust. "Isn't that right?"

Gregory's upper lip began to sweat. "Whatever do you mean?"

Victoria placed her hand on his arm. "I heard him humiliating you last week. At that antique shop."

"You were there?" Gregory's voice squeaked.

Victoria nodded. "I heard you tell him he was dead to you."

"That's j-just a figure of sp-speech," Gregory stammered.

"What did he say that upset you so?" Victoria pressed. "Did he confess that he'd sold *Lady of the Lough*?"

"I didn't kill him," Gregory said.

Kevin whirled on him. "Did you know?"

"Yes," Gregory said. "I went to find out more about the *Lady of the Lough* and I could tell right away that my questions upset him. He told me it was no longer for sale."

Victoria and Kevin both took a step back. Gregory wiped his lip with his sleeve. "I didn't kill him," he repeated. "I've never hurt a fly."

"I haven't had a chance to learn much about the *Lady of the Lough*," Tara said. "I take it she's quite valuable?"

"She's rumored to be off a sunken ship," Gregory said. "And she'd been submerged for over fifty years. That was enough to pique my interest."

Victoria stepped in and lowered her voice as if someone might be listening. "I was told she belonged to a very wealthy family back in the day, and she's originally from Rome."

"I come to every sale Andrew has," Kevin said. His

shoulders slumped. "Poor Hastings," he said. "Murdered over a slab of stone."

Victoria grabbed Tara's arm. "Can you tell us – how was he killed?"

The other two scooted in, their eyes wide with interest.

"I'm going to leave that to the guards," Tara said.

"Could it have been a heart attack?" Gregory said.

Tara shook her head.

"There was blood," Victoria said. "We all saw it."

"True," Gregory said. "But perhaps whilst having a heart attack, he fell and hit his head on a stone." He looked to the others for confirmation.

"Plausible," Kevin said.

"No," Tara said.

"Was he shot?" Victoria asked. "Stabbed?" She sounded somewhat excited.

"She said leave it to the guards," Gregory said. "She doesn't trust us." He sucked in his cheeks which made his already gaunt face look downright skeletal. Tara could easily imagine him blending in with one of the stone sculptures.

"Us?" Kevin turned to Tara and jabbed his finger at her. "You were the only one who was alone with him."

Tara took a step back. "I wasn't alone with him. I'd only just arrived."

"We only have your word for that," Kevin said. He looked at Gregory who shrugged.

"It's her shop," Victoria said. "Do you really think she wants a murder on her premises? She'll be lucky if she ever gets another customer."

Gee, thanks. "It will do us no good to argue," Tara said. "I have nothing to hide, but when I do tell what I know it will be to the guards."

"She's right of course," Victoria said. "And to think. It could have been one of us!"

Whether she meant one of them had killed him, or one of them could have been killed, Tara hadn't a clue. It was surreal, that a living human was dead because of an inanimate object. The depravity of human beings never failed to horrify her.

Just then lights and sirens could be heard, and soon the guards were pulling up to the curb. Tara recognized the tall Detective Sergeant with the weary eyes.

"Ms. Meehan," he said with a tip of his cap.

"Detective Sergeant Gable," Tara said. "I'm so relieved to see you."

Sergeant Gable glanced at her visitors, then rubbed his chin. "Please tell me you've called me out here under false pretenses and there's not a dead man anywhere in the vicinity."

"I would," Tara said. "If only I could."

∼

SERGEANT GABLE HELPED Tara suit up with protective boots and gloves so that she could walk him through the scene while they waited for the Technical Bureau to arrive. First she pointed out the partially wiped prints on the floor inside her shop. She reminded him that the killer would have had to exit the same way.

"Odd," he said.

"The killer made an attempt to disguise his or her footprints," Tara said.

Gable removed his garda cap and scratched his head. "Why not just wipe away all of them?"

"I suppose the killer was in a hurry," Tara said. "If I were you, I would ask our three suspects to hand over their shoes for examination."

"Our three suspects?" Gable thumbed toward the entrance. "That lot outside?"

"Yes. They were all hoping to purchase *The Lady of the Lough*." She took out her phone and pressed play on Andrew's message.

Gable's brows furled as he listened.

"What if one of them is the horrid client?" said Tara.

"Hastings said he had no choice," said the sergeant. "You have no idea what he meant?"

"I didn't when I first listened to it. But now I wonder if he was being physically threatened."

Gable nodded his head, conceding it was a possibility. "Do you think he was leaving the message while this person was threatening him?"

Tara chewed her lip. "It's possible."

"But if he was giving this person what he or she wanted, why was Andrew Hastings killed?"

"Maybe after he hung up he changed his mind." No one liked to be bullied. It was human nature. "But you're right. It doesn't really fit, does it?" As a designer, she always needed patterns to fit. Her theory was slightly off.

Gable's face looked as if it carried the weight of the world. "Is this 'Lady Sculpture' on your patio?"

"I haven't a clue," Tara said. "I didn't remove the sheets."

"Show me."

Tara took him to the patio. She gestured to the six sculptures covered in white sheets. "The sundial isn't mine either," she said, pointing to the stone pedestal it was mounted on near the bench.

"Not much use for a sundial today," Gable remarked, tilting his head to the gray skies.

Tara sighed. "We were supposed to do this on a sunnier day, but one of them had to change dates at the last minute because 'only today would do'."

Gable tilted his head. "Do you think that has something to do with his murder?"

"Again. At the time I didn't, but now I'm questioning everything."

"You would have made a fine detective, Ms. Meehan," Gable said as they headed for the body.

The compliment meant a lot coming from him. They hadn't always seen eye-to-eye. As a designer, Tara was highly attuned to patterns. And the tiniest new element could either make or break a design. Investigations were no different. One had to take in the entire picture and then try and figure out what didn't belong. *Or who...*

Gable neared the body. "His throat was slit," he said. "Most likely from behind."

"The two men are about his height," Tara said. "But Victoria is much shorter." Even in three-inch heels.

Gable surveyed the stone wall that surrounded the patio. "Couldn't this be a random attack? Perhaps a drunk that wandered by?"

"Nobody 'wanders' over a ten-foot stone wall. And there's barely room for one person on the other side." Tara glanced in the bushes where she saw a tiny flash of white.

"What's that?" She approached and pointed to it.

Gable crossed over, then lifted out another white sheet. It was covered in dirt, and leaves and blood. There were two medium-sized holes cut out of it, shoulder-length apart.

"What in the world...?" Gable said.

Tara surveyed her patio until she spotted a path clear of debris. She was starting to see a picture form. "Can you take the sheets off the sculptures?" she asked Gable.

He put his hands on his hips as if she were putting him out. "What will that prove?"

"I want to see if *The Lady of the Lough* is here."

"And if she is?"

"Then my theory might be wrong."

Gable sighed. "And if she isn't?"

"In his message he indicated that even though the Lady was 'spoken for' he needed to come and remove her because of one particular client." *Horrid* was the word he'd used. "So not only did he sell her, he was still going to show her off."

"Until one of his clients became so irate he realized the folly of his decision."

"Exactly," Tara said. "But this client was determined to get *The Lady of the Lough* before he had it carted away."

"Do you really think someone would commit murder over a garden statue?"

"You tell me Detective. Do people always have sane reasons to murder?"

His face fell. "I'm beginning to regret asking you to accompany me."

"This is a rare antique sculpture. Rumored to belong to a rich Roman family back in the day. While being transported to Ireland it fell off a ship, and was submerged for fifty years before she was recovered." Tara threw open her arms. "The wild and eerie story alone makes it invaluable to a collector."

Gable shook his head as if he thought that was madness. And of course, it was. But no more mad than anything else humans killed each other over. Whether people collected coins, or stamps, or trains, or garden statues – collectors could become feverish – and indeed so feverish one might even kill for it.

They passed the sundial and stone bench on their way to the first garden sculpture. He whipped off the sheet. Beneath it was an angel.

He approached the second one. A Celtic Cross.

The third was a sculpture of a hooded monk.

The fourth a pair of cherubs.

The fifth was a roaring lion.

The sixth was a large stone face.

None of the other sheets had blood or holes cut in them. Seven sheets. Six sculptures.

"Well?" Gable said. "Have you cracked the case?"

"I have," Tara said, ignoring his condescending tone. "But I'm going to need you to get her confession."

His mouth dropped open. "Her?"

"I believe Victoria Martin is our killer."

Gable crossed his arms. "Indulge me."

"There appear to be only one set of prints into the shop. They were partially wiped away."

He nodded. "Go on, so."

"There's a reason our killer only needed to partially wipe away the prints. I'll get to that in a minute." Tara pointed out the path that was clear of debris. It led from the stone bench to the body. "I believe Andrew was standing here when his throat was slit." She demonstrated by standing next to the bench with her back to it. "He was placing a white sheet on the last of the sculptures." She pointed to the sundial. "That's not mine." Using gloved hands, she removed the crude metal piece that made up the dial in the center of the pedestal. It was sharp. A red splotch dotted the end.

"Is that blood?" Gable asked.

"I believe it's Andrew's blood. And I believe this sundial belongs to the killer."

"This I've got to hear."

"It's the murder weapon, Detective. She was standing on this bench, covered in a white sheet when Andrew approached."

"She."

Tara nodded. "I believe Victoria Martin is our killer. When she learned Hastings was surrendering the sculpture to someone else, she became enraged. She must have been waiting for him at the shop – slipped in after him."

"The holes through the sheets," Gable said.

"Arm holes," Tara said. "Standing on the bench in her heels, she would have been able to lean over and slit his throat. She then used the sheet to drag his body to a new location."

Gable followed the path where indeed it looked as if something had been dragged. "Why did she need to move the body?"

"She was hoping we'd overlook the bench and the sundial. She was hoping you'd think that no murder weapon equals a random killer who escaped with it. That you'd be on the lookout for a madman with a knife. But this dial is old and quite sharp. It would do the trick."

"And the footprints?" he asked.

"She only needed to wipe part of the prints, the tip of her heels on the floor. The dot from the heel would blend in nicely with Hasting's muddy boot prints."

"Fascinating," he said.

"Before you arrived Victoria Martin let it slip that she played poker with Andrew Hastings. I believe he lost *The Lady of the Lough* in a poker game. That's what he meant by he had no choice. She must have planned this murder in advance, knowing she'd use the sundial as the perfect murder weapon. That's why she wanted to do it on a day we were expecting a storm. Who would notice a sundial on a stormy day?"

Gable blinked hard. "What does she get out of this? If he already sold the sculpture?"

"He sold it, but he was still going to let them have a gawk at her, remember?"

"But it's not here," Gable said.

Tara held up a finger then stood on the bench and peered over the wall. There on the other side was a sculpture covered in yet another white sheet. Most likely swiped from the Galway Inn. "She's here," Tara said. "Waiting to be picked up."

"You've amazed me," Gable said. "But I assume Ms. Martin wore gloves. How do we prove it?"

"Do you want the hard way or the fun way?" Tara asked.

Gable couldn't help himself. He laughed. "Let's hear the fun way."

"Have another guard come back here, safely remove the statue, hide behind the sheet, and wait for Victoria Martin to come to *you*."

∽

TARA SPRITZED CLEANER on the cloth and wiped down her glass counters. A month had passed since the murder, and she was having a do-over. Soon many of Andrew Hastings collection would be on sale. But this time his killer, Victoria Martin, would not be in attendance. She was behind bars where she belonged. The scream she'd let out when she'd snuck back behind the wall to fetch *The Lady of the Lough*, only to find Detective Sergeant Gable hiding beneath the sheet, was something Tara would never forget. She'd been given such a fright that her confession poured out of her all at once.

Tara's patio had been power-washed, and in the spot where Hastings had been so brutally murdered, Tara had placed one her other favorite sculptures from his collection: a stone angel. Andrew of all people would not want his murder to shut down Tara's shop. Their shared passion for architectural salvage was stronger than any horrid client could ever be. She flicked on the patio lights, then turned back to put on the kettle. The sun was making a rare appearance, and cookies fresh from her oven at the mill sat on the counter, emitting an enticing aroma. A purple and yellow butterfly flitted around the angel statue, then gently landed on one of her wings. It was a grand day for a garden sale.

ABOUT CARLENE O'CONNOR

Carlene O'Connor is the USA Today bestselling author of The Irish Village Mysteries, Home to Ireland Mysteries, and the new County Kerry Mystery series. Her mysteries have been translated into German, Estonia, and UK markets thus far and the Irish Village Mysteries have been optioned for television. Readers are encouraged to get in touch via Facebook, Goodreads, Book Bub, or through the contact form on CarleneOConnor.net. An admitted wanderer, Carlene spends as much time in Ireland as possible while currently residing in California and Chicago. She is always up for joining events via Zoom or in person.

8

BLOOMS AND BLACKMAIL

LONDON LOVETT

"That is a fog to beat all fogs, and I've seen fog as thick as my mother's Christmas gravy." Les swept his slightly gnarled fingers across the shoulders of his coat as if the fog had left flakes like snow. While his left hand dusted off the invisible fog particles, his right handed me a mocha latte. Les's coffee shop was located quite conveniently (and by convenient I meant just thirty steps from my flower shop; yes, I'd counted them) next door. Les winked. "Added in a dash of cinnamon, just for you. It'll help take the chill out of your bones."

"You're the best coffee barista a girl could have." I took a sip and had to wriggle my nose to rid it of the cinnamon smell. Don't get me wrong. I adore cinnamon, with its holiday-ish nostalgia and ability to liven up any sweet treat, as much as the next person, but my nose has superpowers. At least, that's what my fiancé, James Briggs, calls it. He's the local detective, and I'd helped him, on more than one occasion (a humble brag), solve a murder by using my extreme sense of smell. Unfortunately, my talented nose also tended to amplify every fragrance, aroma, and smell. Even the good ones like cinnamon.

Les caught my nose wriggle. His brows hopped up like fluffy gray caterpillars that had had too much caffeine. "On no, did I overdo the cinnamon? I always forget about – you know—" He tapped the side of his own nose as if the whole super sense of smell was to be kept secret from my nose.

I laughed. "It's alright to talk about it in front of my nose."

He blushed. "You're right. Silly of me. I think some of that fog has entered my brain."

Les startled briefly when Kingston, my pet crow, decided he needed to be part of the conversation. He landed on the work island and paced back and forth, hoping he'd be noticed. As if it was possible to ignore a large, shiny black bird in the middle of a flower shop. "I think King wants a treat."

Les hurried around to the shelf under the work island where I kept a can of the peanut butter flavored treats his sister, Elsie, baked especially for my bird. Elsie's superb shop, the Sugar and Spice Bakery, was thirty-three steps in the opposite direction of Les's coffee shop. My flower shop, Pink's Flowers, was squeezed between fluffy baked goods and frothy, hot coffees. Not too shabby, eh?

The door pushed open and Lola stood there. The fog that had rolled in from the beach to all but smother Port Danby curled in around her black boots. "What is with that fog?" She didn't brush fog off her coat, but she did stomp her boots a few times as if shaking off the cold, damp weather.

My shop was also located directly across the street from my best friend Lola's antique shop. It was both good and bad, depending on whatever mood Lola was in. She'd just gotten back from a two-day trip up the coast where they were having a massive antique sale, so I was happy to see her. Her husband, Ryder, was my shop assistant. He was off on his own adventure for a few days, camping with his father.

"How was the trip?" I took another sip of coffee.

"I found some things that I think will sell fast, but boy-oh-boy are those sellers up north hard-nosed about bargaining. Had to pull out my bad cop-good cop act."

Les looked up from feeding Kingston his treat. "What is that?" he asked before I could shake my head and tell him not to ask.

Lola was only too happy to explain. "See, I come in with this polite, naïve persona. I call her Lolly because she's sweet like the candy. I act as if I have no idea what something is worth or, for that matter, what the item is."

"In other words, Lolly is clueless." I circled back around the work island to finish arranging a crocus bouquet. As cut flowers they tended to be difficult because they had short stems, but the customer had insisted they were his wife's favorite.

Lola tilted her head side to side. "I suppose you could call her that. As Lolly, I beg and plead to get the price marked down – the whole, oh, but my mother would love this for her birthday and I only have a little money because my car broke down or some such thing. When Lolly's big, teary eyes don't work—" Lola paused to show Les her pleading look "—See that, like a puppy dog wanting a treat. But if the seller's heart is made of stone—"

I paused my flower arranging. "You do realize that the whole Lolly story is fake, right? Chances are the seller is seeing straight through your academy audition."

Lola waved off my comment. "Anyhow, when that doesn't work, I tuck Lolly away and bring out Lucy, named after my favorite *Peanuts* character. Let's just say she's a no-nonsense, very pushy, know-it-all. I quickly let the seller know exactly what their antique is and how much it is worth on the wholesale market. Then I point out all the flaws that will make it hard to sell, and with enough persistence and a few angry glares—" This time she stopped to show Les her serious glower expression.

Les glanced over at me. "It's crazy, but at the same time, I'm impressed."

"You see," Lola said with a satisfied grin. "And it works too. I bought myself this necklace. Although I never had to bring out Lucy. After Lolly, the seller practically gave it to me for free. I think it's from the Edwardian era." Lola lifted a gold necklace out from under her sweater. An Art Nouveau, curvaceous gold heart adorned with three pearls hung from a glittering chain.

I circled around to get a better look. "That is pretty. Is it real gold?"

"Sure is. I saw it in her case and asked her to pull it out for me. She got this weird look on her face, as if I was asking her to touch something radioactive. She lifted it out of the case like it might burst into flames. Weirdest thing ever. When I asked her how much, she told me three dollars. I had to ask her twice because I felt as if I was stealing it at that price. When I hesitated, she dropped the price to a buck. I gave her the dollar, and she handed it off as fast as she could."

"Maybe it's stolen?" I asked. "That seems very strange."

Lola tucked the necklace back under her sweater. "No, I think it has more to do with the curse. Her assistant followed me out of the booth and warned me that the necklace was worn by an old matron at the turn of the century. Her husband murdered her while she was wearing the necklace, and supposedly there's been some bad luck for previous owners, but it's all a bunch of silly superstition." She headed toward the door. "Come over later and look at this sweet little oak tea table I bought. You were talking about adding some antiques to the décor in here. I think it'll look great in the window with some flower vases on top." With that, Lola stepped out of the shop and back into the fog. Seconds later, tires screeched out front.

Les and I raced out the door. Lola was still on our side of the road breathing hard as if she'd just run a marathon. A car had come to a sudden stop in front of the shop. The driver rolled down the window. "I didn't see you in all this fog. Are you all right?"

Lola waved a shaky hand at the woman. "Didn't see you either." The woman drove on but at a snail's pace.

"Lola, that was close." My heart was pounding. All three of us stood at the edge of the sidewalk, looking both ways to make sure there were no cars coming. A shaken Lola stepped cautiously off the curb and hurried across to her shop.

Les and I looked at each other. We didn't say a word, but I

knew we were both thinking about the same thing: the cursed necklace.

～

Elsie popped over with a sample of fudge brownies. Elsie's brownies, in fact everything she baked, were nothing short of sublime. Each brownie melted in your mouth in a magical mix of butter, sugar and cocoa. "So good." I closed my eyes to get the full effect. "Between you and your brother, I'm the most spoiled florist in the world."

"Speaking of spoiled, I made more treats for your crow." Elsie walked over to refill Kingston's treat can. The crow was doing a dance on his perch as he heard each crunchy bite fall into the tin can. Elsie finished by bringing Kingston two of the treats. My bird wouldn't like to admit it, but his takeoffs for a quick jaunt around the neighborhood were getting a little slower and unwieldy. Elsie's treats were a big part of his less than graceful liftoffs. "I'm making spinach dip for girls' night."

"Girls' night?" I asked, then just as quickly remembered. "That's right. I've been so busy, I nearly forgot."

"We could cancel. I mean the fog is pretty bad out there and—" Elsie sounded disappointed at the prospect of canceling girls' night. She'd recently separated from her long-time spouse, a man who traveled so much we rarely saw him. She always looked forward to girls' night, and frankly so did I.

"No, I'm looking forward to it," I said. "I'm going to bring some white wine, and I'll get chips for the spinach dip."

"Not necessary." Elsie patted Kingston on the head. He was too busy with his treat to notice. "I'm making homemade pita chips for the dip. You could bring some veggies and onion dip. I thought we'd make it a dip night. And I've got the movie *Pride and Prejudice* all cued up."

"Yay, a P and P night. Colin or Matthew?" I asked.

"Matthew," she answered. "The last time we tried Colin, we all fell asleep by the fourth hour and missed the famous swim across the pond and wet shirt scene. Lola just about threw a tantrum. Speaking of Lola, did she make it back all right?"

"Yep, back in fine form. She brought back a table she thought I might like. I'm going to close up in a bit and go see it. This fog has really dampened any enthusiasm for flower shopping." My phone buzzed on the counter.

It was a text from Lola. *I just found the strangest thing in my travel bag. I need my super sleuth friend to come look at it.*

"Guess I'll close up now. Lola found something strange in her travel bag."

"Lola, the woman with the largest collection of old hats and rock and roll t-shirts thinks something is strange? I've got to see this."

I turned the shop sign to closed, and Elsie and I cautiously crossed the road to the antique shop. It was unusual for a heavy fog to stick itself so firmly to the coast, but it didn't seem to have any intention of dissipating. Long swirls resembling smoke curled up from the rooftops and the warm asphalt beneath our feet.

Lola popped up from behind her front counter when we walked inside. She hoisted her blue nylon travel bag onto the counter. Beneath the glass there were trays of antique lighters, jewelry, and beaded handbags. She pulled an envelope free from the blue bag.

"I think this all has to do with the funnel cake," Lola began. My friend often started talking in the middle of a topic. I was used to it, but Elsie was confused.

"You found a funnel cake in your travel bag?" Elsie asked.

"No, I think the thing in her bag has something to do with her eating a funnel cake." I turned to Lola to see if I was correct.

"Actually, I never got a chance to eat the funnel cake," Lola said.

Elsie and I stopped at the counter. Realizing asking questions was only going to make this whole thing more confusing, we waited for Lola to explain.

"Here, look at these." She handed over the yellow envelope.

I reached in and pulled out two glossy photos. One showed a man with white hair and a long gray coat leaving a jewelry store with a pretty blonde on his arm. The man looked old enough to be the woman's father, but something told me that wasn't the case. The next photo showed the same man through the front windshield of a Mercedes. He was kissing the young woman, which confirmed my thoughts about the first photo.

"Oh my, someone is being followed by a private eye or suspicious spouse," Elsie said.

I pushed the photos back into the envelope. "Now, leaving the funnel cake situation out of it, please tell us in easy to understand terms (yes, I had to make that clear for

Lola because she tended to do the opposite) why you have someone's private eye or blackmail photos."

"I'll tell you, but the funnel cake is an important chapter." Lola was wearing her favorite Pink Floyd t-shirt. The new necklace dangled right over the center of the triangular prism on the shirt. It seemed the near accident this morning hadn't prompted her to rethink the curse possibility. "I'd just finished sprinkling powdered sugar on my funnel cake. I turned around with my travel bag in one hand and my cake in the other. I smacked right into a man who was moving at a fast pace through the place. We crashed hard. I dropped my bag. My cake flew off the plate and landed right on his coat. He was covered with boysenberry syrup and powdered sugar. He put down whatever he was holding in his hand, this envelope I assume, and snarled at me as he tried to wipe the berry syrup off his jacket. He was quite angry, but I told him it was his fault. I didn't want to stick around and get yelled at, so I snatched up my bag and walked away quickly. By that time I'd had enough of the whole flea market, so I headed straight to my car to begin the drive home. Never saw the man again."

Elsie looked over at me. "That story could only come from those lips."

I nodded. "I agree."

"What should I do with the photos?" Lola asked.

I took the envelope and looked all over it for some kind of address or name. There was nothing. "I'd just throw them away."

Lola took the envelope and dropped it into her trash can. "There. I hope he worked hard to get those. He was a terrible, rude man, with a big ugly scar right across his cheek." She shivered her thin shoulders. "Now I'm glad I didn't stick around to get berated by him. What time is girls' night?" she asked.

"Seven at my house," Elsie said.

"I thought it was at my house this time," said Lola. "I even mopped the kitchen floor so that Miss Persnickety here—" she motioned toward Elsie "—wouldn't have anything to complain about."

"All right," Elsie said. "We'll meet at your house. And I'm not persnickety, am I?" she asked me.

"I have the right to remain silent, and I'm going to take it. See you girls later."

THE FOG HAD STUCK around like a wet, heavy cloak. It was the kind you could feel deep in your bones. Kingston must have felt it too. Once we got home, he headed straight to his cage for the night. Nevermore, my cat, was curled deeply into the throw blanket on the couch as I bid them both good-bye and headed down the road to Lola's for girls' night.

Elsie was already there, setting up her spinach dip and homemade pita chips when I walked in with my veggies and wine. She had also brought along some of her marble cupcakes for dessert. You never left from girls' night hungry with Elsie.

Lola was still wearing the necklace. It glittered against her dark blue sweater. It was pretty and delicate and didn't look the least bit cursed. Lola was already munching on a pita chip as I set down my vegetables. "I was telling Elsie about the Mr Darcy statue in Cheshire, England. He's standing in a lake in his wet shirt." The pita chip crunched between her teeth.

"I think you're making that up," Elsie said. She poured herself a glass of wine and looked at me to side with her.

"She's not," I said. "There's a large statue of a wet Colin Firth in the middle of an English lake."

"See, told you." Lola picked up her phone. "I'm going to show you." As she scrolled through her phone, the power went out. We were standing in pitch dark, my least favorite place to stand. I'd always had a bit of fear of the dark. All right, it was more than a bit. More like a smidgeon. A very big smidgeon, if I was being honest.

The three of us had the same idea. We all turned on our phone flashlights.

"Where is your breaker box?" Elsie asked.

"It's on the side of the house," Lola said.

A noise on the front porch made us all freeze.

"What was that?" Elsie asked.

Lola shook her head. "Sounded like someone standing on the front stoop."

I lowered my phone flashlight and grabbed an umbrella from the antique umbrella stand Lola kept by the front door. Weapon in hand, I crept quietly toward the front window. I pushed the curtain back. A pair of dark, menacing eyes stared back at me. I gasped and stumbled away from the window.

"What did you see?" Elsie was now armed with a frying pan, and Lola had grabbed a kitchen knife.

"A man." I had my phone out and was speed-dialing Briggs before I could take my next breath. I groaned in disappointment when I got his voicemail. "James, it's me. We're at Lola's for girls' night. The lights went out, and there's a strange man on the porch." I hung up and gasped again. "I can't believe I just left that message on his voicemail. He's going to freak out." And freak out he did. Never had I had such a quick return on a message.

He didn't waste time with greetings. *"Get in a locked room and don't open the door for anyone. I'm in Mayfield, but a patrol car is on its way."* His voice held that edge of glacial fright I rarely heard from my overly calm fiancé.

I repeated what he'd said, not needing to tell them more than once. We all hurried to the guest bathroom. It had a lock and was in the middle of the house, so no windows. We all stood huddled together in the small space with our phone lights casting ghostly glows on our faces.

"What did the man look like?" Lola asked. "Maybe it was just my neighbor, Mr Dudley. He knows I'm alone this week, and if the power went out—"

"I've met Mr Dudley. This man had a menacing look in his dark eyes and—" I hesitated, not entirely sure I should divulge the rest.

"Well, don't keep us in suspense," Elsie prodded.

"I only saw him briefly, but his face was at the window." I shuddered thinking how scary it was to look out and have someone staring back at me. I looked at Lola. "It was dark and all that, but I think he had a scar on his cheek."

Lola nearly dropped her phone. Her fingers trembled as

she reached for the necklace. "He's after the cursed necklace," she said with a heavy dose of drama.

"What? No, Lola, I think he's looking for those photos."

She released the necklace. "Oh right, that makes more sense. But I don't have the photos. They're in the trash at the antique shop."

A loud knock on the front door startled all of us. We moved closer together. "Not exactly the girls' night I was picturing," Elsie said.

My phone rang, giving us all another startle.

Lola giggled nervously. "Guess we're all a little on edge."

It was Briggs. *"Everything all right?"* he asked.

"We're locked in a bathroom."

"The officers are at your door. They're doing a full sweep of the property."

Light seeped beneath the door. I turned on the bathroom lights. "Thank goodness, they must have flipped the breaker. The power is back on. James, thanks for sending someone so fast. We think we know who the stranger was. Lola accidentally ended up with some photos in an envelope when she was at the flea market. They were photos that looked as if they'd been taken from a secret angle. It was an older man and younger woman caught in some sort of tryst."

"Where are the photos now?"

"Lola put them in her trash can at work." The officer knocked again. "Is it safe to exit the bathroom?"

"Yes, I just got the all clear. Tell the officers I'll call them in a few minutes for further instructions. And I'll drop by Lola's shop in the morning to pick up those photos. I think it'll be safer for Lola if she no longer has them in her possession."

I motioned for the girls to leave the bathroom. We walked out single file, still with a good dose of caution. The unexpected intruder had scared us all plenty. "Thank you, James. I think we're good now."

"I'll have them patrol the street intermittently through the night. Maybe it'd be better if Lola spent the night at your house."

"Good idea. And thanks again. This was a girls' night to remember."

~

LOLA INSISTED she'd be fine in her own house, as long as a patrol car was making the rounds every hour. It had been a disquieting night to say the least. That face staring back at me through the window had given me a flurry of nightmares. I didn't get a good night's rest.

I was just feeding Nevermore his breakfast kibble and Kingston his hard-boiled egg when my phone rang. It was Lola. I sensed something was wrong when I heard her breathing fast through the phone.

I dropped the hard-boiled egg I was holding. Kingston looked sternly at me from his perch, then swept down to eat the broken egg. "Lola? What's wrong? Where are you?"

Lola took a deep breath, but it was shaky and frail sounding. "Someone broke into the antique shop. I just got here, and the glass on the front door was shattered."

"I thought you had an alarm," I said.

"I hate setting that thing, and sometimes I forget to turn it off and I enter the shop, tripping the alarm and the police show up five minutes later and it's a whole, big embarrassing ordeal.

Besides, I've never had anyone break in before. I'm going to go inside and see what they took."

"Wait, Lola," I said urgently. "What if they're still in there?"

She paused. *"I hadn't thought of that."*

"Walk straight down to the police station and let James know what's happened. He can send Officer Chinmoor to check the place out. Then you can give him a list of what was stolen."

"I'm taking off this darn necklace. That shop assistant was right. It's cursed. I was reading up on cursed jewelry and possessions. You can't just throw the thing away. You need to pass it on to another owner so that the curse can continue. That's why the seller basically gave it away. She wanted to be rid of it. What am I going to do?"

"First of all, let's not get too caught up in the curse hysteria. I think your funnel cake has more to do with all this bad luck." Something had occurred to me as we spoke. "Lola, something tells me the only thing you'll be missing from your shop is that envelope of photos. That man is intent on getting them back. I'll bet they're worth a pretty penny to the man in the photo. Or maybe his wife is building up a good divorce case where she gets everything because he cheated."

Lola groaned loudly enough that I had to pull the phone away from my ear. *"Why does stuff like this always happen to me. How many people crash into a guy with blackmail photos while just trying to enjoy a funnel cake?"*

"I'm going to go out on a limb here and say just one. You. I'm finishing breakfast. I'll be there soon. In the meantime, get down to the station and let them know what's happened."

"Heading down there right now. See you in a bit."

~

My sleuthing skills were still top-notch. I'd been right about the break-in at Lola's shop. The culprit broke in, rummaged around in Lola's office, then snatched the envelope of photos from the trash. Lola was just as happy to be rid of the pictures. They'd caused her no small amount of trouble. The glass company came to repair her door after the police grabbed some fingerprints. But there was no big mystery about who broke in. It had to be the man with the scar. Officer Chinmoor took down a description, so if he showed up somewhere they could take him in for questioning.

Ryder was still out in nature with his dad. He had no idea what had been happening at home. I had the shop to myself as I arranged some pink and yellow tulips for a birthday bouquet. All seemed right side up again in our fair little town, until the door burst open and Les stumbled inside, pale and out of breath.

I dropped my pruning scissors. They clattered on the counter. "Les! What's wrong?"

Les leaned over and rested his hands on his thighs to catch his breath. "I think – he's dead," he said between gulps of air.

"Who's dead?" Adrenaline surged through me.

"A customer." Les pointed back over his shoulder with his thumb. "He's slumped over one of my tables." He was still trying to catch his breath. Les's sister, Elsie, had been making him eat healthier, but she'd been unable to talk him into more exercise than bowling and the occasional golf round. Of course, we were all out of shape compared to Elsie the marathon runner.

I raced out the door, phone in hand, ready to call whoever needed to be called. If Les was right, then it would be Detective Briggs.

I heard Les's plodding footsteps and still slightly labored breathing behind me as I reached his outdoor seating area. The tables were empty except for a spilled cup of coffee.

"I don't understand." Les sounded stunned. "He was right here at this table." It was the one with the spilled coffee. "I poked his shoulder to see if he was okay, but he didn't move. I was sure he was dead."

I circled the table to look for evidence, and my nose jumped into action. I sniffed the cold air a few times. "Aftershave. What did the man look like?"

"He had kind of a dark, scowled appearance. Oh, and he had a mean looking scar across his cheek. I was about to ask him where he got it, but he didn't look like the type for friendly banter. He ordered his coffee, extra strong and black, then he carried it out to the table to drink. He kept looking at his watch, and once or twice he looked back behind him as if worried someone was following him. Then I went into the storeroom to grind coffee beans. When I came back to the front of the shop, I noticed he was slumped over the table. His coffee had spilled." Les still looked pale.

"Let's get you into the shop for a glass of water." I took his arm and led him toward the door. "You didn't happen to notice if he was carrying a yellow envelope?" I pulled open the door. The heavy scent of coffee washed over me. It tended to be overwhelming in the morning, but it was late now and most of the coffee had been brewed.

"He wasn't carrying it, but he had it tucked in his coat. I noticed it when he reached inside for his wallet. Is he the man? The one who broke into Lola's shop?"

"Seems that way. I wonder what happened to him? Maybe he just passed out. Did you smell his aftershave when he was standing in the shop? I can't smell any now, and it was strong enough that I would still smell it."

Les shook his head. "All I smell is coffee. I don't think I noticed any aftershave, but then I don't have a super nose like you."

"Right. I wonder if there's any aftershave lingering in Lola's shop. Call if you need me, Les."

"Thanks, Lacey, and sorry if I scared you."

"I think my heart is finally getting back to its normal tempo." I winked and hurried across the street to Lola's. She was in her office straightening up. The office was a small, poorly ventilated space. It seemed the thief had spent a good amount of time in the office searching for that envelope. My nose would still be able to catch a few molecules of the strong aftershave hanging around.

Lola looked up from her desk. "What a mess, and the stupid thing is, all he would have had to do was ask for the darn envelope. I'd have handed it over without question." She paused and looked at me. "Why are you wiggling your nose in the air? I showered this morning."

I laughed. "It's not you. I'm looking for aftershave."

Lola tapped her cheeks. "Didn't need a shave this

morning, sorry." I was happy to see that all the traumatic events of the last twenty-four hours hadn't wiped away her good humor.

"Actually, I was hoping your thief was wearing it when he broke into the store. But I've got to say, there's not a trace of aftershave anywhere in this office."

Lola shoved a bunch of papers into a file folder. "Guess I'll have to go back through and organize everything. But not right now." She pointed to her neck. "Did you notice? I left my new treasure at home because apparently it carries with it a curse to beat all curses."

"Not sure if Howard Carter and Lord Carnarvon would agree about that, but I don't blame you. It's been a rough few days." I decided I didn't need to add to her angst by mentioning the slumped-over man at the coffee tables across the way. In Lola's mind he had gotten what he came for and was long gone from Port Danby. I knew better, but she didn't need to hear it.

It was a wonder he'd stuck around after committing an obvious crime. Les had mentioned he kept looking at his watch. It was possible he was waiting to catch a bus or a ride to the bus stop, or maybe even a plane. I'd also concluded that he was assaulted by a man wearing a lot of aftershave. And if I was a betting woman (which I really wasn't) I'd bet that the one with the aftershave was the older man in the photos. Now he'd gotten what he came for too, and we'd all be best off if they both took their tawdry dealings out of town.

"I'll see you later." I waved as I walked out.

I crossed over to my side of the road. As I swept past

Elsie's table area, the usual smell of brown sugar, butter and everything wonderful wafted my way, only this time the sweet bakery fragrance carried with it something distinctively not baked goods. It was aftershave.

I followed my nose right to Elsie's door. She was busy chatting with a man wearing a dark sports jacket. He had a gray fedora pulled down low over his white hair. He was wearing dark sunglasses indoors, but Elsie didn't seem to notice. She was filling a pink box with some of her cookies; a treat, perhaps, for his young sweetheart.

I stepped to the side of the door and pulled out my phone. I got lucky. Briggs answered. "James, I'm standing outside the bakery. There have been two men hunting down that envelope of photos – the one who lost them in the first place and the subject in the pictures."

"Yes, I know," he said. *"I've got the man with the scar in the interrogation room. He said he was assaulted, a bump to the head. He gave me the name of the man who hit him."*

"Yep, and he's standing in Elsie's bakery buying cookies right now."

"I'm sending Chinmoor down. Lacey, do not approach him. He struck a man, so he is dangerous."

"Me? Approach a dangerous character?" I asked teasingly.

He groaned. *"Yes, you're the reason for my gray hairs. Chinmoor is on his way."*

"Great. I'll just keep an eye to make sure Elsie's all right."

Seconds later, Officer Chinmoor pulled up in the patrol car and hopped out. The man was exiting with his cookies just as Chinmoor took out his badge. "Lawrence Oster? I'm taking you in for questioning in connection with an assault."

Lawrence took off in my direction. I stuck out a foot. The man stumbled forward. The cookies flew out of his hand, and the yellow envelope fell from his coat.

Officer Chinmoor nodded his thanks.

"Excuse me, Officer Chinmoor, could we not mention the last few seconds to Detective Briggs?"

"Sure thing," he said with a knowing smile.

After all, it wasn't my first time thwarting the getaway of a fugitive. And it probably wouldn't be my last.

ABOUT LONDON LOVETT

London Lovett is a cozy mystery author and connoisseur of delicious baked goods. Many readers have called her Port Danby Cozy Mystery series a 'new favorite'. Port Danby features a small town florist with a powerful sense of smell. Lacey 'Pink' Pinkerton uses her impressive nose to help solve crimes as an amateur sleuth alongside her detective boyfriend, James Briggs. Blooms and Blackmail is a Port Danby short story.

9

SECOND-HAND MURDER

J. NEW

"Dead?" shrieked Gertrude.

"As a Dodo," Maude replied solemnly.

"What do you mean? How?"

"Well, it became extinct."

Gertrude stared at her friend, open-mouthed. "Not the bird, Maude! I mean Arthur Wilkinson."

"Oh. Sorry. Yes, I'm afraid he's dead, too."

"Where is he?"

"In the changing room."

Gertrude shoved past Maude and barrelled down the long aisle to the curtained-off cubby hole toward the back of the shop and flung aside the drapery. Maude was right. Arthur Wilkinson was no more. She grasped the string of fake pearls at her neck and leaned against the wall, trying to catch her breath and slow her hammering heart.

The shop motto, BREATHING NEW LIFE INTO OLD CLOTHES, which she'd proudly hung on the wall when they'd opened barely a month ago, now seemed like a cruel cosmic joke. Especially since it had fallen off and was lying on Arthur's foot.

"Do you think he had a heart attack?" Maude whispered from Gertrude's right shoulder.

"No, Maude, I don't."

"Really? How can you tell?"

Gertrude turned to her friend in disbelief. "For goodness' sake, put your glasses on."

"I don't know where they are."

Gertrude delved into Maude's unruly mop of white hair and plucked out her varifocals, thrusting them into her hand.

"Oh. Sorry. Thank you, Gertie."

With her glasses now firmly fixed on her nose, Maude peered back into the changing room and gasped. Sticking out of Arthur Wilkinson's scrawny neck was a No. 6 knitting needle.

"Oh dear, you're right, Gertie. Not a heart attack." She paused. "Perhaps it was an accident?"

"Maude! What on earth is wrong with you today? Did you leave your wits at home this morning?"

Maude's face flushed an angry mottled pink, highlighting the liver spots on her forehead and cheeks. "There's no need to be so hurtful, Gertrude. I was only making a suggestion."

"What? That Arthur accidentally stabbed himself in the neck with a knitting needle?"

"Well, maybe he did it on purpose. You know..." she trailed off.

Gertrude narrowed her eyes and studied her friend's

mournful face for a moment before realising what she meant. She swung back to the body, viewing it with a renewed focus. It was possible, she supposed, but what an awful way to go. And why on earth would he choose to do it in her shop, of all places? She stared at the scene a moment longer before resolutely shaking her head.

"No, I can't see it, Maude. Arthur wouldn't do this. He was happy. Besides, there are far easier ways if he *was* that way inclined. Pills, for example. Have you ever heard of anyone ending it with a knitting needle?"

"To be honest, I've never heard of anyone ending it at all, Gertie."

"Cooee!" a distant voice called from the front of the shop as the bell above the door tinkled.

Gertrude and Maude shared a horrified glance and sprung together in fright.

"It's Mary, Gertie!" Maude squeaked, clutching her friend's arm.

"I'm aware of that," Gertrude hissed back.

"Whatever shall we do? We can't let her see Arthur like this."

"Quick, Maude. Close the curtain and drag that rail of clothes over the front. We'll say the changing room is off limits today because of a flood. I'll greet her. Hurry!"

"But there's no water in there," Maude said. However, Gertie had already gone and failed to hear her. Maude did as Gertrude asked, wondering why it was always her who had to do these tasks. The clothes rail was heavy, and Gertrude was both taller and stronger than she was. It would have taken her much less time.

∼

"Mary, how lovely to see you," Gertrude said, just as Maude staggered up beside her, red in the face and gasping for breath. "Can I help you with something?"

Mary took off her headscarf and put it on the counter, along with her handbag. She looked at Maude with curiosity. "Are you all right, Maude?"

"Oh, yes, fine. Just been moving some ... er ... stuff. A bit heavy, that's all."

"Have you come to buy something, Mary?" Gertrude asked hopefully. Customers were few and far between on a good day, but Tuesdays were pitiful.

"Actually, I've come with some news."

"Oh?"

"Yes. Arthur's numbers came up."

"Mary! How did you know?" Maude blurted out and received a venomous glare from Gertie.

"I got a telephone call last evening."

"Last evening? Did you really?" Gertrude said, eyeing the brand-new handbag.

"But that would mean—" Maude began.

"Maude!" Gertie interrupted loudly. "Perhaps you could put the kettle on and make us all a nice cup of tea?"

"Tea?"

"Yes, tea. Mary, you'd like a cuppa, wouldn't you?"

"That would be very nice, Gertrude. Thank you, Maude."

"So, what's this news you've got to share with us?" Gertrude asked once Maude had stumbled to the little kitchen behind the counter.

"I'll wait until Maude gets back. No point saying it twice."

Gertrude eyed her friend with interest. She was positively vibrating. Whatever she was about to share must be monumental.

Maude returned five minutes later with a tray on which sat a selection of second-hand china with more chips than a computer shop, and a teapot wearing a moth-eaten knitted cosy shaped like a sheep. Gertrude frowned at the mess of a tray. This really wasn't how tea should be served.

"Shall I be mother?" Maude asked, starting to pour without waiting for an answer.

Gertrude turned once more to Mary, studying her closely. She was wearing a brand-new coat, one from that designer boutique on the corner if she wasn't mistaken. "Well?" she said.

"Arthur won the lottery."

There was a tremendous crash as Maude dropped the pot. She looked up at Gertrude. Her bottom lip beginning to quiver and her fringe dripping with tea.

"Don't worry, Maude," Gertrude said through clenched teeth. "It was an accident. You can clear it up later."

"Gertrude is right," Mary said. "It wasn't your fault. Nothing to get upset about. I'm the same with heavy objects now. It's the arthritis I suppose, is it? Yes, I thought so. It's only to be expected at our age. Look, why don't you go and clean yourself up, and Gertrude and me will deal with the mess."

"Oh. Well, if you're sure," Maude stammered out, wiping droplets from the end of her nose and looking myopically at Gertrude through tea splashed glasses.

"Yes, yes. Off you go. Mary and I will sort things out here."

Maude darted around the counter and scuttled off toward the far end of the shop where the storeroom and staff toilet were. By the time she returned, over fifteen minutes later, the wrecked china and vast pool of tea was history and a newly replenished tray, replete with fancy doily, was sitting on the counter. Gertrude had replaced the teapot cosy with one she'd knitted herself in the shape of a royal crown. *Much better*, she thought. She'd no idea where that ghastly sheep one had come from, but it was now in the bin.

"Everything all right, Maude?" Mary asked, filling the cups.

"Oh, yes, thank you, Mary."

"You didn't burn yourself, did you? Scalding tea can be quite dangerous."

"No, no. I'm fine, honestly. Luckily, I didn't make it that hot."

"I suppose congratulations are in order, Mary," Gertrude said. "We're very pleased for you both, aren't we, Maude?"

"Oh, we are. Is it... Is it a lot of money, Mary?"

"It's more than enough. Thank you, ladies," she replied with a smile. "By the way, I don't suppose you've seen Arthur today, have you? He said he was popping in for a suit he liked the look of. It's his club night tonight and I think he wanted to dress up a bit."

"He wanted to buy a second-hand suit when you've just won the lottery?" Maude asked in surprise.

"Oh, come now, Maude, we've all been friends for donkey's years. You know what Arthur's like. Short arms and long pockets. He won't spend a ha'penny more than he has to."

"Well, we haven't seen him, have we, Maude?" Gertrude said, elbowing her friend none too gently in the ribs.

"Er, no. We haven't. Sorry."

"Oh well, I'll find him in the village, no doubt. By the way, is your heating on the blink? It's freezing in here?"

"Maybe," Maude said, nodding sagely. "We've had a flood. In the changing room. That's why it's closed."

Gertrude closed her eyes for a second, muttering "God, give me strength," before taking a deep breath and plastering on a rictus smile. "Never mind that, Maude. I'm sure Mary has got better things to do than listen to our little problems."

"I'd love to stay and chat actually, Gertrude, but you're right, I'm afraid I can't," she replied, retrieving her scarf and hat. "I have an appointment with the bank manager, so must be off. Thank you for the tea. Oh, and if Arthur does happen to pop in, tell him I'll see him at home, would you?"

"The lottery, eh?" Maude said wistfully, once Mary had gone. "Who would have thought it?"

"I think we need to close the shop."

"Close the shop?" Maude tittered. "*We* haven't won the lottery, Gertie, and don't forget we've sunk all our savings into the place. We can't afford to close."

Gertrude gave her friend yet another withering stare. "Have you forgotten we've got a dead body in the dressing room?"

"Oh. Yes. I'll get the key."

Gertrude shook her head in disbelief. She sometimes wondered if her oldest friend was losing her marbles. But she did have a point. They really did need to make a go of this place or they were at risk of losing everything, including their home. Both spinsters, they'd lived together for years, and Gertrude felt quite nauseous at the thought of having to start again elsewhere at her age.

∼

"Did you see Arthur come in today, Maude?" Gertrude asked several minutes later. She was leaning against the kitchen cupboard, arms folded and a puzzled frown on her face, while Maude washed, dried, and put away the tea things.

"No. I thought you must have. Didn't you?"

"No, I didn't. How did he get in without either of us seeing him?"

"Or hearing him. The bell above the door would have rung. But you opened up this morning, Gertrude, if you remember, as I was at the doctors. Could he have come in during that half hour, do you think?"

"No, Maude. I would have seen him. I'm not blind."

Maude dried her hands on the tea towel, hung it neatly on the rusty nail which acted as a hook, and followed Gertrude back out to the shop, where they stood in silence. Anxiously looking at one another as the reality of the appalling situation dawned on them.

"Mary's right," Gertrude said suddenly. "It's like an ice box in here. Where *on earth* is that draft coming from?"

She set off back down the aisle like a tank charging into battle and a minute later yelled, "Maude! Maude, come here!"

Maude gave a resigned sigh and set off at a slow, shuffling trot to the far end of the shop, fervently wishing they'd bought a building that wasn't the length of a football field. "What is it?"

"Did you leave the back door open?"

"No, of course not. I'm not a complete idiot, Gertrude."

Gertrude opened her mouth, intending to argue the point, but, uncharacteristically, shut it again. She glanced round at the storeroom, which, unlike the shop, was miniscule, and across to the open lavatory door. "Well, if there *was* someone here, they certainly aren't now."

She slowly approached the open door and quickly peered along the cobbled street beyond, where a sea of large wheelie bins belonging to the shops greeted her. Satisfied there was nobody out there, she shut and locked the door, putting the key in her cardigan pocket.

"Would you like another cup of tea, Gertie? You're looking very pale."

"I'd rather have a stiff brandy; I'm getting one of my heads." She removed her glasses and closed her eyes, pinching the bridge of her nose for a second. Then, with a groan, she grabbed her friend's arm. "Come on, Maude, we can't delay things any longer."

Gertrude approached the changing room with Maude in tow and quickly pushed away the rack of clothes. She took a deep breath and pulled aside the curtain. Then, with an audible thump, promptly keeled over in a dead faint. Maude cried out in surprise. The changing room was empty. Arthur Wilkinson was gone.

Gertrude came round to Maude, whimpering and slapping her cheek in increasingly heavy blows. "Maude, will you stop that!"

"Gertrude! Oh, thanks heavens, I thought you were dead."

"Of course I'm not dead, I—" She shifted onto one elbow and peered back at the empty changing room, her eyes wide with fear. "Where is he?"

Maude shook her head. "I don't know, Gertie," she whispered. "He's vanished."

"Quickly, help me up."

Maude took Gertrude's arm and tried to lift her. Pushing, pulling, shoving and dragging, but her skinny frame was no match for Gertrude's corpulent one, and eventually she had to give up.

"I'm sorry, Gertie. I can't."

"Oh, for heaven's sake," Gertrude spat, clumsily rolling onto all fours and crawling to a nearby table which displayed an array of outdated hats and ancient fur stoles. She gripped the edge, gritted her teeth, and with great difficulty heaved herself upright.

"I'm going home, Maude," she said wearily.

"But what about Arthur?"

"What about him? He's gone, Maude, in case you haven't noticed. He's not our problem anymore."

Maude wrung her hands. "But shouldn't we call the police?"

"And say what, exactly? That we found Arthur Wilkinson

stabbed to death in our changing room, yet somehow he managed to get up and walk away? Use your brain, Maude."

Maude nodded. "Yes, of course, you're right, Gertie. Let's go home and forget all about it. I've got some nice finny haddock I'll do for tea before you go to your group."

"I'm not going. I'm far too upset for that, Maude. I just want to go home and rest."

~

THE NEXT MORNING, while Maude was bustling about making breakfast and Gertrude was at the table reading the morning paper, there was a frantic knocking at the door. Maude answered it and found a dishevelled Mary on the doorstep.

"Mary, come in. Are you all right?"

"Not really, Maude," she answered, entering the kitchen. "Arthur didn't come home last night."

"Come and sit down, dear. I'll get you a cup of tea," Maude said, glancing quickly at Gertrude. She had attempted earlier to broach the subject of what had happened the day before, but Gertrude had resolutely refused to discuss it.

"I'm putting it down to a very mean practical joke, Maude, and I have no wish to discuss it further," she'd said. And that was the end of the matter. Until Mary turned up. Now Gertrude looked shaken.

"Perhaps he had a bit too much to drink at the club last night and stayed with someone?" she suggested.

Mary shook her head. "I've already telephoned them. He never arrived at the club. No one has seen him since he left home yesterday morning on his way to your shop." She burst into tears and scrabbled about in her handbag for a handkerchief. "Where is he?" she wept. "I can't understand why he would just disappear like this. It's not like Arthur at all. Something awful must have happened. I'm sure of it."

"Now, now, Mary," Maude said gently, patting her hand. "Let's not think the worst."

"I can't help it, Maude. It's so unlike him not to tell me where he's going."

At that moment, the hall telephone began to ring and Maude got up to answer it. She was gone only two minutes, but returned looking pale and frightened.

"What is it, Maude?" Gertrude asked.

Maude gulped and shot a quick glance at Mary. "That was the police. They're on their way here."

"I knew it," Mary wailed to a fresh bout of tears.

"But why are the police coming here?" Maude asked quietly.

"Did you tell anyone you were coming to see us, Mary?" Gertrude said, a little sharply.

"Only Hyacinth next door. Just in case Arthur came home and wondered where I was. But now he'll never be coming home," she sobbed.

"We don't know that, Mary," Gertrude said in a no-nonsense tone. "He could have had an accident and simply be in hospital. Let's wait until the police tell us what's actually happened before jumping to conclusions. Maude, we'd best see them in the drawing room. Go and check it's tidy, will you? I'll put the kettle on."

Maude stood gaping at Gertrude's fortitude, before

shaking her head and hurrying off to do her bidding. Not long after, the front doorbell rang. This time, Gertrude answered it.

∽

Detective Inspector Thornaby had a face like a basset hound, and Gertrude silently prayed he didn't have the character traits of his canine counterpart. He was accompanied by a young, uniformed female police constable, by the name of Rhodes. After Gertrude had introduced herself, she escorted them both to the kitchen, where Mary Wilkinson was still sitting at the table crying softly into her now sodden hankie.

"Miss Bickel," DI Thornaby said quietly to Gertrude. "Perhaps you'd be good enough to leave for a moment while I speak with Mrs Wilkinson?"

"Oh. Yes, I suppose so. I'll be in the drawing room."

"Gertrude, what's happening?" Maude whispered as soon as she entered.

"They must have found Arthur, Maude, and are just telling Mary."

"What shall we do?"

Gertrude grabbed her friend's arm, causing Maude to wince slightly as strong fingers pinched her flesh.

"Nothing, Maude. Do you understand? We mustn't tell them anything or we'll get the blame."

"But we didn't do anything!"

"Of course we didn't, but the police won't believe us. You mark my words, if they even get a whiff that we know more than we're letting on, they'll be trouble. Promise me you'll watch what you say? In fact, say as little as possible. You're like a leaky faucet when you get going."

Maude nodded. "I promise, Gertie."

"Good. Now, quickly, tidy up. The place is a mess."

"Ladies," said a voice from the doorway, causing the two women to nearly jump out of their skins. It was the inspector. "PC Rhodes is escorting Mrs Wilkinson home and will stay with her for the time being. I'm afraid she's had some bad news. I'd like to ask you both some questions, if I may?"

"Please, come in, Inspector," Gertrude said in her posh voice. "Have a seat."

Maude dashed to the red velvet chair and removed the large basket of knitting paraphernalia. She stood holding it, casting her eye wildly around the room for a place to put it. But, with every available surface choc-a-block with knick-knacks and doodads, she didn't know what to do.

"Maude, will you put that down! I've said time and time again I don't like you touching my things. You make such a mess of everything."

"Sorry, Gertie," Maude said, her colour rising. She dumped the basket in the hearth next to the Inspector's foot and scurried over to perch next to Gertrude on the sofa.

"You're not a knitter, Miss Utley?"

"Oh, good heavens no," Maude replied, turning pinker. "I'm all thumbs, I'm afraid. It's Gertrude's. She's very good, as you can see."

She waved an arm around the stuffy, dark room, indicating the woollen doilies, antimacassars and protective head rests on the furniture, and the row of knitted toys on the sill below the net curtains. Gertrude preened.

"Yes, I am rather good," Gertrude agreed. "My Tuesday night knitting club members are always asking for my patterns and advice. I just seem to have a knack for it. Sadly, Maude can barely thread a needle. Isn't that right, dear?"

The inspector smiled thinly and nodded before clearing his throat and getting down to business. "I'm afraid what I'm about to tell you will be upsetting, but Arthur Wilkinson was found dead this morning."

Maude's hands flew to her mouth and Gertrude gasped.

"Oh, poor Mary," Maude said.

"Dead?" Gertrude said, as a strong wave of déjà vu washed over her. "How? What happened?"

"Might I ask where you both were yesterday?" Thornaby asked, ignoring Gertrude.

"At the shop. Isn't that right, Maude?"

"Oh yes. We were at the shop. I had a doctor's appointment first thing, though I was only half an hour late."

"That's New to You, the second-hand shop on the village's main street?"

"That's right," Gertrude said.

"And you were there all day?"

"Yes," Maude nodded. "Well, until—" She froze, looking like an animal caught in headlights.

"Until?" Thornaby prompted.

"Until I got one of my heads," Gertrude finished. "I suffer dreadfully from headaches and I'm afraid I got one yesterday. Maude can't manage on her own, so we closed up and came home."

"I see," Thornaby said, making notes. "And did you see Mr Wilkinson at any time yesterday?"

Both women shook their heads.

"We didn't see anyone," Maude said. "We don't really get many customers, I'm afraid. It's a bit worrying, actually." She looked down and plucked a bit of fluff from her tweed skirt.

"That's not quite true actually, Inspector," Gertrude said. "Mary came mid-morning and stayed for a cup of tea."

"Oh yes, I'd forgotten that," Maude said. "Sorry. I'm still shocked at what has happened."

"Yes, I understand," the inspector said, making more notes.

"Detective Thornaby," Gertrude asked in an unusually conciliatory tone. "Might I ask why you're questioning us in particular? Arthur and Mary have many other friends here, too, you know?"

"I was under the impression he was on his way to your shop for a suit. Is that not correct?"

"Oh, I see. Yes, apparently so. Mary said as much. But, obviously, he never arrived."

DI Thornaby attempted to lean back, but the six frilly chintz cushions prevented any reverse movement. He shuffled uncomfortably for a moment, then, seemingly having made up his mind about something, spoke again.

"There is another reason, actually. Arthur Wilkinson was found dead outside the back of your shop."

"What?" Gertrude gasped. "But that's impossible."

"And why do you say that, Miss Bickel?"

"Well, it just is," Gertrude spluttered, trying not to panic. "I mean ... why would he go to the *back* of the shop? There's nothing out there except— Oh, Good Lord! That's where you found him, isn't it? In the bin?"

DI Thornaby's silence and grave facial expression spoke volumes.

"Oh, how awful," Maude said.

"Dreadful," Gertrude agreed. "Oh dear, I feel quite sick."

Maude jumped up. "Hang on, Gertie, I'll get you some water." She dashed to the kitchen and returned seconds later with a full glass.

Gertrude gulped it down noisily and handed the empty glass back to Maude, who put it on a knitted coaster on one of the occasional tables.

DI Thornaby stood.

"I'm sorry to have brought you such distressing news. I'll take my leave now, but if there's anything you remember, please give me a call," he said, glancing at Gertrude, who was wafting her rubicund face with the television guide. He handed his card to Maude.

"I'll see you out," she said, putting the card on the sideboard. With the inspector on his way, she returned to the drawing room and asked Gertie how she was feeling?

"Perhaps a sherry, Maude?" Gertrude said, slumping back against the mound of overly stuffed floral cushions and closing her eyes.

"Um, isn't it a bit early, Gertie?"

"No, it isn't. My nerves are in shreds. That was simply dreadful. I felt like a criminal in my own home. Make it a large one, Maude."

"You recovered well from that little slip," Maude said, handing her a brimming glass of golden liquid.

"What do you mean?" Gertrude said sharply, then shook her head. "Never mind. Do you think he noticed? It's usually you who opens your big mouth; I can't think what came over me. It must have been the shock. Oh, Maude, what shall we do? That detective is far more astute than he looks, I'm sure of it. Oh, how stupid of me! He made me all flustered. I couldn't think straight."

"Now, now, Gertie, don't get yourself all in a bother. You recovered well by saying Arthur would never come to the back door. I mean, why would he? He's never done it before and if he wanted to buy something he'd have come to the front like any normal customer. I don't think the detective noticed at all. Honestly."

"Do you really think so? Yes, I expect you're right. I am good at thinking on my feet. Besides, we were upset at hearing the dreadful news, weren't we? It's no wonder I was all of a tizzy. Policemen are notorious for tricking you and trying to catch you out, you know."

"Are they?" Maude asked.

"Indeed they are. I've seen it on the telly. Even when you're innocent, they make you feel guilty and try to make you confess. They ask you the same question over and over in different ways until you can hardly string a sentence together and get all confused. I've seen it, Maude. It's a well-known tactic. Yes, that's what he was doing. I've never in my life been questioned by the police. Oh, the shame of it. Goodness knows what the neighbours will think. It's hardly surprising he threw me off balance, is it?"

"No, of course it isn't. Well, as long as you are feeling better, Gertie."

"Actually, I've got one of my heads coming on. I'm going to lie down for a while. You can call me when lunch is ready. What are we having?"

"I thought cold cuts with a salad."

"All right. And dinner?"

In her mind, Maude rapidly pictured what was ready in the freezer. "Shepherd's Pie?"

"Yes, that will do."

As Gertrude laboriously made her way upstairs, Maude returned to the kitchen to prepare the food. She was glad of something to do. It had been a very trying morning, and she was feeling the beginnings of a headache herself. Perhaps a walk and some fresh air would do her good? She was halfway up the staircase, with the intention of letting Gertie know she was going out, when the sound of loud, rumbling snores reached her ears. Gertrude wouldn't be pleased if she woke her, so Maude left a note on the kitchen table instead and, grabbing her coat, left the house.

∾

MAUDE FELT her body begin to relax and the tension drain away the further she walked from her home. She'd known Gertrude since they'd been children and had lived with her for nearly eight years. She was used to her overbearing and tactless personality. But now, with her being all at sixes and sevens after the visit from the police, she was even more truculent. She'd made the right decision to escape, even if it was only for a short while. She hoped Gertrude would be in a better mood by the time she returned.

Maude wasn't a fast walker: the arthritis in her wrists also extended to one hip, so she tended to limp and list slightly to one side. But she was enjoying the freedom and peace so much she was out for longer than intended. It was nearly two hours later when she unlatched the garden gate and found Gertrude blocking the doorway while arguing with Detective Inspector Thornaby. Her heart sank, and she felt the anxiety she'd managed to walk off return tenfold. Something was terribly wrong.

"Maude!" Gertrude yelled. "Finally! Where have you been?"

"For a walk. I left a note on the kitchen table. Didn't you see it?"

"Obviously not. But never mind that. Come and help me. This policeman wants to come in and search my house, Maude! I told you, didn't I? I told you they'd be up to their trickery."

Maude edged into the doorway beside Gertrude and looked questioningly at DI Thornaby.

"We have a search warrant, Miss Utley," he said, handing her an official looking paper.

She searched her pockets for her glasses, trying to ignore Gertrude's impatient sighs and tuts of annoyance, and put them on. She shook out the page and began to read.

"Well?" Gertrude demanded. "It's all nonsense isn't it, Maude? He can't just come barging into someone's private property and start searching through their belongings, can he?"

Maude swallowed and returned her glasses to her pocket. "I'm sorry, Gertie," she whispered. "But it looks like he can.

This is a legal document. Look, it's been signed by the court. I don't think we have a choice. We have to let him in or we'll get into dreadful trouble."

Gertrude stiffened for a moment then deflated before her eyes, slumping heavily against the door jamb.

"I don't know how much more I can take, Maude. Honestly, I don't."

"Come inside, dear, I'll make you a cup of tea. The neighbours are beginning to stare."

Maude was aware the mention of nosy neighbours guaranteed her friend would hurriedly move indoors. She couldn't abide being the subject of petty gossip, let alone something as serious as a police investigation. She gave the inspector a quick nod over her shoulder as she guided Gertrude into the kitchen and sat her at the table.

"Try not to worry, Gertrude," Maude said ten minutes later as she poured the tea. "I'm sure it's all a terrible mistake."

They could hear the sound of Thornaby and his officers rifling through the rooms upstairs and in the drawing room.

"Worry, Maude! I'm not worried, I'm angry. There are strangers in my house snooping through my belongings. It's appalling the way I'm being treated."

"They're searching my things, too."

"Don't split hairs, Maude. What on earth are they expecting to find, that's what I want to know?"

"I'm sure they won't find anything, Gertie. We have nothing to do with any of this."

But Maude was wrong, as DI Thornaby informed them when he entered the kitchen a moment later.

"Miss Bickel, I'd like you to accompany me to the station."

"I beg your pardon?"

"You need to come to the station for a formal interview under caution, with regard to the death of Arthur Wilkinson."

"Certainly not! I have absolutely nothing to do with him dying. How can you think such a thing?"

"Then I have no option but to place you under arrest."

Gertrude gasped, and all colour drained from her face. She struggled out of her chair and went to stand next to Maude, clutching her friend's arm.

"What does he mean, Maude? He's arresting me for murdering Arthur? But I didn't do it!"

"I don't know, Gertrude. But I think you had better do as Detective Inspector Thornaby asks or you'll be in even more trouble. Do we know a solicitor who could help?"

Gertrude shook her head.

"If you don't have a solicitor, one will be provided for you," DI Thornaby said. "Now, if you'll get ready to leave. I don't have time to waste."

"Maude! Maude, do something. Help me!"

"I will try, Gertie. Just go to the station and I'll have a think. It's obviously a horrible mistake. I'm sure the police will realise it too. Just try to remain calm and tell them what you know."

A few minutes later Gertrude was bundled into her coat and escorted to a waiting police car. The last image Maude had of her friend was the stunned face staring at her from the back of the vehicle.

MAUDE WATCHED the car until it disappeared around the corner. She was about to raise her hand to wave, then realised how inappropriate it would be, so went back inside, head bowed to avoid the shocked gazes of the neighbours. She stood in the middle of the kitchen, feeling a bit bewildered. The house felt empty without Gertrude's larger-than-life personality. Even when she was silent, which Maude admitted wasn't very often, she still seemed to fill the place just by being present.

Maude's intention had been to get ready and go to the police station in a show of moral support for Gertrude, but Thornaby had informed her, just before he left, that it would be a waste of time. She wouldn't be able to see Gertrude. Maude had tentatively asked what he'd found in the house, but again he was unable to tell her anything. Apparently, they weren't allowed discuss an ongoing investigation. But Gertrude's solicitor would be given all pertinent information he'd told her, which was some solace, she supposed.

She stood for a moment longer then shook herself out of her reverie. "Come along, Maude," she admonished herself. "It's no good standing around like a lemon; you need to keep busy."

She first cleared away the old tea things, then made herself another pot, which she drank while eating a solitary lunch. With that done and the washing up finished, she tentatively approached the hall telephone, thinking she should perhaps call Mary. Then again, having just lost her husband she was probably busy and being comforted by other friends and family. Not to mention PC Rhodes was probably still there. No, she shouldn't impose, she'd call another day. Instead, she climbed the stairs to see what a mess the police search had wrought.

From the way Gertrude had talked about the police Maude had expected a shambles, and the remainder of her day to be spent tidying up. So she was pleasantly surprised to see things were generally tidy. She righted a few ornaments and plumped the cushions on Gertrude's bed, then moved to her own room. There was very little in her tiny room that had been disturbed, so she went back downstairs. A quick glance in the drawing room revealed the same, so she put the kettle on.

That evening she opened the television guide and found a repeat of a program she'd been hoping to watch, a railway journey throughout the British Isles. She'd missed it the first time as Gertrude was fond of soaps and watched every single one, including all the repeats. They weren't really the sort of thing Maude liked, so, more often than not she retired to her small box room early and spent the evening reading before retiring properly. The only time she was able to watch something she liked was when Gertrude was out at her group meeting. But that was only once a week.

Tonight, however, she relaxed on the sofa and switched off her mind from the awful things that had happened and simply enjoyed the program. It wasn't until it had finished and she was about to go up to bed that she realised what was missing from the room. There was a space on the hearth. The police had taken away Gertrude's knitting basket.

As was her wont, Maude awoke early the next day and was already preparing breakfast for two before she remembered Gertrude's absence. She put away the duplicated items, switched on the wireless for some company, and put some bread in the toaster. She wondered briefly if she should have a bacon sandwich, but dismissed the idea just as quickly. When Gertrude came home and found she'd used her bacon, she wouldn't be best pleased. No, she'd stick to her usual muesli and toast. But, perhaps, just a little strawberry preserve as a treat.

She'd just finished the hoovering and was about to call the police station to see how Gertrude was when she was interrupted by a knock at the door. She found DI Thornaby on the doorstep.

"Oh, Inspector, is there any news? How is Gertrude? When will she be coming home?"

"Perhaps I could come in, Miss Utley?" Thornaby asked gently.

"Oh, dear me, I am sorry. Yes, please do come in. Would you like a cup of tea, or perhaps coffee?"

"Coffee, please, if it's not too much trouble."

Maude shuffled down the hall to the kitchen and put the kettle on, spooning coffee granules into two mugs. She rarely drank coffee, but judging from the look on DI Thornaby's face she thought it would be a good idea this time. Putting a milk jug and sugar bowl on the table she handed him a mug. As she did so the sleeve of her cardigan rose, revealing a nasty bruise. Thornaby raised an eyebrow and Maude followed his gaze.

"Oh, it's nothing. Gertrude doesn't know her own strength sometimes. And I tend to bruise easily." Maude said, pulling down her cuff and taking a seat. "Can you tell me what's happened?"

"I'll bring you up to date shortly, Miss Utley, but first I'd like to ask you some questions to confirm a few things. Is that all right?"

Maude nodded in mute resignation.

"Can you tell me about Miss Bickel's knitting club?"

This wasn't a question she had expected.

"The knitting club? Well, I don't know very much about it, I'm afraid. I don't attend you see. It's on a Tuesday evening and they take it in turns to be the host. I think there are five of them, including Gertrude. But I don't know any of the others. I'm sorry."

"Has the group ever been here?"

"Only the once, and quite a long time ago. I'm afraid one of the ladies was careless with a hot cup of tea and left a dreadful mark on Gertrude's favourite table. She was quite furious. She stopped them coming after that. Made an excuse."

"Oh? What was the excuse?"

Maude blushed. "Me. She told them I didn't really like crowds and preferred to have the house to myself. It wasn't true, of course, I quite like meeting new people, and I seldom get the chance. But if it helped Gertrude…"

Thornaby took a gulp of his coffee, eyeing the woman thoughtfully over the rim of his cup. "Miss Utley, I've spoken with the other four group members. Would you be surprised to learn that Miss Bickel hasn't attended a meeting for several months?"

Maude stared at him for a moment. "She hasn't? No, I don't think that can be true, Inspector. She's gone out every Tuesday as normal. Where else would she be going? I don't understand."

"How well did you know Arthur Wilkinson?"

Maude was a little taken aback at the sudden change of direction but answered, nonetheless.

"We were all at school together. Gertrude, me, Mary, and Arthur. So I suppose reasonably well. Arthur and Mary started courting in our final year and eventually got married. We've been friends ever since."

Thornaby nodded and retrieved his notebook from his pocket. Thumbing through the pages he asked, "I am correct in thinking Arthur was also a member of a club, aren't I?"

"Yes. It's a working men's club in the village. He usually goes on a Tuesday." Maude's voice faltered. "Inspector?"

"I'm sorry, Miss Utley, but according to several members and the barman at the club, Arthur hasn't been seen there for several months either."

Maude shook her head and wrung her hands. "It must be a coincidence," she said with very little conviction.

The inspector shook his head. "Miss Bickel has confessed to the affair during questioning."

Maude shook her head, unable to speak. Taking a handkerchief from her pocket she removed her glasses and dabbed her eyes.

"I can't believe it," she said quietly. "Oh goodness, does Mary know?"

Thornaby nodded. "Yes. I broke the news to her just before I came here."

"How is she?"

"Shocked, as you can imagine. And hurt obviously. She had no idea. I daresay she'll run through the gamut of emotions over the next few days. Apparently, according to Miss Bickel, Arthur Wilkinson intended to leave his wife and move in here."

"What? But that would be dreadful. How would it work with three of us?"

A look of sympathy appeared on the inspector's face and there was no need for him to say more.

"She was going to ask me to leave? But this is my home. Where would I go?"

"I am sorry, Miss Utley."

"Tell me exactly what she said. Please, Inspector."

"Are you sure? It will only be hurtful, and it's obviously not going to happen now."

"I am sure. I thought Gertrude was my friend but ... well it doesn't matter. However, I do need to know what she said for my own peace of mind."

Detective Inspector Thornaby nodded and, clearing his throat, began.

Gertrude had told him she and Arthur had originally been a couple for a while in school, but the relationship had petered out and he'd moved onto Mary. She hadn't minded in the slightest, but several months ago their love had been rekindled, and they both realised they should have stayed together. About a month ago they decided Arthur would leave Mary and move in with Gertrude. They would have to ask Maude to leave, but there were some very nice flats for rent in the nearby town, and Gertrude was sure she'd find somewhere quickly.

"The town?" Maude said. "But I don't want to move all that way. I love this village. I'd get lost in town. Besides, I don't have any money. Gertrude used it for the shop."

"You don't have to move now, Miss Utley, remember?"

"Oh, yes. Sorry. Please, carry on."

Unexpectedly, a fortnight ago Arthur had informed Gertrude he'd changed his mind and wouldn't be leaving his wife after all. Gertrude was upset at first, then angry, and demanded to know why he'd had a change of heart. It turned out Mary had won the lottery, and he wasn't going to give up all that money. It was what he deserved after having put up with her for so long. But he said it meant he could still come and see Gertrude and treat her every so often.

"Oh dear, she wouldn't have liked that," Maude said. "He told her about the lottery win two weeks ago?"

"According to Miss Bickel, yes. Why do you ask?"

"That was the news Mary came to tell us. I recall Gertrude being surprised, but now you tell me she already knew." Maude shook her head in amazement. "She was so convincing. What happens now, Inspector? When will Gertrude be coming home? I'm afraid I feel quite nervous at the thought of still living in the same house, you see. Knowing she doesn't really want me here."

"You have no need to worry on that score, Miss Utley. Gertrude Bickel will not be returning home. Her knitting basket contained the matching needle to the murder weapon, and both had only her fingerprints on them. Arthur Wilkinson must have paid her a sneaky visit at the shop when you weren't there. She has officially been arrested for his murder.

∼

ONE WEEK later in an exclusive and well-heeled tearoom in the nearby town, a doctor and his wife were partaking of afternoon tea. The room was adorned with tall screens and large potted ferns making the privacy of its clients a priority. But there was another pair sitting at the other side of the screen who could hear every word.

The doctor shook out the paper and spoke to his wife. "Did you see this article about the local murder?"

"Yes, I did. Isn't it dreadful? Mind you, he was quite cruel to his wife by all accounts."

"Mmm, it says as much here."

"It's that poor elderly lady, the companion to the accused, I feel sorry for. She was also verbally and physically abused as well. Apart from being treated as a serf to boot. Poor thing."

"They're calling it a crime of passion."

The doctor's wife scoffed. "More to do with the large lottery win I should think."

"Yes. The root of all evil." He folded the newspaper, drained the last of his tea and turned to his wife. "We better get a move on. We don't want to be late."

The two eavesdroppers waited until they were alone before speaking.

"Obviously there was no problem moving the body into the changing room that morning?" The first murmured quietly.

"None at all," the other replied in the same low tone.

"And to the bin later on?"

"No. Everything worked out perfectly. It's amazing what some people will do for work nowadays. And the fact he had been in prison and was still on probation made all the difference. That and a hefty payment of course."

"It worked out well with everyone being at the front of the shop when he snuck in the back."

"A newly unlocked door and a pot of cold tea was all it took."

"And a *misplaced* knitting needle."

"Indeed."

"And talking of tea, shall I be mother, Mary?"

"That would be very nice. Thank you, Maude."

ABOUT J. NEW

J. New is the author of The Yellow Cottage Vintage Mysteries. Immerse yourself in country house murders, dastardly deeds at English Church fetes, daring escapades in the French Riviera and the secret tunnels under London, in the award-winning series readers call, 'Miss Marple' meets 'The Ghost Whisperer.' She also writes two contemporary mystery series: Tea & Sympathy featuring Lilly Tweed, former Agony Aunt now purveyor of fine teas and Finch & Fischer with mobile librarian Penny Finch and her rescue dog Fischer at the helm.

Jacquie lives in the North of England with her partner and an assortment of rescue animals.

10

THE LADY OF THE HOUSE

FLORA MCGOWAN

Charles took a second to compose himself. After all, selling a house was a serious business, especially if the occupant had resided there for some time. He could not deny however (with a very small accompanying grin), that he enjoyed his work. This part, particularly. Trying to persuade defenceless old dears that their pride and joy, the home in which they had lived since the year dot and lovingly taken care of was, in fact, merely a pile of bricks and mortar, and the only value it contained was that of the sentiment they themselves attached to it. No-one else would "view" it quite the same. Despite himself he chuckled at his own pun.

Eddie, his best mate from school, had suggested to Charles almost 10 years ago that they embark on this enterprise and go into business together. And while they still worked out of the same small office in a modest part of town, it belied the fact that business was doing well. More than well really, considering other concerns had closed down over the years, while they still had a steady stream of clients.

The two friends had concentrated their endeavours on a particular type of property and client – bungalows belonging to the elderly. These, they had discovered, were excellent properties to have on their books – always in demand as few new ones were built, and frail old dears who cannot manage the stairs in their houses need to move to more suitable accommodation. With limited ground floor flats available, and the ground rents and service charges of apartments with lifts rising quicker than you could say "penthouse please", bungalows were the property of choice. With independence and a nice little garden of one's own to boot. Plus the fact that the elderly were more likely to visit a bricks and mortar estate agent than a "virtual" online company.

The two friends had worked out a nice system between them. Nice solid dependable Eddie manned the office: the guiding force behind the partnership. He had a plain but pleasant countenance with short dark hair, and sported little round glasses. Old ladies took to him and found him well-mannered and charming. To them he was Edward, a man they could rely on to get them the best price for their property. He made arrangements for valuations and viewings, produced the nicely coloured details, and was always on hand to answer any questions and sooth away doubts. The fact that he had actually been christened "Dwayne" was something he kept well hidden. He had soon realised, after initially introducing himself by his given name, that many of his prospective clients looked at him with a hint of suspicion, an accompanying frown and queried "*Who*?" Whereas "Edward" portrayed a person with whom they could more much easily relate.

Similarly, both men always referred to their clients in a respectful manner, as Mr or Mrs So-and-so, or Miss on occasion. Charles had noticed one day, whilst waiting in line at his local building society, that the female employees always spoke to their customers in this manner; whereas the sole male member of counter staff would smile and try for a more friendly approach, calling the customers by their first names. However, when it came to appointments for mortgages or applications for other accounts, work that might accrue a productivity bonus, it was the women, with their more respectful approach, who had by far the most custom.

Charles, (known by his parents as "Calvin" and who had gone through school taunted with various nicknames such as "Pants" or "Grits" and had decided that "Charles" portrayed more of a *presence*) with his boyish good looks, a head of wavy blond locks and twinkling blue eyes, undertook those valuations and viewings. He could cajole the most forbidding old matron into believing her beloved kitchen was outdated, her bathroom archaic, and her dining room décor antiquated. Then, all that was needed was her signature on the details and he could almost feel the money in his custom-made pocket. The property was priced well under market value ("But *those* properties have *modern* fitted kitchens...") and a quick sale was in the bag. Moreover, with a fixed rate of commission the fee he earned was the same as that for a more expensive, more realistically valued house owned by a person less easily hoodwinked.

Only last week Eddie had made an appointment for Charles to value Mrs Jenkins' property. She had hesitantly enquired about the possibility of a visit, her husband having recently died and she was finding it difficult to manage the place on her own.

Edward had understood. On the one hand she had her memories, which at times were painful, and on the other, she was unable to cut the grass or replace the light bulbs when they blew, and was loath to pay someone to do all the little jobs that needed doing.

"Besides," she had confided, "it can be so hard to find an honest man these days. So often they cut the grass, but *don't* trim the edges. Or you find the cuttings strewn all over the flower beds where the wind has blown them and they have not been tidied away. And once—" here she had leaned across the desk and lowered her voice even though there was no-one else in the office to overhear, "—once I went outside to find that my delphiniums had been dug up."

Charles straightened his tie, (both he and Eddie always wore modest three-piece suits), ran a hand over his hair to ensure it was not too bouncy and virile, and knocked on the door. He then took a step back so as not to crowd the old dear on her own doorstep, and waited.

His eyes widened in surprise. He realised his mouth was open but no sound coming out when he saw the woman who opened the door. He had to mentally get a hold of himself and take charge of the situation.

"Good morning. I'm Charles from Smithfield Estates," he introduced himself. "To see Mrs Jenkins about a valuation."

"She's resting. I'm her granddaughter."

Charles was a little taken aback by the brusqueness of her tone. However, as the woman standing before him was quite possibly the most stunning creature he had seen in quite a while, he decided to overlook it. She was of a willowy slim build in everyday jeans and a plain white scooped neck T-shirt that fitted her curves like a second skin. Moreover, her complexion was flawless, the real peaches and cream he had only read about in books, with long shiny blonde hair reaching to her shoulders. She also had cold blue eyes fixed on him, and a mouth that was just a grim line outlined in girly pink.

"Nice to meet you." He extended his hand in greeting. "I'm Charles," he repeated, still a little flustered, then amended it to "Charlie. And you are?"

"I already told you. I'm her granddaughter," the woman replied sharply, and a tiny arrow of ice pierced him vaguely in the region of his heart. She glanced down at his proffered hand with an expression akin to scorn, then turned her back on him, saying over her shoulder, "You had better come in, then."

Regaining some of his poise, Charles carefully and in something of an exaggerated manner wiped his feet on the doormat, before stepping over the threshold into the hallway where the woman was impatiently waiting for him. He looked up as she uttered a tetchy sigh and decided, perhaps, he was overdoing it a bit.

Silently she led the way into the main living room. Charles followed meekly, his mind frantically thinking of things to say. He normally had a whole stock of well-practiced phrases, but these he used on the old grannies he was trying to impress with his knowledge, whilst at the same time convince them that while they might love their home just as it was, others might not.

"Well, this is a very lovely home," he finally elected to say. "Very nice." He nodded as if in agreement with himself as he gazed around, noting the walls painted in pastels shades and not covered in wallpaper featuring huge garish flowers, or painted anaglypta from several decades ago.

If he had expected to find the old lady sitting in an armchair calmly awaiting his arrival he was disappointed, and decided therefore she must be reclining in another room.

Feeling a little self-conscious under his companion's unrelenting gaze he strode into the middle of the room, produced his mobile phone and proceeded to take photographs of various salient features, turning ninety degrees each time to ensure he snapped the entire room. Next, he took digital measurements of the length and breadth of the room, and all the while the woman stood silently, arms folded across her chest, her eyes narrowed in a frown, watching.

Why is she making me feel guilty? Charles thought. I have not done anything, yet.

When Charles had finished in the living room Mrs Jenkins' granddaughter led him into the kitchen. Again, all his previously used stock phrases regarding outdated units froze on his lips as he contemplated the understated room.

"Very nice," he muttered weakly, feeling he should say something. While not new, the cabinets were in a country style of muted greens, and well cared for. His eyes could detect no scuffs or scratches. The stainless-steel sink with mixer taps had been polished until they gleamed. The floor tiles in rustic browns appeared freshly washed. Even the windows sparkled as if they had just been wiped over not five minutes previously.

In the bathroom, once again his prepared speech remained unspoken. The bath looked to be an original enamel tub which had been lovingly cleaned after each use. The large mirror taking up most of the wall facing the bath was spotless. On the towel rail hung fluffy pale aquamarine towels.

The woman led him back into the hallway and he expected her to take him into the kitchen where he had noticed a door leading out to the back garden. When he mentioned this, she spun around and asked, somewhat surprised, "Don't you want to see the bedroom?"

Taken off guard he merely nodded, then muttered, "But I thought you said your grandmother was resting?"

"She is. But not here."

A vague notion that he was being kept from speaking to the old lady crept over him. He wondered afresh where she was. Had all his dubious practices been spotted? Instead of an old-age pensioner used to having a husband do all the paperwork, sign the legal stuff, pay the bills – a woman whom he could easily hoodwink – was he now having to deal with her granddaughter? A *young* woman whom he felt sure would drive a very hard bargain indeed. No low asking price for a quick sale on this property; she would expect the going rate.

There *were* flowers on the wallpaper in the bedroom, not

large roses but tasteful sprigs of lavender and violets which complemented the curtains and the candlewick bedspread. The carpet on the floor was a thick plush pile in a complementing pale pink.

Finally, he thought of something to say. "Are you taking the carpets and curtains? Or leaving them."

She looked down at the floor beneath her feet as if seeing it for the first time, then glanced from the bedspread to the matching curtains before replying. "Leaving the carpets. But not the curtains."

"In all the rooms?"

She nodded, then added in a voice that brooked no argument, "Yes."

Outside in the garden, which like the house was well tended – the lawn weed-free and evenly trimmed (perhaps someone was paid to do the garden, he thought, maybe there was a cleaner as well) – the flower beds were a riot of colour. He recognised a few of the plants, a lavender bush, some roses and rhododendrons, but there his gardening knowledge ended. He ought to have picked up more; he had been in enough gardens during his time valuing properties.

As he wandered around, he strayed into an area shaded by a large tree. Despite wearing a suit in the warm weather he shivered at the sudden change in temperature. *Her frostiness must be catching*, he thought. *Or else I am close to the location of some bones.*

He caught himself studying the ground, looking for any signs of a large, recently dug hole.

Casually he opened the shed door and peered inside. Although it was dark and gloomy he could see enough to know there was no body stashed away. The old lady really must be resting somewhere; the girl's limited conversation had left him uneasy.

Back inside the house once more, no skeletons (literally) having been found in any closet, Charles was just beginning to relax. When they returned to the living room he made to sit down while removing some papers from his pocket.

"Sorry they're a bit crumpled, but I had to fold them," he explained. "I brought your gran some details for a couple of nice retirement apartments she might care to look at." He smiled as he laid his presents out on the coffee table, although it was more for his benefit: thinking of the joy he always had when he made a double sale with matching commission.

"There's no need. She's coming to stay with me."

The reply had been instant. Charles heart sank. And not for the first time that afternoon, as he realised that although his initial reaction on meeting Mrs Jenkins' granddaughter had been one of pleasant surprise, his mood had subsequently become gloomier. Not only with each well-presented room they had entered, but whenever she opened her mouth (which was not soft as he had originally thought, but hard and cruel) in rebuttal. His earlier feelings of attraction had gradually melted away with her continued chilly demeanour.

This was no goddess or angel whom he might want to serenade, but a harpy intent (and succeeding) on making him feel uncomfortable. When he looked into her cold blue eyes she had the power, like Medusa, to turn his potential ardour to stone. No, he decided, she was a Siren, attracting him with her long blond hair and shapely figure, only to dash all his hopes of a profitable sale on the rocks of her granite-like heart. Deflated, he returned the retirement property details unseen to his pocket.

"Well," he said, resigned to the fact that this valuation had not gone according to plan, not to his plan anyway. "We'll get the details typed up, then your grandmother can approve them and sign all the necessary. Then we can get the show on the road." He gave his much-lauded smile, which again failed to reach its target. Charles rose. Silently he wished the old woman (wherever she was) joy of her graceless granddaughter. He took his leave, surprising himself at the urgency with which he vacated the premises.

∼

EDDIE WAS RELAXING in the office while striving to look busy. Every now and then he would take a stack of papers (partially blank) from one folder and slip them into another, before reversing the process some minutes later. He would peer at his computer screen, type furiously for several minutes, then pick up the telephone receiver (the old dears loved an estate agent who still retained an old landline) and go through the motions of placing a call only to "discover" that the intended recipient was not at home.

Today was a particularly slow day. Sometimes it went like that on a Monday. Prospective clients tended to make arrangements on a Saturday. Even pensioners who had to fill Monday to Friday with something tended to do their grocery shopping on Mondays, having left supermarkets free at the weekends for those who worked during the week.

Therefore, he greeted the woman who entered the office late morning with rather more enthusiasm than he might have done, considering she was both flustered and upset in turns. After his cheery, "Good morning, madam! How can I help you today?" he noted her dark clothes, pale face and general distressed demeanour, and decided to tone his approach down a little. He replaced his grin of joy at the presence of a potential customer with an empathic smile of one who wishes to help if he can.

"Please, take a seat," he suggested, while arising from his own and walking around the desk to guide her towards a comfortably plush chair. That was another of his business practices – customers spend more money when they are comfortable. Provide only hard chairs and people do not stay in the office long, but leave for other premises.

"Oh, thank you," murmured the woman, lowering herself into the seat. She retrieved a tissue from her handbag and gently blew her nose.

"And how can I help you today," Eddie repeated. As she bowed her head to compose herself he grinned at Charles, lurking in the back room without her noticing; a grin that signalled: this should hopefully be an easy sale. Charles grinned back, but stayed out of sight of the woman, confident that his colleague had it all in hand.

"I'm sorry, but I should have come before," the woman began. "Only—" She paused and sniffed into her tissue again. Eddie waited for her to continue. He sensed a bereavement sale in the offing if he was not mistaken. Always good for a cheap sale, as those who had inherited the building never wanted a long-protracted affair, but money in the bank now. Especially if proceeds were to be split between several heirs. Neither did they want the place to be standing empty, getting damp, attracting squatters, losing its value.

"I was going to come in before the funeral," she began again, and Eddie had to bite his lip to stop the smile from spreading across his face. "But there was so much to see to: the vicar, the flowers, informing everyone. Making sure people had somewhere to stay. Where to have the wake, then who's going to do the catering and whether there should be alcohol or just a sherry, and—"

Eddie could tell that now the floodgates were opened, it might be difficult to stop the woman from talking. Perhaps he should guide her towards the matter in hand, whatever it was.

"And the house?" he prompted, guessing the type of property in question. After all, "house" covered various types of dwelling – single storey bungalow, multi storey, a townhouse, semi- detached, cottage.

"Yes exactly, the house," the woman agreed.

"Mrs?" Eddie prompted again.

"Mrs Hargreaves," the woman supplied. "Although, it's not my house, or rather it wasn't. Although it is now." And over her head Eddie and Charles exchanged grins once more. "So, I did mean to cancel—"

And suddenly, simultaneously, with that one simple word, the smiles froze on both Charles' and Eddie's faces.

"Cancel?" Eddie repeated, a little uncertainly.

"Yes, well, you see, as Mother was taken ill and then

rushed into hospital there was no way she would be able to see you for the valuation she had arranged. I meant to come in and well, not cancel it, not at that time, anyway. Just delay it for a while. But then she died, and I forgot all about it, until I started sorting out her things, you know, cancelling the milkman, telling the phone company. And I remembered she mentioned coming to see you to make an appointment for a valuation. She did not want to live in her house on her own any more after Father died. She decided she wanted to make a fresh start. But ... but—" Mrs Hargreaves withdrew her tissue once again and dabbed at her eyes.

Eddie decided to try and take control of the situation, "But won't you want to sell it now?" he asked. "If the house if vacant."

"Oh no, we've decided to move into it ourselves. My husband and I are going to downsize, and a nice little bungalow is just what we need – with all these rising bills, heating and so on. I've decided I can cope with the memories, after all it was my girlhood home. I lived there once before."

And before Eddie could ask if her current house needed selling, she added, "And so we're selling our house in Gloucester and moving back here. Permanently. We've been living in the house since Mother was taken ill and we've decided we're going to stay."

For once Eddie was speechless. He was also minus his normally happy face that attracted customers.

"So, as you see," continued Mrs Hargreaves, although just at that moment neither Eddie or Charles did see. As far as they could fathom, she had come into their office not to arrange to buy or sell, or even rent a property at all. "I should have come in and informed you of Mother's illness and subsequent death. Which was why, when you went to do the valuation that had been arranged the other week, there was no-one there. Mother was in hospital at the time."

Eddie turned to consult his computer screen regarding appointments for valuation. He did not remember any failed appointments. He glanced at Charles, who shook his head in puzzlement. He had successfully valued all the properties he had been booked to visit.

Then Eddie noticed the file on his desk, containing the details of Mrs Jenkins' bungalow, the nicely coloured page describing the property. All that it needed was for Mrs Jenkins to give the sheet the once over and approve the sale by signing on the dotted line. It had lain unsigned on his desk for almost two weeks now, possibly longer.

"And your mother's name was...?" Eddie began hesitantly.

"Jenkins. Beryl Jenkins."

Eddie's mouth silently opened and closed. His fingers shook slightly as he withdrew the paper from the folder.

Charles decided it was time he made his presence felt. "But we valued – *I* valued – Mrs Jenkins' bungalow," he asserted.

"Oh, no, Mother was in hospital."

Charles remembered the woman telling him the old lady had been "resting."

"But her granddaughter—" Charles began. He got no further as Mrs Hargreaves' face crumpled and she searched for her tissue once more.

After a few minutes Mrs Hargreaves composed herself enough to say, "We buried Mother next to my daughter."

Charles shivered, remembering the old wives' tale of someone walking over your grave at such a moment. He recalled the girl's reply when he had offered to show her details of a nice little retirement apartment—

"She's coming to stay with me."

ABOUT FLORA MCGOWAN

Flora McGowan is the author of the Carrie and Keith Mysteries, novels and short stories. Her stories combine a mix of mystery with the mystical and supernatural, often with an historical element as well as a touch of humour and a dash of romance. Flora was born in Dorset and has spent most, but not all, of her life there, and many of her stories are based in this locale. Flora enjoys travelling, taking inspiration from the places she visits. You can catch up with Flora via Goodreads, her blog, Facebook, Instagram or BookBub.

11

REQUIEM FOR A VIOLIN

GERALDINE MOORKENS BYRNE

Mrs O'Brien set the violin back into the battered case with extreme care. The instrument's body was a dull, reddish brown. The scroll was delicately carved, with gold-tipped ebony pegs. The bridge was worn and slightly warped, and the strings were far too old – but Mrs O'Brien felt sure that all the old thing needed to make it sing was a little tender care. O'Brien's Music Shop was just the place to make that happen.

"You realize what this is?" She peered over her glasses at the customer, a fresh-faced young woman, tall and slim, with long dark hair and soft brown eyes.

"No... I mean, Grandad always said it was a good instrument."

"Do you play yourself?"

The young woman nodded. "Well, yes. I play with the Symphony, actually. The Hibernian Symphony." She smiled shyly. "I'm second chair at the moment, but I hope – well,

Grandad always said with this instrument I could be as good as anyone in the orchestra. I know it sounds silly, but I hoped it was true."

"There's nothing silly about that," Mrs O'Brien said. "Being a professional violinist isn't easy, as you well know, but with one like this..." She touched the wood reverently. "If this didn't inspire you to play, there'd be no hope for you."

"Is it really that good?"

"It's a Perry, my dear! The only true Irish master-maker. This was made around seventeen ninety-five, and it's in excellent condition." She picked it up again, turned it over and showed the girl the button at the base of the neck. "That's the number, and underneath, Perry, Dublin."

Tears filled the soft brown eyes. "Oh! Grandad would have been delighted! My uncle Dan used to laugh at him, said it was nothing but junk. Hah! Grandad would be crowing now."

"Well to the untrained eye, I suppose one old violin looks much like another."

"Oh, but he isn't untrained! He's a conductor. He used to play violin too, only he wasn't made first violinist, so he quit. He's better as a conductor— Oh! I don't mean that the way it sounds. But, honestly, it's true. He is quite well known as a conductor, so it all worked out."

She reached out and caught Mrs O'Brien's own hand in hers. "Can you possibly fix it up? How much would it cost to do it really well?"

"It doesn't need much work. Only a bridge, the pegs need some care, and a new set of strings." It would all depend on the strings, Mrs O'Brien thought. To do it justice, it needed a really good set, and even half-decent ones were expensive. She named a figure and wasn't surprised to see the girl look downcast.

"Oh. That is expensive. But I know that brand is the best." She looked ready to cry. "It's just a bad week for it. I'll get paid next week. Would it be possible to leave it with you, and pick it up then?"

The shopkeeper hesitated. In nearly fifty years behind the counter of O'Brien's music shop she had seen every type of customer. The jobbing musician who worked hard to scrape a living; the privileged ones with trust funds and private means who never had to worry about money… A sudden image came to her: this young woman strolling into the orchestra with a Perry under her arm, knocking spots off all the rest. She made up her mind.

"What's your name, dear?"

"Lisa, Lisa Kennedy."

Mrs O'Brien filled out a docket listing the name, the instrument, the repairs to be undertaken. She asked for a phone number and added it to the list. But in the box where the estimate should be, she listed a figure far below the price quoted.

"I'm charging you for the bridge, Lisa. I have a few sets of those strings that the sales reps have given us. We'll give you a set, as long as you write a wee review for me. That sound fair?"

Lisa stared at her for a moment, then quite literally danced on the spot, clapping her hands. There was something so childlike in her delight, Mrs O'Brien had a hard time hiding her laughter.

"Yes, thank you! Oh, I can't thank you enough. I wonder if I can use it this weekend? We have such a big concert—"

She chatted away happily while Mrs O'Brien tagged the instrument with the docket. However, her exuberance faded as the bell jangled, and a man pushed the heavy old door open. Lisa glanced at him, and her face fell. She looked imploringly at Mrs O'Brien, who quietly lifted the violin in its shabby case down from the countertop and out of sight.

"Lisa?" The man spoke with an affected accent, one that Mrs O'Brien immediately categorized as "put on." He looked around the interior of the tiny shop and his mouth twisted into a sneer. "Oh. It's very small in here, isn't it? I thought you always went to our local music shop. But of course, things are probably cheaper in a small place like this…"

Mrs O'Brien grinned to herself. "You won't get a rise out me like that." She was justly proud of her establishment. The shop might be small, but it was over one hundred and fifty years old, and very well respected. Her late husband had been considered Ireland's finest restorer and luthier, and his replacement upstairs was young Michael, with two gold medals for making violins and a list of minor awards. So, she just smiled comfortably and addressed herself to Lisa.

"Well, I'll give you a ring when we have those items,"

Lisa was quick on the uptake. "Oh thanks. Just let me know." She gathered her bag and scarf and turned towards the man. "Are you on your way to the concert hall, Uncle Dan?"

He gave her a long, hard look, but replied civilly enough, "Yes, I spotted you as I went past, and thought I'd walk back with you. Rehearsals start promptly at eleven, you know."

Lisa didn't reply, but left with her uncle, giving the older woman a last, grateful look as she went.

Mrs O'Brien took the precious violin and brought it into the office. Michael would be in soon, and she knew he would be delighted to get his hands on such a rare and lovely piece. But she found herself frowning at the thought of 'Uncle Dan.'

"Nasty man," she muttered to herself. "I expect he bullies that young girl."

∽

THE SHOP DOOR jangled open again, and she stepped out to the counter. To her surprise, the very man she had been thinking about had returned, this time with a smile on his lips and a calculating look in his eye.

"Mrs O'Brien?"

"That's my name," she said agreeably.

"I'm Daniel Kennedy." He paused, apparently expecting some twitch of recognition from the woman. She didn't give it to him. "Hmm. Well, I'm the uncle of that young girl that was in here half an hour ago. She left an instrument for repair."

Still no response. Mrs O'Brien hadn't reared three kids without learning the art of silence as a weapon. He tried again, this time with a slightly waspish tone. "You remember her, I presume? Young woman, dark hair, tall and slim. She brought in a— I mean *my* violin."

His violin? She tutted to herself. It wasn't hard to see where this was going. She recalled Lisa saying how her uncle had sneered at the violin, claiming it was worth little or nothing. It seemed he was more aware of its value than he cared to admit.

"I'm sorry, I'm not following. Can I help you with something specific?" Her tone was glacial.

Danial Kennedy started and began to babble in a far less assured manner. "I just— I mean, I need to collect the violin. We – that is, I – have decided not to go ahead with the repairs at present." He rallied a little, and with a return to his old manner, added, "I assume you won't refuse to return an instrument that hasn't even been worked on yet?"

"Of course not," She smiled broadly. "Give me the docket and I'll sort it out for you."

His jaw clenched. "Docket? What docket?"

"The repair docket. I'm sorry, you can't collect a repair without it." She shrugged elegantly, "I'm afraid you need the docket."

He glowered at her for a long moment, then without so much as a goodbye turned on his heel and stalked out of the shop. He slammed the door so hard that several of the instruments shifted in their glass cases, making a discordant chorus to send him on his way. She looked around her little shop space. It might be untidy, and it was definitely small, but it was packed full of beautiful instruments, from cellos to ukuleles.

"Don't mind him, my loves. He's a nasty, angry man."

A short while later, Michael Clancy arrived into work. She glanced up at him fondly. The young luthier had been a godsend after the old man had passed away; cheerful, enthusiastic, and talented. He made a good living working out of the repair rooms upstairs and he was generous with his time when customers needed help.

"Howya, Missus" He greeted her and threw himself into the office's only other chair. The battered violin case caught his eye. "What on earth is in that? It looks about a hundred years old."

"The case is probably at least that old. The violin is older still."

He perked up like an inquisitive puppy. "Really?"

"Open it and look."

He did so, and his reaction was all that she had expected.

"Perry," he breathed. "And a perfect one, at that." He glanced at the docket and nodded. "Yes, bridge and strings. I'll adjust the pegs too. They'll need it after so long. But there's not much needed. It's a beauty."

"I thought we'd help out the owner," She gave a succinct account of her morning. "She's a nice young girl, and he's a wretch."

Michael whistled. "I think he knows fine well how good it is. I assume it is hers? I mean, the grandfather didn't leave it to the uncle, and she's trying to swipe it?"

"I'm sure. She was very genuine."

"Wait a moment! Did you say Lisa Kennedy?" He took out his mobile and began to scroll frantically. Thrusting the screen at her, he asked, "This Lisa Kennedy?" A smiling picture of the violin's owner was on the screen with a brief biography underneath.

"Graduate of the Sorbonne Academy, Paris, and winner of the *Prie D'Or* at the International Violin Competition, Lisa is a valued member of the famous Hibernian Symphony Orchestra."

"That's her. Why, do you know her?"

To her surprise the young man blushed bright pink. "I met her briefly. She was playing in my sister's chamber group. She was just filling in for one of the regulars but..." He gazed into the distance. "She was amazing."

"Well, she'll be even more amazing if you get that violin done for her. She needs to play it in before Saturday."

"I'll have it tomorrow," he said firmly, and ran upstairs clutching the violin to his manly chest.

∽

NEXT MORNING, true to his word, Michael presented her with the newly tended Perry. Its wood now gleamed in earnest, grime and resin removed to reveal a stunningly grained maple. The pegs had been adjusted, the new bridge perfectly cut. With the new strings, of the best quality, the instrument had come alive. It seemed to want to sing, catching and echoing every sound.

"It's ready," he said simply.

Mrs O'Brien dialled the number Lisa had provided. The girl answered immediately, and asked anxiously *"It that O'Brien's?"*

"It is. I have good news for you..."

Lisa gurgled with delight! *"That is amazing, I can't thank you enough. I have rehearsals all day, but I will get to you as soon as I can..."*

Mrs O'Brien became aware of Michael's frantic signalling.

"Tell her I'll drop it over to the concert hall for her." He avoided her eyes. She rolled hers.

"Lisa, would it help if we dropped it over to you? I think our luthier would like to hear it being played properly…"

"Of course! And you too, please. I'd love you both to come and hear the rehearsal." And before she knew it, Mrs O'Brien had agreed to shut for an hour to go hear the instrument.

"Ah well, life is about more than work." She winked at Michael. "Come on, you. Let's go hear the lovely Lisa play."

~

THE PUBLIC AREA of the concert hall was deserted except for a lone usher, who waved them through once they explained their errand.

"I know where to go," Mrs O'Brien led the way. "It's not the first time I've been here. I've had to deliver many an emergency set of strings. There's a shortcut here through the dressing rooms."

Lisa was to meet them at the stage entrance, to try the instrument in the superb acoustics of the concert hall. They made their way to the narrow corridor which housed the dressing rooms. Even in the middle of the day it was gloomy in the staff areas of the concert hall; there were no windows and only a set of elderly light fittings cast a dim glow. Michael had never been backstage before and he was intrigued. There were doors along the length of the corridor on both sides, each with a name plate. One was marked

Ursula Graves, a famous flautist, and another bore the name Paulo Cassatta, a tenor of international renown. Both were due to perform that weekend with the orchestra.

Most doors had lists of names pinned to them, four on each. Obviously, the regular players didn't get private dressing rooms and instead had to share. He noticed Lisa Kennedy's name on a list with three other players. She shared with Ollessa Obu, a violist, and Clara Fitzpatrick, a cellist. The last name was Marianne Devlin, first violinist and first chair of the orchestra – titles which made her next in importance to the conductor. Michael had attended enough symphony concerts to recognize the name. She had appeared on Irish television, too. A tall woman, with brown hair and a slim build. A formidable player, famous for her Bach.

As he passed, he couldn't help noticing that the door was open. Without thinking, he glanced inside. His employer stopped and looked back. She saw Michael, the violin case in one hand and the other pointing towards the open dressing room door. He looked frozen on the spot, his face rigid with shock. She walked briskly back towards him and glanced into the room.

"What's the matter with you?" She asked, followed rather quickly by "Oh—!"

A woman was sprawled on the floor, face down. A large metal rod protruded from her back, its tip deeply embedded. She had long brown hair and was dressed in the black dress worn by the ladies of the orchestra for performances. Mrs O'Brien could just see her profile by bending down and peering closely.

"What – what is that?" Michael pointed to the wicked looking metal bar.

"That's a German nickel cello spike," she answered. "And I think she's dead…"

∼

HALF AN HOUR HAD PASSED and now the dressing room was filled with police and forensics. Several young women, among them Lisa, were in tears. Michael was still shocked, but he no longer looked as if he might be sick. Mrs O'Brien watched the scene carefully. She was shocked by the murder, of course she was, but there was a part of her that couldn't help being interested. The dressing room was the province of the Gardai now, but it was the scene in the corridor that occupied her thoughts.

She knew most of the orchestra by sight and many were customers. You get to know a lot about people from behind a shop counter. Especially a music shop. Kind people who loved music were always easy to deal with. It didn't matter if they were amateur or professional. On the other hand, there were those who had great reputations but treated shop staff like dirt. They could be the most famous musician in the world and spend money hand over fist, but if they were mean and snobbish, then to Mrs O'Brien they were bad customers.

She glanced at the unfortunate victim. Marianne hadn't been her favourite customer – a bit abrasive and very slow to settle her account. But once, when the late Mr O'Brien had undercharged her for strings, she had come back into town on the bus to rectify it. That went a long way in Mrs O'Brien's opinion. Just as she thought this, a slight commotion caught her attention. The door from the main public area swung open to reveal Daniel Kennedy, clutching a takeaway coffee.

"Let me in!" he was protesting to the young Garda on duty. "Do you know who I am?"

The Garda looked worried, and half turned to consult his superior, who was deep in discussion with the pathologist. Before he could attract the Inspector's attention, Lisa stepped forward and caught her uncle's arm.

"Uncle Dan, calm down!" She added politely to the Garda, "My uncle is the conductor."

"Lisa!" He looked around rather wildly. "What – what has happened?"

"I'm afraid there's been … a death" Lisa said.

Dan gaped at his niece, his face quite ashen and his eyes wide. "What? What do you mean – who died?"

"Marianne," A thin young man who had introduced himself as Peter, interjected. "Poor Marianne. She ran back to the dressing room to get some paracetamol tablets for a headache. She was only gone a few minutes when we heard someone shouting for help. Mrs O'Brien found her."

Dan's eyes bulged even more. "What? What were you doing here?"

"I was delivering an instrument." Mrs O'Brien said in her mildest tones. "Michael here happened to look in as he passed. The door was open, and the poor woman was beyond help."

"It was murder," someone said, and a shudder ran through the assembled musicians.

"But who could have done it?" Lisa appealed to her colleagues. "It's just horrible."

"Maybe she disturbed a thief?" Michael spoke for the first time since finding Marianne's body. "If she found someone riffling through the dressing room – maybe they panicked and stabbed her?"

"How would they get in?" Peter shook his head. "Sorry, I can't see it. You have to get past the lobby to access this corridor. Surely they'd have noticed a stranger?"

"Not necessarily, Peter" Daniel replied. "I've always said they were far too lax up there." He threw a pointed look at Michael. "They let in anyone with half an excuse."

Lisa reddened and took a step closer to where Michael and Mrs O'Brien were seated. "I told Una to let in Mrs O'Brien. They were delivering my violin to me. Una isn't lax at all; she would definitely ask a stranger for ID."

The Garda abandoned his aloof attitude to join in. "Is there no other way in here then?"

"None,"

"Then either they got in through the lobby or—"

He broke off abruptly and looked hard at the group. There was a moment's silence as each person turned it over in their mind and reached the same conclusion. If it wasn't an outsider, then one of them had murdered the First Chair.

The Garda Detective chose this moment to step out into the corridor. One shrewd look around the assembled staff told him a lot. Half of them were here as spectators, in his estimation. What was needed here was a cull.

"Who was on the stage rehearsing when this happened?"

The woodwind and timpani sections all raised their hands, along with roughly half the strings.

"Right, if you were on stage and hadn't left it in the fifteen minutes that the victim was absent, please return to the main hall and a Garda will take your statements. Everyone else, remain here."

Dan Kennedy went to follow the former group to the stage area, but Peter stopped him.

"You weren't on stage," he said firmly. "I was in the storeroom sorting this lot out." He waved a bundle of music sheets. "You weren't on stage. And you weren't in any of the rehearsal rooms, either."

"Well?" Dan snapped. "I wasn't in the building at all. I was out for a walk. I stopped on the way back for a coffee. Here!" He waved the coffee cup around alarmingly. He took a sup, winced at the hot liquid, and added, "I trust that clears it up?"

"Stay here the moment, even so." The Garda Detective had a pleasant voice and spoke with an air of quiet authority. "Now, I'd like to know your names."

One by one the remaining members of the orchestra gave their names, then he turned to Mrs O'Brien. Forestalling his enquiry, she gave a brief but accurate summary of events, including her name, Michael's name, and what they were doing there. She was rewarded by a warm smile and a nod of approbation.

"Well, I'm Detective Malachy Flynn. Miss Kennedy, why were you absent from the rehearsal hall?"

"My friend, Ollessa – she was due to rehearse next but her dress kept twisting. It's this material, it bunches up and make you miserable playing. I was in the Ladies' Toilet in the seating area, helping her fix it."

"I'm Ollessa," said a young woman with brown curls set around a sweet face. "It's true."

"I had intended to meet Mrs O'Brien by the stage door, but I was delayed fixing Ollessa's dress," Lisa finished.

"I was in the music storeroom," Peter repeated, adding rather smugly, "I was there five minutes before Marianne left the hall."

"Okay. And Mr Kennedy was out getting coffee?"

They all nodded, Dan adding "I don't see how any of us could be involved then."

Detective Flynn ignored him and turned to the last person, a large older man with sparse fair hair and a cheerful face. "What about you, sir?"

"I'm Charles McKay, Detective. Double Bass player. I was in rehearsal room B. Before you ask, I saw no one, and heard nothing – the rooms are soundproofed. I only came out when someone banged on the door."

Detective Flynn nodded. "Right. The question now is – who would have wanted to kill this lady?"

The baldness of the question left them all silent. Finally, Mrs O'Brien spoke.

"It's hard to speak ill of the dead, Detective. I'm sure her colleagues don't want to be rude about the poor woman. I've known her for twenty years, as a customer. For what it's worth, I found her difficult – very exacting, very much a perfectionist. Her music was her life, as far as I could see. But she was honest, and she was fair."

Lisa Kennedy nodded. "She was very tough. She would

openly criticize anyone in the orchestra if she felt they weren't up to scratch. But she really cared about the Symphony. She wanted us all to do well. She was delighted about my Perry, said it would make all the difference for my career." She realized the Detective was looking bewildered and added, "My violin that Mrs O'Brien came here to deliver. It's a really good, old handmade Irish instrument, by a maker called Perry."

"I see. And you, Mr Kennedy, how did you get on with the deceased?"

"Me? Marianne and I were on excellent terms. She was a most esteemed colleague."

Charles McKay snorted. "I would hardly say you were on excellent terms!"

Dan's face turned a bright puce. "How dare you, you old fraud!"

"You and Marianne were going at it earlier," Charles said firmly. "I overheard you, and I'm not the only one. I couldn't hear it all, Detective, but Marianne shouted at him that he was a jealous old goat, and he called her an interfering wagon."

Detective Flynn smiled at Dan. It was not a pleasant smile.

"That's the second time someone has had to correct your evidence, Mr Kennedy."

"It's – it's not how it sounds. We are musicians. We are passionate. Sometimes we argue, it's perfectly normal. But we don't take such things seriously. For that matter, Charles wasn't her favourite colleague either, were you? Marianne thought you were lazy, and she was right. I'm telling you,

Detective, she argued with everyone. She openly said that Peter here wasn't up to his job."

Peter flushed but shrugged. "She didn't like me, and I didn't like her."

Charles smiled. "I hate to agree with Dan, but she really didn't like young Peter here. She thought he was untrustworthy. She did say he should be replaced, at least once every rehearsal."

"And had she any power? What I mean is, could she have fired anyone?"

"No," Peter said. "Well, she could complain to the management, but I doubt they would take her complaints seriously. She complained about everything and everyone."

"She told me she was looking into grounds for dismissal." Charles snapped.

As the trio of Dan, Charles and Peter bickered, Mrs O'Brien took her opportunity.

"Is Peter really that useless?" she asked Lisa.

"To be honest, yes. He's as lazy as sin, and just between us, I've heard he has a gambling problem. Marianne thought he was light-fingered."

"Bear with me now. Are you always in that dressing room? And do you share with the same people each time?"

"Oh yes, that's our normal room. Ollessa, Clara and I always share when we can."

"And Marianne?"

"As a matter of fact, Marianne would normally have her own room, but because we needed two rooms for the stars, she came in with us."

Mrs O'Brien nodded. "And I notice, you all wear similar dresses. Not identical, but similar."

"Yes, it's the rule. Men in black tie, women in black dresses."

Looking very pleased with herself, Mrs O'Brien had one more point to clear up.

"Excuse me." She walked past Daniel Kennedy, still engaged in a war of words with Charles. "Ooops!"

Her elbow caught the hand holding the takeaway coffee cup and it dropped to the floor, spreading a puddle of liquid. A good quantity of it splashed on Dan's hand and trouser leg, and he swore in annoyance, but continued arguing. Some of it landed on Mrs O'Brien's arm, but she didn't seem a bit put out. In fact, she smiled.

"Detective Flynn," she called out. "Could I talk to you for a moment."

The Detective looked surprised but nodded.

"Mr Kennedy here arrived back with his coffee less than twenty minutes ago. We all saw him sip it, and wince at the heat. Yet if you check what I spilled just now, it's stone cold!"

Detective Flynn's eyes narrowed, and he looked from her to the conductor. "That's very interesting, indeed."

"Another interesting fact. Peter claims to have been in the storeroom all that time. So how did he know Marianne left the hall five minutes after him? Unless he was in the corridor on the lookout for someone."

Peter began to bluster, but a look from the detective silenced him. Mrs O'Brien continued unperturbed.

"See, there was one person who was meant to leave at that time: Lisa Kennedy. She should have been at the stage door to meet Michael and me. But she stopped to help Ollessa, and by sheer bad luck Marianne left instead. Another tall brunette, with hair arranged in a similar style to Lisa's, wearing a dress so similar one can hardly tell them apart."

She looked Daniel Kennedy in the eyes. "You tried to steal that Perry from Lisa once already. Coming back to my shop and pretending it was yours. And if we had handed it over here, you could hardly claim it for yourself. You pretended to slip out and get coffee, but in fact all you did was hide an old cup. You paid Peter here to tip you off when Lisa was alone in the corridor – he's an unscrupulous wretch, but I don't think he has quite the stomach for an actual murder. But he didn't mind helping, eh?" She shook her head in disgust. "Marianne looked enough like Lisa from the back, so Peter called Dan here and told him she had popped into the dressing room."

"It was all him!" Peter shrieked. "I didn't know what he was up to, I thought he just wanted to steal the violin. If it went missing from the concert hall, no one could blame him. That's what he told me."

"Shut up!" Dan snarled.

"Uncle Dan—" Lisa choked back a sob. "How could you?"

Daniel Kennedy swung around to face her, his face livid with rage. "It should have been mine! My stupid father hoarding that instrument, saying he was waiting for a worthy player – have you any idea how that felt? If I had had that instrument I would have been successful, but he hid it away and then gave it to you!"

"You killed an innocent woman,"

"I killed an interfering baggage."

"You would have murdered your own niece," Mrs O'Brien said sharply. "Marianne was just in the wrong place. Your plan all along was to kill Lisa. Otherwise, you could have just stolen the violin at another time. But if she was dead, you could claim it as her next of kin. Or just pretend it was yours, all along."

She turned to Peter, an avenging angel in full flight. "As for you – you can pretend all you want, but you knew what he had planned. Answer me this: where did he get a sixteen-inch German nickel cello end rod from?"

"We keep them in the music storeroom," Ollessa said, pointing at Peter. "You gave it to him!"

Peter crumpled, shrieking over and over, "No, I didn't know!", but the Detective shook his head grimly.

"Save it for your solicitor. Garda Clarke, hold that man" He himself took charge of Dan Kennedy, grasping his arm firmly. "Daniel Kennedy, you are under arrest for the murder of Marianne Devlin—"

∼

HOURS PASSED before Mrs O'Brien and the other witnesses were able to go home. It was over a week before the press interest and public curiosity died down. Mrs O'Brien kept her shop closed, and spent a quiet week with her eldest son and his family. Michael texted her to say he had taken Lisa out to dinner "to cheer her up," and Detective Flynn sent her a very complimentary email, thanking her for her quick-witted intervention.

But at length it was time to get back to normal. The old doors of the shop reopened, the shutters went up and business as normal resumed. They were back to work for almost another week when Lisa rang.

"Call around to the Concert Hall, please! And bring Michael."

When they arrived they found a small group seated in the auditorium, including Ollessa, Charles and other members of the orchestra. Taking a seat next to them, Mrs O'Brien and Michael were greeted warmly, but Ollessa put her fingers to her lips and shushed them, pointing to the stage.

A lone figure stood in the centre, poised to start playing. Mrs O'Brien held her breath, as the bow touched the strings of the Perry. The opening strains of the exquisite *Méditation* by Massenet filled the air, and she closed her eyes. She saw her late husband, smiling over his work, her children and her grandchildren, and finally she thought of her own parents, their comforting presence as tangible as that of Michael, her young protégé. As the final notes lingered on the air, everyone applauded. Mrs O'Brien wiped a tear from her eye, and joined in the cheers.

She had been right, all the Perry had needed was a little tender care.

ABOUT GERALDINE MOORKENS BYRNE

Geraldine Moorkens Byrne is an Irish mystery writer, poet and educator. She lives with her family in Dublin where many of her stories are set, especially The Caroline Jordan series. When not dreaming up modern murder mysteries, she knits, crochets and teaches classes on Irish folk traditions. Until 2021 she owned Ireland's oldest family owned music shop, the basis for "Requiem for a Violin." Mrs. O'Brien and friends will return in their own series in 2023, The Music Shop Mysteries.

She also writes a magical cosy mystery series, The Old Bat Chronicles under the pen name Nina Hayes.

12

NIGHTLY NUISANCE

KATHRYN MYKEL

Too excited to sleep any longer, Sarah rose early. She dressed and walked the half mile to her new business – and Taunton, Massachusetts' very first Quilt Shop.

Once she arrived at Quilter's Haven, Sarah scurried around the large open area preparing for the grand opening tomorrow, setting the air conditioning to stay at sixty-eight degrees every day from nine to six. The snack corner near the husbands' seating area was fully stocked, complete with a mini fridge filled to the max with refreshing bottled water.

Her hands were shaky with first day jitters and Sarah dropped the class fliers, scattering them around the floor. As she bent over to pick them up, she hesitated with a pang of regret that her fiancé, Brad, couldn't be there for the opening. He'd been instrumental in helping her set up. His police training had shined when he meticulously arranged the fabric bolts on the color wall; and of course she leaned on his strength for moving the display racks around. Once she had the papers up, Sarah straightened the pile and set them on the checkout counter. She glanced at the clock repeatedly as the minutes ticked by. Her final task was to finish setting up the class displays – eager to entice customers to sign up – she'd spent months getting ready. Making samples for each class, including patchwork bears, small pillows and travel-size pillowcases, cloth books for kids, and even a full-size Rail Fence quilt project.

As she was mentally checking off her to-do list, Sarah was startled by an unexpected voice.

"Wow, the place looks great!" Ginny, her real estate agent, said as she entered through the unlocked front door. She swiveled around, her eyes widening at each new space she looked at. For Sarah, it was like watching a child in a candy store.

"Here, these are for you," Ginny handed Sarah a small vase, full of fresh daisies.

"Thank you. That's sweet. I hadn't realized the time; the morning has flown by." Sarah smiled appreciatively at the daisies, before leaning in for a quick hug. Such a thoughtful gesture. Though she'd hired Ginny to find the perfect retail space to rent for her new quilt shop, Sarah hadn't really gotten to know her very well.

Sarah looked around for the perfect place to display the flowers and Ginny followed. "Now, remember the deal with the landlord. You are not to go into the attic," Ginny commented in a serious tone and eyed the trapdoor in the ceiling above.

"I haven't," Sarah replied, her eyes also darting to the

trap door. "But I overheard some gossip from ladies in the salon – that the previous tenant went missing in this very shop." Sarah grimaced. "They said he went into the attic and never came back down. I'm sure it's just chatter and has nothing to do with why the landlord urged no one go up there." She stiffened suddenly. "You don't think he's still up there, do you? Like his body? Because that would be creepy!"

"No, no, don't be silly. That's just your imagination running wild," Ginny said, shaking her head which made her bouncy gray curls bob back and forth.

Sarah felt goosebumps rise on her skin and changed the subject. "Oh, check out this medallion that I found when I was cleaning." She walked to her desk and pulled out the round disk for Ginny to inspect.

Ginny got close and held out her hand. "Let's see what you've got here." She squinted to get a better look at the metallic object. Sarah, in the meantime, decided the fresh flowers would look perfect on her desk and set them down next to her computer.

"Do you think it's good luck?" Sarah asked. "It looks like a fleur-de-lis symbol, and I always thought those were for good fortune, right?"

"I don't know," Ginny responded, turning it over in her hand. "It's a mystery to me."

"Maybe it was from the magician. Ooh, maybe it's a clue?" Sarah grinned and winked.

"I don't know. I've seen nothing like it, but I'm no expert! Hang onto it." Ginny handed back the unusual medallion.

Sarah walked to the classroom and flopped into one of

the chairs just as her stomach growled. "Do you have time for lunch?" she asked Ginny.

"Yes, let's go to that new cafe in town – The Daily Grind. I've heard they have the best tomato soup there."

"I could also go for a strong cup of coffee." Sarah peered around. The morning had flown by, but the shop was in good shape. "I think everything is all set for tomorrow." She grabbed her coat. and flicked off the lights, engaged the alarm system, then locked the deadbolt on the front door.

∼

THE FOLLOWING MORNING, Sarah arrived early again, eager for her grand opening. She inserted her key into the deadbolt unlocking the door and pushed it open with her shoulder. Balancing a package in her arms, she flicked the light switch on – and shrieked. The entire place was in disarray: bolts of fabric were on the floor and the cutting table – there was trash everywhere!

A multi pack of scissors was open on the counter. She picked up the pack and saw that a pair was missing from it. As she scanned the length of the room, she noticed a chair was knocked over in the back. She walked the entire store – putting the stock back in place and picking up empty water bottles and wrappers while doing a mental inventory. She frowned at the realization there were things missing!

Her eyes pricked as she squeezed the single patchwork bear, wondering where the other had gone. She had worked endless hours making the set of bears.

Walking over to the display next to the remaining bear,

Sarah counted the pre-cut packs. Ordered in quantities of twelve, she counted only ten now.

Who would do such things in a quilt shop? What kind of thief is this? Maybe I should call Brad at the police station? Or the insurance company?

A spool of bright yellow thread distracted her, and she bent to pick it up. She chased the unraveled strand across the gray carpet. As she tugged on it, she saw a sewing kit under the foot of the display. Kneeling down on the floor, she reached her arm under the wooden cabinet, but when she pulled out the sewing kit, she found it was empty! Not a needle or piece of thread left behind –completely empty! Now that was really strange.

She fished her phone from her handbag to snap a couple pictures and realized she'd left it at home. Darn it!

Checking the back door, though she'd never used it, Sarah found it was locked and the little red light on the alarm panel blinked, alerting her it was alarmed. She walked back to the front to make a note of the missing items and found there were customers already waiting outside.

"Good morning." Her voice croaked as she greeted the women. "I'm sorry—" she cleared her throat. "I've had a bit of a morning."

The women all gave her a reassuring smile in response.

"Please let me know if I can help you with anything," Sarah said, eager to get to her notepad and write down what had gone missing. She scribbled down the list on the back of one of the class fliers.

. . .

2 PRE-CUT *charm packs*
 1 pair of scissors
 1 patchwork bear
 1 sewing kit
 waters and snacks

A BUS TOUR arrived just before lunch. Thirty happy quilters chatted about the store as they piled up bolt after bolt on her cutting counter, keeping her busy until well after closing time. She had no time to think any more about the strange mess she had walked in upon this morning. Long after the last customer left, and Sarah had reorganized the entire store, everything was cleaned up and ready for the next day. She turned off the lights, set the alarm, locked the front door behind her and gave it a powerful tug just to make sure.

Exhausted, she mulled over her day as she walked home, Sarah was no closer to figuring out what could have happened, and she couldn't wait to be reunited with her cell phone. It wouldn't have been a critter. They don't have opposable thumbs to open water bottles. A person. But who? Ginny? Why would Ginny let herself in and make a mess? She shook her head to clear the errant thoughts as she checked the mailbox at the end of her driveway.

∽

THE NEXT MORNING, Sarah was uneasy about what she might find. She unlocked the front door and disengaged the alarm. She took a deep breath and flicked on the lights.

"Argh," she groaned. "More trash on the floor." This time she found patterns had been pulled off the hangers and there was one open on her desk. "I know I didn't leave it like this yesterday."

She walked over and plopped down in her office chair and repackaged the pattern in the zip-lock bag.

From this vantage point, she could see the scrap bin overturned across the room. It looked like Master Quilter Eleanor Burns had been here, tossing every scrap in the bin over her shoulder onto the floor! What a mess!

She walked the whole shop, doing another mental inventory. She frowned when she noticed the children's cloth book was missing, as well as the small pillow and the travel pillowcase. Now, she was short four samples for her classes!

"Two days in a row," she grumbled under her breath.

She found a pen in the drawer of her desk and added the additional missing items to the list on the back of the class flier from the day before.

WATERS AND CANDY *bars*
   small pillow and travel size case
   cloth book

BEFORE SHE COULD PULL out her phone to call the police, a rapping on the door made her pause. She stood up, smoothed her hair, checked her watch, and took a deep breath.

Just five minutes before opening time and I still need to clean up, and snap some pictures.

Sarah reluctantly opened the door to let the customers in early.

"Good morning," she greeted the elderly couple. "You may come in, but please be careful and excuse the mess. It appears someone was in the shop causing mischief last night." She frowned and waved her hand around.

"Oh dear! Let us help you clean up," the woman said, giving her man a nudge towards the mess.

"No, that's not necessary, it's not much. Just give me a few minutes to pick up and let me know if you have questions, or if you need me. I'll just be right over here," Sarah said, gesturing to the fabric scraps strewn all over the floor.

"How fun." The woman cheered and clapped her hands. "Let me! I love to paw through scrap bins. I'll go through them and put back whatever I don't want."

"Oh no, you mustn't. I can't have you picking up scraps off the floor," Sarah said in horror.

"Nonsense. I had nine children. You leave it to me, dear," the woman hummed. She whisked up the scraps, like a much older version of Mary Poppins.

Despite the evening's mischief, business was booming again, and Sarah was quickly distracted. Several large groups of women from the local quilt guilds visited throughout the day. She no sooner had the place tidied up after one group before another would enter, and the cycle of cut, fold, cash out and clean up, would repeat all over again.

Sarah rubbed her sore shoulder. *I might have to hire*

someone to help. She chuckled. What would they think of coming to work every morning to find the store a mess?

Today she had taken a few bites of her sandwich, so at least her stomach wasn't growling on top of her aches and pains. She glanced at the clock on the wall. "Wow, it's already five thirty-five!" With less than a half hour until closing, she had little time to straighten up, but no time to make a call to the insurance company, which she was sure would be closed by this time.

Rapping her fingers on the cutting board, she stared at the list of missing items. *What is going on? Was it the previous tenant? The gossip was that he was a magician. I don't recall this being a magic shop previously.* She scurried around the store straightening up. *Was he haunting the store? Don't be daft Sarah, why would a magician take or need quilting supplies? Besides, you don't even believe in ghosts!* Goosebumps erupted down her spine as she thought it.

She rubbed her arms and shook off the uneasy thoughts of missing tenants and creepy magicians. Once the shop was presentable again, Sarah followed the same closing routine as she had done the previous two nights and gave the door an extra tug to make sure it was locked.

∽

This morning, Sarah was chuckling as she flicked the lights on, thinking of how silly she'd been with her theories of ghosts and haunted quilt shops. She stopped short, her eyes bulging. The store looked like a cyclone had hit it again today.

Bottles of water and empty cookie packages littered the floor.

Whoever this is, sure is a slob. She trudged farther into the shop, only to find more missing items. Sarah grabbed her pen and notepad and added a package of batting and a quilt label to her growing list of missing supplies. If she didn't know any better, she'd think the magician's ghost was making a quilt. Now you know that is crazy thinking.

She pounded her fist on the counter and winced at the strike of pain which shot through her wrist. "I'm going to find you!" she yelled at the ceiling.

The ceiling – the attic. She heard Ginny's words ring in her ears as she walked toward the trap door: *Don't go in the attic*.

"Don't go in the attic, missing magicians – my foot!" she mumbled as she pulled the chain for the attic door. She coughed and waved her hand to clear the cloud of dust that filled the air in front of her face.

Sarah was tugging on the handle for the ladder when she was suddenly startled by someone clearing their throat. "Eh hm." Her friend Paul was standing behind her, his arms crossed with a quizzical smile. She was so focused on the attic, she hadn't even heard him come into her shop. "Whatcha doin'?" he asked.

"Ah, nothing!" She covered her eyes with her hand, already feeling dust fall from above. "I'm probably just being silly anyway," she said as she pushed the ladder back up, then turned with open arms for a much needed hug.

"How's it going?" Paul asked, squeezing her.

"Can't breathe," she croaked.

He released her and coughed. "What's all over your shoulder?"

Sarah looked down to see the offending fabric dust. "Everything is great ... except for the slob haunting my shop at night!" she said, brushing her shoulder clean.

She flushed as she saw the *This chick is nuts* look that crossed Paul's face.

"Haunting? You don't really believe in that, do you?"

"No. But I've been so busy during the day, I haven't had time to report it. By the time I close up it's too late in the day."

"Why isn't Brad on the case?" Paul asked.

"He's on an undercover assignment, so he doesn't even know what's going on yet." Sarah sighed and slouched into one of the classroom chairs.

"Should you call someone, now, while we have a minute?" Paul asked.

Sarah grimaced, seeing the look on Paul's face when she mentioned what was happening. She wasn't looking forward to repeating the strange events to anyone else. "Never mind. It's nothing I can't handle. How are you?" she asked and gestured for him to sit across from her.

"Tell me what's really going on, Sarah."

She scowled at him as he tried his best to keep a straight face while she told her story. He started laughing, and Sarah swatted him playfully. "It's not funny."

"Hey, why don't you pretend to leave tonight, but wait and see what happens instead," Paul grinned.

"That's a great idea. You'll stay too?" she eyed him.

"Oh no, you're on your own," he winked.

"Some friend you are!"

∽

RIGHT AT CLOSING TIME, Sarah followed her nightly routine, except this time she didn't leave. She waited by the snack area with her phone on and a giant flashlight that Paul had let her borrow.

She heard footsteps overhead. *What was I thinking? This is dangerous, being here alone!*

Silent and with as little movement as possible, she pressed *911*, kept her finger hovering over the call button, and waited stiff as a statue. After what seemed like hours, but was really just a few minutes, she heard the stairs from the attic door creak as they unfolded. She could just make out a small poof of dust, followed by a dark shape descending the ladder. "I've got you now," she yelled as she clicked on the flashlight and beamed it straight at the stairs – but there was nothing there. *Are my eyes playing tricks on me?*

She moved along the wall to the light switch, flipped it, and the fluorescent lights lit up every corner of the shop. Still nothing. She walked the entire store twice, but there was no sign of anything or anyone. The ladder was down – she now knew it had to be a ghost! She grabbed her purse and keys and bolted out the front door. She didn't even stop to engage the alarm.

∽

Since Brad was on assignment, Paul had agreed to go back to the shop with her after dinner. With a hearty meal fortifying her, she was calm and had regained her senses, disregarding her ghost theory again.

The two could see that the lights were still on as they pulled into the parking lot. Peeking in the window, Sarah said, "There's no mess inside, but the ladder is back up and the trapdoor is shut."

"You must've scared it," he mocked her.

"Me? Scared it? I don't think so." She shook her head.

Inside, with the lights still on, Paul pulled down the stairs. "Wait for me." Sarah reached for him, just as a cloud of dust enveloped them both.

"What is that dust?" he asked before sneezing. They both wiped their faces before climbing the ladder.

"I think it's lint, from the precut fabric packs. They make a huge mess, you know."

Paul smiled. Twice her size she urged him to go up first with the flashlight. He was waiting at the top of the steps and helped her up into the attic. Once inside, Sarah stood still for a minute, giving her eyes time to adjust to the diminished light. She blinked several times then stared ahead. Unbelievable. A magical glow emanated from the window at the far end of the attic. She tapped Paul's shoulder and pointed.

Paul shined the flashlight in the direction where the roof sloped. The beam of light illuminated a small pile of blankets and old clothes. She wiped her eyes and, like she had before, blinked a few times. *Are my eyes playing tricks, again?*

Paul whispered, "Is that a—?"

"A gnome," Sarah said, finishing his sentence.

Sarah believed in magical creatures, thanks to her Scandinavian grandmother Farmor Estrid, who taught her about the *tomtes*. Grandmother Estrid had believed the little woodland creatures, which we now call gnomes, protected her family and their livestock from misfortune.

No longer afraid, Sarah tiptoed quietly towards the gnome until she stubbed her foot against a wooden crate. "Ouch!"

The two-foot-tall creature woke with a fright and jumped back, knocking its head against the rafters of the slanted roof. Rubbing its head, it wobbled, and Sarah instinctively reached out a helping hand.

Brad is never going to believe this!

"Don't touch it,"' Paul yelled. The little creature cowered and bumped its head again.

"Don't worry, little one, we won't hurt you," Sarah cooed and turned to Paul. "It's okay, I'm sure it won't hurt us."

Paul huffed.

"My name is Sarah, and this is Paul," she whispered, slowly waving an open hand towards her friend. "Will you tell us what you're doing here?"

The gnome spoke in a melodic tone. "My name is Birger. I am looking for a missing amulet. An enormous creature called ... umm—" The gnome paused. "Magician, yes, I believe that is your word for such a creature. The large magician came to our land and stole our amulet, only to do harm." The gnome's voice trembled as it told its story.

Well, that explained the round object I found ... and the missing magician. Ha.

"I'm here to find the amulet and bring it home. If you help me find it, Birger the Helper – that's me – will always protect your home and family," the little creature said in a soothing tone.

Sarah knew just where the amulet was. "Before I find your amulet and return it, I have one question."

"Oh yes, I'll answer any question in return for my missing amulet," Birger replied.

"What have you been doing with the items which you took from the shop downstairs?"

"This Bjorn has kept me in splendid company," he said, pointing to the patchwork bear. "And I have read this cloth fairytale book, to my delight. I am homesick for my dear Asta, and the beautifully encased pillow comforted me – though it was not as soft to lie on as the grasses from my land," Birger said with a look of remorse.

"And the quilting supplies, what could you possibly need those for?" Paul snapped.

"I have worked hard to make you this gift for leaving me food and drink every night." The gnome patted the beautiful quilt on his makeshift bed. "It will bring you good fortune and prosperity all your life, I promise you this."

∽

THAT NIGHT, Sarah returned the round metal coin to the curious gnome and was overcome by mixed emotions as the charming creature left her attic for good. With the mystery solved, she slept easily that night and was filled with renewed peace. The next day, she was light on her feet as she opened her shop's door, confident in what she would find. For the first time in days she felt fully prepared to greet her customers, an unexplainable sense of ease washed over her. And, of course, the shop was pristine, just as she had left it the night before!

ABOUT KATHRYN MYKEL

Kathryn Mykel is the author of the Award-Winning Sewing Suspicion - A Quilting Cozy Mystery. Kathryn is inspired by the laugh-out-loud and fanciful aspects of cozies.

Kathryn Mykel aims to write lighthearted, humorous cozies surrounding her passion for the craft of quilting.

Born and raised in a small New England town—Kathryn is an avid quilter.

13

THE GIFT OF DRAGONS

ACF BOOKENS

T*was the night before Christmas and all through the bookstore,*
  The doggies were snoring. It was quite an uproar.

THAT WAS AS FAR as I'd gotten into my attempt at a holiday poem for my bookstore, All Booked Up, but I liked it. "Accurate and charming," I said to myself as I put down my pen and finished up the closing chores for this last night of the holiday season.

We'd had a great year, the best yet, and I was thrilled about that. But there was always something a little melancholy about Christmas Eve for me. Maybe it was the slowing down of the frenzy – something I appreciated but also felt a bit of a disappointment – or maybe just the fact that grief dances close to the sparkling lights this time of year. In any case, I was a little down.

Fortunately, Mayhem and Taco, my dogs, were okay with that, as they sawed logs on their dogbeds in the front window. Taco had even managed to tolerate the Santa hat over his floppy basset hound ears for the entire day. "Come on, guys," I said in the tone that never failed to spark them to life, since it was the same one I used for dinner.

The two of them popped up like they had springs for legs and bounded over, their excitement even greater when they saw the leashes in my hands. Next to food, these two loved walks best of all, and on a cold, snowy night, they loved it even more. You'd think they were Newfies or Bernese Mountain Dogs instead of short-haired hounds, what with their enthusiasm for the cold.

I got the dogs leashed up and started toward the front door when Mayhem stopped short, her nose in the air. I gave her a minute to sniff what I presumed was the lingering waft of baked goods from the café, then tugged her gently toward the door. She wouldn't budge. Then, she started to growl.

Mayhem wasn't much of a growler, or a barker for that matter, but when she did either I paid attention. Now, she had the low, growing growl of a dog who really didn't like what he was smelling. And her worry brought the basset hound to full attention, and soon enough both of them were growling with their noses in the air.

Unfortunately, I'd had a lot of rather unpleasant encounters over the years, so even though I was very eager to get to my fiancé Jared's for our Christmas Eve dinner, I knew better than to ignore this moment.

Quickly, I let the dogs off their leashes and watched. They both rushed over to the fiction shelf that sat nearest the front door and sniffed and growled intermittently. A moment later, Taco hefted his considerable girth up onto two legs and stretched his long body up as high as he could go toward the top shelf. Mayhem, apparently the one of the two silently assigned to stand guard, growled and kept her eyes fixed on the shelf.

"What is it, you two?" I said, now a little annoyed since I was hungry and eager to eat Jared's amazing macaroni and cheese. "They're just books. What in the world?"

I walked a bit closer and stared at the top shelf, the As of the fiction section, and that's when I saw it. A very big, very old leather-bound book. "Oh," I said, and bent down to scratch the dogs' ears without taking my eyes off the book. "That's weird."

My attention clearly directed, finally, in the right direction, both dogs laid down on the floor and waited to see what I was going to do about this very strange – and apparently strange-smelling – addition to our store. I only sold new books; so to see an old book, especially a leather-bound one on my shelves was very, very odd. Odd and intriguing.

I reached up and pulled the volume off the shelf, and took it to the register. It was immensely heavy, like ten times as heavy as a normal hardcover. The leather was very old, and the gold-colored printing on the front too faded for me to read. Carefully, I turned the book on its spine and could just read the words, OF DRAGONS.

Now, I was an immense fan of dragons of all sorts, and secretly hoped that one day I would meet one. What I could read of the title made me very excited and very curious. *But* the binding looked very fragile, and I didn't want it to break.

Plus, I was now running late for Christmas Eve dinner with a very handsome man.

So begrudgingly, I carefully tucked the book under the register and headed out for my Christmas celebrations.

∽

TO BE HONEST, I kind of forgot about the book for the next day or so. I ate a ton of food and smooched my love. I took the dogs for long walks, and I spent time with the people I loved the most. We exchanged gifts and sang songs with a profound amount of silliness, and before I knew it, Christmas was done, and we had entered that strange liminal time between Christmas and New Year's. People are off work, children are out of school, and we're all just kind of milling about in the aftermath of the holidays and the year. I pretty much love it.

So when I opened the store on Boxing Day, I was in a great mood. We would have a good week in sales, if previous years were any indicator, and I loved how relaxed people were during this week, when pretty much all productivity stopped. It was beautiful.

Marcus came in to open with me because we knew we had a big day ahead, especially since we'd sold a lot of gift cards in the previous weeks. When I met him at the register, he was staring at me with the big old book in his hand. "What is this?" he said.

"Oh, right. That's why I've been dreaming about

dragons," I said, as I thought back to the wild and beautiful dreams I'd had of flying and swimming, Scrooge McDuck-style, in the piles of gold my dragon had procured in her work as a guard dragon. The dream had been very specific, I was now realizing, as I stared at the mysterious book again.

"Forgive me, Harvey, but what do your dreams have to do with this book?" Marcus asked as he studied the fragile book.

"It's about dragons. See?" I said, pointing to the only legible words on the spine. "I found it on Christmas Eve, but I didn't open it because it looked like it might fall apart." I took the book from his hands and studied it again. "But I suppose we need to."

"Did someone leave it here? Maybe we should put it in Lost and Found?" he suggested. He meant our very sophisticated system of an old cardboard box onto which I had scribbled *Lost And Found* a couple years back. Somehow, it didn't feel right to relegate the book to the same space as the odd sparkly mitten and someone's water bottle.

I stared at the book again. "No, it wasn't just forgotten. Someone shelved it." I pointed to the top shelf of the fiction section where I'd found the book. "Taco and Mayhem smelled it and led me to it." I glanced over at the two dogs who hadn't even bothered to so much open their eyes when I'd said their names. The sunbeams in the front window were too magical, I supposed.

"Well, that's odd." Marcus ran his fingers gently over the front cover. "Do you think someone was trying to hide it?"

I shook my head. "I have no idea. But I guess we should take a look inside." I gritted my teeth as I imagined the spine splitting when we opened it.

"Hold on one second," Marcus said and jogged over to the café, where his fiancée Rocky was finishing her morning set-up.

A minute later, he was back with four empty mugs which he turned upside down on the counter in front of us, before setting the book on its spine between them. "This way, we won't open the book all the way."

"Excellent," I said as I looked at the makeshift book cradle. "Here we go." Marcus held one side of the book and I the other as we gently let the spine open and rest against the coffee mugs.

Both of us gasped as the book opened to a beautiful, gilded illustration of a blue dragon flying low over a landscape of green, rolling hills. "Holy sh—, holy cow," I said, catching myself. "This is amazing."

Marcus slid his pointer finger gently over the image. "It's hand-drawn," he said. "Cate needs to see this."

"Everyone needs to see this," I said and took out my phone. "And we need an expert opinion. I'm going to reach out to this rare book dealer in Virginia. He specializes in this kind of thing." I opened my camera. "Help me find a few more images to send to him?"

After snapping as clear a photo as I could of the pictures and the text, which seemed to be in Latin, I looked up the rare book dealer in Charlottesville, a man named Fitzhugh Diamond, and gave him a call.

He answered on the first ring, and I quickly explained what I had found and asked if I could send him some images. *"Oh yes, please, do. My niece Poe is here for the holidays, and this sort of folklore text is her speciality. We'll take a look and get back to you immediately."*

"Thanks so much," I said and quickly emailed the images over to the address he'd given me. "They'll get back to us soon," I said to Marcus as he came back to the counter after unlocking the front door. "In the meantime, we have a store to run."

"We do," Marcus said, "and I may have also told our friends about the book." He gave me a cheesy grin and shrugged. "I can't keep amazing news like this to myself."

I smiled. "That's awesome. Everyone coming by?"

Just then the bell over the front door rang, and Cate and Lucas came in. Cate was an artist and Lucas a historian, so it was no surprise they were the first two people to arrive. "Let me see," Cate said and hip-checked me out of the way so she could look down at the book on the makeshift stand we had moved to a small table behind the register. "Whoa," she said.

Lucas peered over her shoulder. "Man, that's beautiful." He gingerly turned a couple of pages and stared at the beautiful text – all hand-written – and another image of a small, white girl in a long skirt, and a pail in her hand. "Look at that detail," he said as he leaned in.

"Whoever did these images is a real master," Cate added. "Where did you find this?"

I told her about the dogs and the bookshelf. "Someone left it here, intentionally," I finished.

"As a gift, maybe?" Lucas suggested. "Maybe a secret admirer?"

I rolled my eyes. "I doubt it. I think it's more likely that someone wanted to hide it here." I looked over at where I'd found the book. "The question is, why?"

A customer came up to buy a copy of *The Ex Hex* by Erin Sterling, and my focus shifted to work. The next time I had a break, I saw that Marcus and Stephen, another dear friend, were leaning over the book at a table in the café. Stephen's husband Walter was nearby talking with our friends Myrna and Bear, her husband, and all of them kept looking over at the book. Apparently, our friends were all fascinated with our find.

I started to head their way, but Jared came through the door and intercepted me. "So let me see this book," he said with a smile.

His presence made me realize that maybe this was a more serious matter than I thought. "Oh, goodness. Should I have reported this to you and Tuck?" I said.

Jared frowned at me. "Why would the sheriff's office need to know about a book that was left in your shop? You didn't steal it." He winked at me. "Did you?"

I swatted his arm. "Of course not, but what if it is stolen?" I winced as that possibility sank in. Maybe that's why someone had tried to hide the book here.

"If you find out it's stolen, then we'll figure that out. But it's not your responsibility to find that out, Harvey." He hugged me quickly. "Just enjoy the book, okay?"

I stared at him a minute as I tried to figure out if he was encouraging nonchalance because it wasn't a big deal, or because he didn't want me to, again, get involved in something criminal that was really none of my business.

After a moment, I decided it didn't matter. He was right. I was just going to enjoy the book.

As Marcus headed back into the shop to run the register, my phone rang in my pocket, and I stepped out into the chilly December air to answer. "Hello," I said.

"Harvey, it's Fitz Diamond. Poe and I have consulted about your text. Do you have a minute to talk?" he asked with a bouncing voice. It sounded like good news.

"Of course," I said, wishing I had grabbed my coat on the way out. It was downright cold out here.

"Well, we believe you have a twelfth century illuminated manuscript. That's what the binding and the illustrations lead Poe to believe. It's a bestiary of sorts, she suggests, a way of recording all the stories that particular community had about dragons."

I nodded, then realized Fitz couldn't see me. "That makes sense. I don't read Latin, but the pictures do look like the ones in picture books. You know, they kind of tell the story beside the words that tell the story."

"Exactly," he continued. "We're not talking about a time when most people in Europe were literate, so the images would have served just that purpose." He cleared his throat. "As you can imagine, this is an extremely rare book, and so, forgive us, but we did do a quick check to see if anything of this nature has been reported stolen."

I sucked in a quick breath. "And?"

"We have found nothing to indicate that is so. In fact, we don't have any record of this book anywhere." He cleared his throat. "You've got a one-of-a-kind volume there, Ms. Beckett. Would you like to know its estimated value?"

"Uh-huh," I managed to say as my heart pounded against my rib cage.

"You're looking at a book valued at between three hundred thousand and five hundred thousand dollars. Perhaps more, when it's authenticated."

I almost dropped the phone. "Um, excuse me? I'm not sure I heard you correctly."

"It could be half a million, if the images are as high quality as these," Fitz continued, as if he hadn't just blown my head off my shoulders with these figures.

I took a long, deep breath. "So what you're saying is that this book that someone randomly left in my store could be worth five hundred thousand dollars?" I cleared my throat. "Is that right?"

"Correct. We can authenticate it for you, if you'd like, but of course, we'd need to see the book in person," Fitz continued casually, as if he was just telling me that it was supposed to be cold tomorrow. *"You can bring it here, or we can come there. Just let us know if you need us."*

"Um, okay," I said and then just sat there.

"Happy Holidays, Ms. Beckett."

"Oh yeah, right. Happy Holidays," I replied, then just stood there with my phone in my hand while my brain tried to catch up to what had just happened.

I was still dumb-founded and frozen in place when my parents came up the sidewalk. "What's wrong, Harvey?" Mom said. "You're pale. Are you feeling okay?"

I came to myself just in time to block her hand from feeling my forehead. I nodded and moved to go back into the shop.

"What's this about a book?" Dad said as he opened the door for me.

I couldn't even form words, so I just walked over to where Jared and our friends were looking at the book before going to Rocky and miming lifting a mug to my lips and then scribbling something on a pad of paper. She pursed her lips but then passed me a pen and notepad before turning to steam milk for my latte.

I wrote *$500,000* on the pad and then walked over to Jared again, handing him the notepad.

He looked at it, looked at me, looked at the book again, then looked back at me. "That book is worth half a million bucks?"

Something about him speaking those words unfroze my brain, and I said, "Yes, potentially."

He stared at me. "Maybe it is stolen," he said.

As if part of a dance ensemble, our friends all took a step back in unison. We all knew better than to touch evidence.

I shook my head. "It's not. They searched to be sure since the book is so rare, and it's not on record anywhere."

The bell over the door rang again, and Pickle, Woody, and Galen came in. "Where's that book?" Pickle said in his usual voice, always a bit too loud for the room.

"Over here," Dad said and shook each man's hand as they came in. "How was breakfast? Sorry I couldn't make it today."

The guys had a usual Boxing Day breakfast that had been a tradition for a number of years. "The bacon was extra crispy this morning," Woody said. "Just like you like it. You missed out."

Dad laughed. "There's always next year," he quipped, as if

they didn't also have breakfast together every Saturday morning. "The book is something. Harvey just learned it could be worth half a mill."

Galen whistled. "Is that so? Wow." He looked at the book from across the café and nodded. "How did you find out its value?"

I told the men about the call with Fitz and his offer to value the book. "Sounds like it might be good to take it over to him," Dad suggested. "Your mother and I are always up for a weekend away if you need transportation services."

I smiled. "Thanks. At this point, I'm just trying to wrap my head around all of this."

Galen smiled and squeezed my shoulder. "Quite a gift someone gave you," he said, then headed off toward the mystery section to get his holiday week's supply of books.

I stared after him as his words sank in. I looked at Mom. "Surely someone didn't leave this here as a gift, did they?" I squinted at her. "You didn't do this did you?"

Mom's mouth fell open, and she shook her head. "I love you, honey, but if I was going to give you a book worth hundreds of thousands of dollars, I would want the credit."

I laughed because it was true. My mom was generous, but quiet humility wasn't really her thing.

"My guess is someone didn't want to carry it around and just put it on a shelf, thinking that with the holidays it would be there when they got back." Mom spun slowly in circles, doing what it had just occurred to me to do – check to see if anyone was looking for the book. But no one was even near the beginning of the fiction section. And while I wanted to check with Marcus, I hadn't really seen anyone near there for most of the morning. If someone was coming back for the book, they sure were taking their time.

I decided to put aside my thoughts about the book as much as I could since the store was getting busier and, honestly, I had no idea what to do with anything worth that much money. Even the house that Mart and I shared wasn't worth that much.

So I made myself busy helping customers and straightening up the store, and it was only two hours later that my mind was brought back to the valuable book. After all our friends – including Elle, who had sprinted over from her farm shop on her lunch break to take a peek – had seen it, Marcus had wrapped it in tissue paper and slid it carefully back under the register.

I discovered Marcus's care of the tome when our sheriff, Tucker Mason, came in with his wife Lu for their own glimpse of the book. "Not stolen, though," Tuck asked. "That's what Jared told me."

"The expert I consulted seemed confident that was the case," I said and hoped he was right.

"Seems to be. I did a search myself and didn't see where the book had ever been publicly recorded, and nothing in the police databases lists anything like it. I even checked Interpol," he added with a grin.

"Ooh, small-town cop goes international," I teased. "Well, that's good then, but it doesn't solve the mystery of how the book got here." I could feel myself getting frustrated because I didn't like having something this valuable under my care.

Lu nodded. "But you love a good mystery, right?" She

winked at me. "At least no one died this time." She was joking, but she was also right.

"I do," I said. "But the thing is I have no idea how to go about solving this one. The book appeared out of nowhere, and short of going through all our sales' slips for Christmas Eve—" I stopped short. "I could do that."

Tuck smiled. "Yes, you could. And I can help. You're closing up early tonight, right?"

I nodded. "We are. No reason to be open in the evenings this week since we won't have much traffic." I looked at him out of the corner of my eye. "What are you thinking?"

"Potluck. We can all help out as you sleuth your way to a solution." He looked at me hopefully.

"I like that idea. I'll ask Mom to take care of inviting everyone and coordinating food," I said.

"I've got the food," Lu said. "Truck's closed this week, and I could use a reason to be in the kitchen." Lu ran the best food truck on the Eastern Shore, and I never turned down an offer to eat her *mole*. "Tacos okay?"

"Always," I said. "I'll get Mom and Stephen and Walter to handle the rest though."

Within a half-hour, everyone knew we were having one of our regular potlucks in the shop. Stephen and Walter were bringing a new cocktail for us all to try, we had Lucas bringing cupcakes, and even Galen offering to come along with paper products. "Fit for the season," he said.

At five o'clock, we rang up our last customers for the day, and Marcus and I counted the till and did our closing chores as all our friends wandered in with their offerings for our dinner. We'd been having these gatherings since I opened the shop, and I loved them because they reminded me I had a big, chosen family of people I just adored.

While Mom coordinated the placement of food and drinks on the tables we'd borrowed from Rocky's café, Jared and I set up another table with the book on it, still carefully perched on the coffee mugs. Marcus had run a sales' report for Christmas Eve and made copies of it for everyone.

And as soon as we had all eaten and gotten our custom Boxing Day Cocktails – vanilla vodka, cranberry, and a sprig of rosemary – from Stephen and Walter, we set to work. I had no idea what we were looking for in the receipts, but we checked each record, trying to determine what might indicate someone had dropped off a book of this value.

Sadly, an hour later, we had no more clues about our mystery book-dropper. No one had made an exorbitantly large purchase that day, something Dad suggested might indicate a person who owned a book of this value, and nothing else odd stood out from the receipts. We were at a dead end.

I got up to ask Stephen to make me another drink, something to stave off my disappointment, but swung by the book to take one more look. This time, after setting down my plastic cup on a nearby table, I hefted the weight of the pages in my right hand and opened the inside cover. I hadn't really examined the book in much detail beyond taking pictures, and I wanted to see if, by chance, there was an inscription or some sort of note on the front end papers.

There wasn't, and I was just about to put the book back to its half-open position on the mugs when I flipped a few more pages just past the title page, which included a tiny red dragon in the lower corner below the title D~racones~ E~uropae~. Just as I went to close the book, the tip of my finger felt a ridge beneath the title page. I turned the leaf over and there sat a small envelope with my name on it.

Shocked, I stared at the envelope for a minute before setting the book down carefully and then picking up the envelope. *Harvey Beckett* it said, clear as day.

I turned the envelope over slowly and slid my finger under the flap to pop it open. Then, with my breath balled up in my chest, I slid out a tiny read card that had a printed *Thank you* on the front. I opened the card and read.

Harvey, you have done so much for St. Marin's, and I know you have always loved dragons. We talked about it once when I was shopping. I know you will value this book for its full worth. Happy Holidays!

For a long few seconds I just stared at the card. I turned it over to look for a signature. I looked at the envelope again. Then I read the note one more time. Finally, tears sprung to my eyes, and I called, "Jared, come here."

He must have heard the distress in my voice because he jogged over. "What's wrong?" He looked down at the note in my hand and then gently took it from me.

"It's a gift," I whispered as I swallowed back the knot in my throat. "To me."

He read the card and then hugged me tight. "A well-deserved one," he said before heading back over to the group and reading the card to them.

A few of my friends teared up as well, a fact I noticed as I studied each of their faces to see if they might be the mystery book giver. Everyone met my eyes and smiled, and no one looked embarrassed or guilty. Still, I couldn't help but ask, "Did one of you do this?"

Tuck laughed. "Do you think any one of us has this kind of money, Harvey? We love you, but girl..." He chuckled again.

Everyone around the group nodded as Cate said, "Tuck is right. All of us would have loved to give you this, Harvey, but there's no way any of us could have afforded something like that."

I sighed. I knew they were right. All of us were solid financially, but no one had the kind of cash required to buy a book that cost half a million dollars. "Well, this is a beautiful gift, and I'm certainly grateful for it." I took a deep breath. "But I'd like to sell it and donate the money to the town so we can get those wheelchair accessible walkways and clearer crosswalks installed."

I glanced over at Jared, and he was nodding. "I figured you'd donate it, Harvey." He pulled me close. "Just one of the many reasons I love you."

"I'll get in touch with Mr Diamond and see if he can't come out and value the book; maybe find out who might want to buy it." I looked over my shoulder at the book. "It really belongs in a museum somewhere."

Tuck nodded. "It does, and that's a beautiful gift to give the town," he said. "Thank you."

I nodded and suddenly felt quite tired in the way that the best kind of days make you tired. "You all ready to head out?" I said.

Within minutes, my friends had cleaned up the dinner things and tidied the store. Marcus had, again, wrapped the book in tissue and slipped in into the tote bag that I carried back and forth each day.

I slipped into the back room to get my coat and scarf and grab the dogs' leashes so we could walk home. When I came out, I saw Jared and Galen talking to each other by the door. They were smiling, and when Woody joined them, I saw the three of them exchange a fist bump.

I staggered back a step as my mind caught up to what my eyes had seen as I glanced over to where Mom, Dad, Rocky, and Marcus were talking by the café counter. They were all beaming. And the rest of my friends were huddled by the register, all laughing and talking very quietly.

I took a deep breath and thought about what everyone had said when they asked if they'd done this. *"Any one of us,"* Tuck had said. And he was right. Not a single one of my friends could have afforded this book. But as a collective…

Quickly, I wiped the tears from my eyes and steadied myself. Sometimes, the best gifts are the ones that come unsigned.

I wrapped my scarf around my neck, called Mayhem and Taco, and whistled *We Wish You A Merry Christmas* as I walked to the front of the store.

THE BOOKS WERE *all shelved with their spines nice and straight*
In the hopes that their new owners wouldn't be very late.

THE BOOKSELLER WAS SMILING *as she turned out the light.*
"Happy Holidays to all and to all a good night."

ABOUT ACF BOOKENS

ACF Bookens lives in Virginia's Southwestern Mountains with two hound dogs and a very energetic preschooler. When she's not writing, she enjoys watching shows with teenagers who are way cooler than she ever was and cross-stitch. You can find her books at acfbookens.com

14

NOWHERE TO HIDE

DEBBIE YOUNG

Tommy burst into Hector's House bookshop, sending the door crashing against the rubber doorstop on the floor. The ladies browsing the bookshelves glowered and tutted at him.

"Anyone seen Bob?"

Hector, perched on his usual stool behind the trade counter, looked up from his computer keyboard. "I think he's on day shift during the whole of half term week, Tommy. Why?"

Bob was the local policeman. Or rather, he lived in our Cotswold village, but was usually based at the police station at Slate Green, the nearest market town.

"I want to report a crime."

Tommy's frequent interruptions to the orderly running of the bookshop usually turned out to be a big fuss about nothing, the fabrication of a bored teenager seeking to create his own entertainment in our sleepy, isolated village. Hector did not stir, so the gangly lad bounded towards the tea-room, where I was wiping the tables and Mrs Wetherley was unpacking her home-made cakes, filling the whole shop with delicious aromas of cinnamon and vanilla.

"What sort of crime, boy?" asked Billy. The elderly odd-job man, who Tommy often helps with his chores, was enjoying elevenses at his favourite table, wiping his cappuccino moustache on the cuff of his ancient tweed jacket.

Tommy pulled out a chair from the adjacent table, where Hector's godmother, Kate, was writing in a birthday card she'd just bought. Tommy turned the chair round and straddled it, leaning his elbows on its back.

"Theft." He paused for dramatic effect.

I stuffed the polishing cloth into my apron pocket. "Someone's stolen something from you? What have they taken?"

I hoped it wasn't his precious new smartphone. Tommy had been the last in his class at the local high school to get his own mobile phone. His single mum, raising him and his little sister Sina alone, was on a tight budget. To my relief, he shook his head vigorously.

"Not from me. From the whole village."

"A park bench perhaps?" guessed a woman by the gardening shelf.

"Surely you don't mean the maypole," suggested another from historical fiction. "That's just been taken down and packed away till next May."

Hector sighed. "Do you have to be so cloak-and-dagger about it, Tommy?"

"Cloak and dagger? There's an idea!" Tommy sprang from his chair and dashed to the trade counter to reach for the fancy letter-opener Hector kept neatly aligned in parallel with his ruler, stapler and hole-punch. It had been a Christmas gift from my parents, the Celtic design on the pewter handle to remind him of Scotland, where they live. "This is a great dagger. Can anyone lend me a cloak?"

Hector covered the letter-opener with his hand before Tommy could grab it. "Just tell us, Tommy. What do you think has been stolen?"

Tommy turned round to broadcast his answer to the whole shop. "The village phone. You know, the big old silvery thing in the red phone box opposite the village shop. It's gone. Someone's nicked it." He paused to let this news sink in. "But I don't know who or why. I mean, who would want to thieve a great heavy thing like that when we've all got mobile phones these days?"

With a proud flourish, he pulled his smartphone from the back pocket of his jeans.

Kate chuckled as she laid down her pen. "Well, you are partly right, Tommy. The ubiquity of mobile phones is the reason the parish council has acquired the phone box for a change of use."

Tommy frowned. "U-whatty?"

"That means mobile phones are everywhere these days, like you said. We've all got them. Which makes the public payphone surplus to requirements, so it's being decommissioned."

Tommy frowned again.

"That means it's being taken out of use," Kate continued. "It's been removed, to make way for the kiosk's new purpose."

Tommy narrowed his eyes. "Are the parish council allowed to do that?"

Kate tucked the birthday card into its envelope. "Oh yes, they're being actively encouraged. BT, who installed all the red phone boxes in the country back in the day, now readily sell them to local councils and charities. There's just two conditions: the new owners must repurpose the phone box for community use, and they must assume responsibility for its upkeep."

Tommy's shoulders slumped. "Oh, I see." He turned to me. "Sorry, Sophie, I know you fancy yourself as a detective. I thought I might have brought you an interesting new case."

I smiled. "Don't worry, I'm not disappointed. I'm just interested to see how the parish council will use the old phone box."

Billy raised his hand. "How about they turn it into a public toilet? That would come in handy when I get caught short on my way home from here. It'd save me having to go behind the bus shelter."

Kate put her hands over her eyes in horror. "I hardly think that's appropriate for a structure with floor-to-ceiling windows on three sides."

Hector's fingers were rattling over his keyboard. "I'm just googling the possibilities," he said. "Using them to store defibrillators seems the most popular application, but we've already got one of those in a case on the wall of the village hall."

Tommy came back to sit on his chair, this time the right

way round. "If no-one else has a better idea, could I have it as a den? Or better still, I could turn it into a Tiny House. Do you know about Tiny Houses? They're a thing now in America. I follow this kid on Instagram who built his own Tiny House when he was twelve."

I was pleased he'd been using his new phone to explore the world beyond the village where he'd been born and raised.

"What's a Tiny House?" asked Billy, who wouldn't have known what Instagram was either.

Tommy's face brightened. "Tiny Houses are brilliant. People save money by building the smallest house possible to live in. They do things like put beds on shelves and their garden on their roof. I'd love a Tiny House of my own."

Kate set her elbows on the table and rested her chin in her hands. "But where would you sleep in it? You've grown so tall lately, Tommy. I can't see how you could fit your bed in a phone box."

The boy was undaunted. "I could curl up on the floor like a hedgehog. It's only a question of geometry. I'm good at geometry at school."

Kate smiled apologetically. "I'm sorry, Tommy, but the parish council has already made its decision. It's turning the phone box into a Little Free Library. That's another American innovation, you know. Since the mobile library service stopped calling here last year, there's been nowhere locally for people to borrow books for free, unless they make the trip to Slate Green. The parish council thinks lots of villagers will enjoy using a free community library, and it'll be open all hours, unlike the public library in town. You might even decide to borrow some books yourself."

Tommy shook his head in vigorous denial. Although he spends a lot of time in our bookshop, the only books he's ever bought have been Christmas presents for his mother and sister.

"Anyway," Kate continued, "Julia Prentice is going to organise it, and if you tell her what sort of books you like, I'm sure she'll get some for you. She's been running the WI book group for years. She's very good at choosing books to suit all tastes."

"I can vouch for that," said one of the browsing ladies, and the others agreed.

Tommy's skinny chest swelled a little. "Julia Prentice is my relation. Second cousin once replaced."

The corners of Hector's mouth twitched. "I think you mean once removed."

"Whatever." Tommy got up from his seat and wandered back to the trade counter. "But, Hector, won't that put you out of business, if they start giving everyone books for free? Why would anyone come to your shop and spend money on books if they can get them for nothing from the phone box?" With a wave of his arm, Tommy dismissed all our thoughtfully curated shelves of brand-new books.

"Thank you for your concern, but I'm sure my shop will be just fine," said Hector. "Public libraries and bookshops have comfortably coexisted for centuries. In fact, they feed off each other. Same goes for charity shops selling second-hand books for next to nothing. People discover new favourite books and authors in libraries and charity shops, and then go to bookshops to buy copies to keep, or to buy other books by those authors that they can't find elsewhere. The stock in Little Free Libraries is even smaller than in public libraries and charity shops, and people are seldom able to find every book they're looking for there. So, never fear, there will always be business for bookshops."

"All the same, Hector," I put in, "it might be worth us posting a notice up in the phone box reminding people that if they can't find a book they like, they can always come to Hector's House for a wider choice, and for special orders too."

"Good idea, Sophie. I'll make one right now on my computer. And Tommy, if you give me a few minutes, you can run along and stick it up in the phone box for me. There'll be a milkshake in it for you if you do."

Tommy's brow furrowed. "A milkshake in the phone box?"

Hector rolled his eyes. "In the tea-room, while you're waiting."

Tommy settled down for a chat with Billy while I headed for the blender to rustle up Tommy's favourite banana concoction.

∼

A COUPLE OF DAYS LATER, Julia Prentice called into Hector's House, deftly manoeuvring an old-fashioned shopping basket on wheels through the narrow doorway. I'd been leaning over the trade counter, taking advantage of the absence of customers to flirt with Hector. (He's my boyfriend as well as my boss.)

Once she'd parked her trolley in front of the counter, Julia turned on a radiant smile, the sort I've noticed Mrs Fortescue use in her role as chair of the WI to persuade others to do favours for her WI.

"Hello, Hector, hi, Sophie. Did you read in the *Parish News* that the council has asked me to set up a free community library in the old phone box?" She didn't wait for a reply. Every grown-up in Wendlebury Barrow reads the *News* from cover to cover. Carol sells more copies in the village shop than all the other monthly magazines put together, and the latest edition had confirmed Kate's news. "I expect you can guess what I'm going to ask you next. Have you any old books you'd like to donate? All genres welcome! Doesn't matter if they're a bit battered. Damaged stock that you can't sell would be fine."

Anticipating her request, Hector had already filled a large cardboard box with books whose covers had faded from spending too long on display in the shop window, or those which had been damaged by careless browsers. He'd also added duplicates of bestselling trade paperbacks from our second-hand department. They rarely fetch more than a pound apiece as there's such a glut of them.

"Here you go, Julia. Happy to help." Hector lifted the box on to the counter, and she began to decant its contents into her shopping trolley, packing them as neatly as a tangram. Perhaps strong geometry genes ran in Tommy's family. "Help yourself if you'd like a few of our promotional bookmarks. You can never have too many bookmarks."

"Nor too many books," replied Julia, cementing her position as one of Hector's favourite customers.

Later that afternoon, a lady of similar age to Julia, but stouter and more expensively dressed, breezed into the shop and headed straight for the counter. Not many customers do that. They tend to circle the shop first, unless they've come to collect a special order.

"Mr Munro." I didn't recognise her, and I didn't think Hector did either. I'd never seen her in our bookshop before. "I hate to be the bearer of bad news." She rested her perfectly manicured hands on the counter and leaned further over it than was comfortable for Hector, obscuring his view of the shop floor with her bulk. "But have you seen what is happening to the telephone kiosk opposite the village shop?"

Hector edged his stool as far back from her as the limited space behind the counter allowed.

"Yes, and I shall be glad to support it."

She pressed her palms against her cheeks to express her horror. "Oh, but think of the business it will take from your poor shop."

Hector bridled. "My shop is not poor, thank you very much, and I have no doubt that it will flourish even more with a well-used free community library as a near neighbour – reminding every passer-by of the joy of books and reading. Now, is there a particular book you are looking to buy here today that I can help you find?"

She glanced warily behind her as if expecting to see a mugger about to pounce. "Good heavens, no. I'm not here on a shopping trip." She turned on the heel of her patent nude court shoe and fled the shop.

"Who on earth was she?" I asked a few minutes later, bringing Hector a restorative cup of tea and setting it on the counter.

He shrugged. "Never seen her before in my life. Perhaps she's new to the village."

Mrs Fortescue approached from the craft section, bearing an expensive hardback collection of vintage *Vogue* knitting patterns.

"Count yourself lucky," she said. "That's Trixie Drake from Boxford: self-appointed arch-rival to dear Julia Prentice in the local philanthropy stakes. She'll be annoyed at Julia for creating a free community library here in Wendlebury, because she'll see it as competition for her own book lending box, and superior too. A few weeks ago she set one up on her front garden wall in a dilapidated old rabbit hutch. Minus the rabbit, of course."

Hector's forehead creased. "Competition? They're hardly commercial rivals if all their books are free. Surely the more free books there are in the community, the better."

As Mrs Fortescue delved into her soft tan leather purse for her platinum credit card, Hector scanned the barcode on the knitting patterns book.

"So any sensible person thinks." She unfolded a bag-for-life and inserted her new book. "But this is just the latest in a string of rivalries that go back to when they were teenagers, and Trixie's ex-boyfriend starting dating Julia. Trixie's been trying to prove herself superior ever since. My sister lives in Boxford, so she keeps me informed about her deranged antics. They would be entertaining if they weren't so pathetic. You see, when Julia runs a charity ten kilometres, Trixie must do a marathon."

I blinked in surprise. I doubted running was in Trixie's comfort zone, although I'd often seen Julia jogging around the village.

"And do you remember last year when Julia cut off her ponytail and donated it to a wig charity? Trixie shaved her head."

Hector tried not to take sides in local feuds, so his reply was diplomatic. "Oh well, all in a good cause, I suppose."

Mrs Fortescue raised her eyebrows. "I suppose so, but you mark my words. One day, Trixie Drake will take this silly rivalry nonsense a step too far."

~

We didn't have to wait long for the next instalment of the phone box library saga. On the Friday, Trixie Drake came bustling into the bookshop once more, dark eyes blazing.

"Far be it from me to accuse Julia Prentice of snaffling books from my community book box to stock hers," she began, with no apparent sense of irony. "But I want to check with you first, Mr Munro, as a purveyor of preloved books, whether you source any of your stock from local free resources?"

Hector's jaw dropped. For a moment, he couldn't muster a reply. Trixie Drake took his silence as permission to continue.

"You see, when I went to restock the free book box on my front wall this morning, almost all my books had gone.

Rarely are more than a couple of books taken at a time, so I can only conclude that someone is lifting them wholesale for their own nefarious purposes."

Hector's eyes narrowed. "Madam." I'd never heard him call a customer madam before. "For a start, I have no idea where you live, so I don't know where your precious book box is. Secondly, if you think you're going to trap me into suggesting Julia Prentice must be the culprit, you are wrong." His tone was getting icier by the moment. "Has it not occurred to you that perhaps you have created in your midst such a bevy of eager readers that demand is outstripping supply? Especially with the holiday season coming up. And isn't that what you want, to send your books out into the community to be enjoyed by others?"

He stood up so abruptly that he knocked over his stool. Perhaps not realising until then how much taller Hector was than her, Trixie Drake took a step backwards, worried what he might do next. I'd never seen Hector so angry. I dashed over from the cookery section, where I'd been shelving new books, to try and calm the atmosphere.

"Mrs Drake, surely there are plenty of other explanations for where your books might have gone?" I suggested, edging in front of the trade counter to stand between her and Hector. "For example, at the recent church fete, someone was running a book tombola. I've also seen fundraisers online offering a Blind Date with a Book Service, where you pay a set amount for an unspecified book, mysteriously wrapped in brown paper. I wondered where they were getting their books from."

Trixie's eyes goggled at these fresh ideas for the

surreptitious diversion of her book stock. Hector cleared his throat to get my attention.

"Sweetheart, I don't think you're helping."

Fearing he was right, I went off at a different tangent. "Anyway, here's an easy way to deter potential thieves in future, and help you identify your books in the wild. Just get some stickers, or a rubber stamp made up, so you can easily mark every book you put in your box as coming from you. It would be a great advertisement for your service long after each book's gone out into the world." I guessed she'd welcome the chance to advertise her philanthropy at the same time.

She clasped her hands. "I see. Erm, yes. Thank you. I think I will do just that." She glanced at her Rolex. "If I dash, I should make it to Timpson's in Slate Green to order a rubber stamp before they close."

Without a word of apology to Hector she left the shop, only to glide past the window a few moments later in a gleaming white BMW coupé, bestowing upon us a quasi-royal wave.

On my way home from work, I called into the village shop to pick up a loaf of Ted's excellent granary bread. Ted, an accomplished baker, was Carol's new late-in-life boyfriend. The shopkeeper herself was poring over a mound of dusty, musty clothes and bric-a-brac, spread over the counter. She was struggling to fasten a silver buckle on a tunic knitted in glittery thread to resemble chain mail. As I approached her with my loaf, she set the buckle down and wiped her hands on her apron. I clutched my loaf to my chest rather than pass it to her for bagging up.

"It's a grubby old business, sorting out the Wendlebury Players' wardrobe," she confided. "But I need to do a stock-take and a spring clean before their next production, and there just aren't enough hours in the day." Her trading hours were far longer than ours at Hector's House. "The props box is not much better either." She nodded to the far end of the counter, where an orange plastic crate held a jumble of crockery and stuffed animals, dog-eared books, and period weaponry.

"Every spring, I ditch anything that doesn't overwinter well," she continued as she rang up my purchase on the till. "Anything made of cardboard or paper tends to go mouldy in the Players' cupboard at the village hall, or else squirrels or mice get in and nest in it. I hate to throw anything away, especially the books, but I couldn't even give these away to some woman who came in begging for old books the other day. Turned her nose up when she saw the mouse-droppings."

I bit my lip. "Posh woman, well-dressed, with an expensive gold watch and fancy sports car?"

Carol frowned. "Sounds about right. Not from round here, is she?"

"Boxford," I replied, privately thinking that I'd have counted the neighbouring village just two miles away as *around here*.

"No manners either, for all her airs and graces. Didn't buy

a thing after giving me the third man about our new phone box library."

She meant the third degree, of course.

∼

Halfway through Saturday morning, I noticed Hector rifling through his habitually tidy workspace. "Sweetheart, you haven't borrowed my letter-opener, have you? You know, the one your parents bought me last Christmas?"

I shook my head. "Not since you took it off Tommy the other day. I haven't been using it to open this morning's deliveries, if that's what you're wondering. I used the plain old one you had before for that."

Hector sighed. "Damn. I was hoping you might have hidden it to keep it out of Tommy's reach. I hate putting temptation in his way. He's far too good at finding it without any help from me."

Right on cue, as if Hector had summoned him up, Tommy came crashing into the shop. I was about to admonish him for his boisterous entry, but his pallid complexion made me hesitate.

"Are you okay, Tommy?" I asked gently.

"I'm okay," he replied. "I'm fine. But in the phone box, there's some lady slumped on the ground, and there are bloody footprints all around her."

"Language, Tommy," said Hector, automatically. "Do you mean her boots were muddy from walking the Cotswold Way? Is that why there are footprints?"

Our village is on the famous National Trail, and we get a lot of walkers passing through.

Tommy frowned. "That wasn't a swearing bloody. It was a descriptive one. The footprints are made of blood."

Mrs Wetherley set down the box of jam tarts she'd been decanting into a glass dome on the tea-room counter and rushed over to lay a motherly arm about Tommy's shoulders.

"Oh, my word, what a shock for you, dear." She glanced meaningfully at Hector and me. "You two go and investigate while I give this boy a cup of hot, sweet tea. He's had a nasty shock."

I could tell Tommy was torn between coming with us and allowing Mrs Wetherley to cosset him, but her grip on his narrow shoulders was too firm to give him any choice.

Hector and I needed no further bidding. We sprinted down the High Street, only slowing when we reached the trail of slender red footprints leading away from the phone box to the kerb in front of the bus stop. They were clearly a woman's prints, with pointed tips, and dots for the heel no bigger than a five-pence piece.

Avoiding the footprints so as not to destroy their evidence, Hector pulled a tissue from his pocket and wrapped it around his fingers before hauling open the phone box door using the brass handle. With another tissue, I took the handle from him to hold the door open while he bent down to check the state of whoever it was in the phone box. As she fell backwards against Hector, I recognised her at once: Julia Prentice. Immediately in front of her were two carrier bags overflowing with old books. She must have been attacked as she was filling the newly installed bookshelves.

Hector leaned forward, using his body as a backstop to prevent her falling any further. Then he laid one hand on the pulse point on her neck and the other on her chest to check she was still breathing. As he touched her throat, she let out a little moan.

"Thank goodness!" I murmured. "She's still with us!"

Without turning round, Hector said to me, "Well, her breathing and her pulse seem normal, as far as I can tell from what little I know of first aid. But there are two patches of blood on the back of her jacket, and possibly elsewhere. I can't see an actual wound, but we'd better phone for an ambulance without delay."

He reached for the back pocket of his jeans. "Oh damn, I left my mobile at the shop." He glanced at the rear wall of the kiosk. "Oh, for goodness' sake, where's a phone when you need one?"

"Don't worry, I've got mine, Hector." I pulled my phone from my skirt pocket and tapped in 999. "Try talking to her to see if you can bring her round."

As I was giving the details to the emergency services call-taker, I was conscious of footsteps running across the road behind me. As soon as I'd finished my call, I turned round to see Carol, who had left her shop to find out what was going on. I was surprised she hadn't been out here sooner when she should have had a clear view of the phone box from her shop.

"Please don't tell me Billy's dead," she pleaded, her voice tremulous. "I saw him messing about over here earlier. But – oh, no, hang on, I see it's a woman."

"Billy?" said Hector and I in unison.

"I know, I never had him down as being a reader either," replied Carol. "But perhaps when there are books to be had for free…"

"That wasn't quite what I meant—" began Hector, but he cut his speech short at the sound of something hard and solid tumbling to the ground as Julia Prentice repositioned herself.

"Oh, my goodness, a knife!" cried Carol. "No wonder there's so much blood on the pavement! Someone's stabbed her." Unlike Hector and me, Carol hadn't taken care to avoid stepping on the bloody footprints left by the culprit. "It's still sticky, too." The sole of her blue canvas plimsoll squelched as she raised it from the ground. Soon there was a second kind of red footprint patterning the pavement. "And to think I missed all the action! I'm sorry, I was distracted by Ted when he brought this morning's bread delivery. Still, at least we are each other's alibi." She gave an awkward laugh.

"Carol, did you see anyone pass by here in the last little while?" I asked. "Before Ted arrived."

She thought for a moment without taking her eyes off Julia, who was now starting to stir a little in Hector's arms. "Tommy's been out and about in the High Street since not long after I opened, then there were my usual customers coming in for their newspapers, of course. I can't say I noticed much beyond my shop window during the morning rush. There were certainly no suspicious customers from beyond the village. Except, now I think of it, that stuck-up madam who turned her nose up at the books I wanted her to take off my hands."

"You mean Trixie Drake?" I asked. "Those pointy

footprints look like the kind she'd leave with her posh court shoes. Whoever it was, I'm guessing that as soon as she realised she was leaving footprints, she removed her shoes to throw people off her trail. Or perhaps she had parked a getaway car here, and she just climbed in and drove away. Either way, the trail goes cold at the kerb."

Hector wasn't listening. He was gazing at the dull grey knife that lay on the pavement to the right of his knee. "I don't think this can be the murder weapon, or rather the attempted murder weapon, because there's no blood on it. Yet I swear it just fell out of Julia's clothes."

Carol took a step closer to him and bent down to peer at the knife. "Well, there wouldn't be," she said, matter of factly. "You'd never draw blood with a knife like that. Look, it's reprehensible."

Ignoring my cry of "Don't touch! It could be important evidence!", she stooped to pick it up from the ground. To my horror, before I could stop her, she'd stabbed herself in the stomach. Hector and I froze in disbelief, our silence broken only by a distinctive pinging sound.

I breathed out. "Not reprehensible. Retractable. It's a retractable knife. A stage knife."

"Isn't that what I said?" asked Carol lightly, waving the knife in the air to demonstrate the reappearance of its blade. "It had got a bit rusty over winter, which has made it too noisy to use convincingly on stage. That's why I put it on my discards pile when I was sorting out the props box yesterday. It was in the box of bits I left outside the shop this morning, with a sign on it inviting people to help themselves."

"So that's why there's no blood on it." Hector peered over

Julia's shoulder at her chest, which continued to move gently and regularly up and down. "The only blood I can see on Julia are those two patches on the back of her jacket. They're just superficial marks, not the result of wounds. Now that I look at them more closely, I think they could be handprints. The two big splodges must be the palms, and the little dots above each one could come from fingertips." He held Julia's shoulders and bent her slightly forward to show us. "I don't think she's been stabbed at all. I don't think this is her blood."

"So whose is it?" I wondered. "It must be very fresh to be such a vivid red. It's as bright as the phone box."

The sound of a vehicle coming to a stop behind us made me turn round to see the ambulance. It had arrived remarkably quickly, given how far Wendlebury is from the nearest ambulance station. Two trim paramedics in pine-green boilersuits stepped out of the van and came over to join us, sporting reassuring yet serious smiles.

"Now, love, was it you who summoned us today?" the taller one asked me. I nodded. "Can you tell me from the top what the problem is here, please?"

His deep voice startled Julia, who opened her eyes and twisted round to see whose arms were still wrapped around her.

"Oh, Hector, I'm so sorry, how embarrassing." She lifted her hands to cover her eyes. "I'm afraid I'm always the same, completely hopeless at the sight of blood. Is that awful woman all right? The one who shoved me in the back while I was filling the shelves, then held up her bloody hands to frighten me? I thought she must have cut herself and come to ask me for help; but then I saw a knife in her hand, pointing towards me. Instead of helping her, I'm afraid I just keeled over. Is she still here? Trixie Drake, I mean. It was Trixie Drake. Was she serious? Was she really about to attack me?"

She gazed at each of us in turn, her eyes a silent appeal for reassurance.

Before I could formulate a reply, another vehicle pulled in behind the ambulance. It looked ordinary enough, but there was a flashing blue light on its roof, attached to a long curly cable feeding into the open window on the passenger side.

"I didn't hear you ask for the police too," said Hector.

"I didn't," I replied.

The police officer in the passenger seat called across to us. "Excuse me, do any of you know whether a number twenty-seven bus has passed this way recently?"

Carol put up her hand, as eager as a child in class to answer their favourite teacher's question.

"Yes, it left a few moments ago, the ten-thirty, heading for Slate Green. I didn't actually see it, as I had my back to my shop window while I was restocking my bread shelf, but I heard the distinctive sound of its neurotic brakes, so it must have let someone on or off. I don't know which."

"She means pneumatic brakes," I explained. "But, Carol, that's brilliant; that's all we need to know. It must have stopped to let Trixie board, just after she'd attacked poor Julia. What an unconventional getaway car."

The police officer's face lit up. "Makes perfect sense to me, miss. That's why we're in pursuit of the bus. The driver radioed in to say he had a passenger behaving suspiciously, boarding with blood stains on her hands and clothes. She snapped at him so sharply when she got on that he was too afraid not to let her on the bus, in case she pulled a knife or a gun on him. But he's not letting her off until we catch up with him. He couldn't say too much, and didn't even give his precise whereabouts, as he didn't want her to twig that he was calling for help, so we're not entirely sure where he is. The satnav tracker's a bit dodgy out here in the sticks." He turned to his colleague. "Looks like we'd better call for a second crew to come and sort out the crime scene here. What do you reckon, lads?"

This last remark was addressed to the paramedics. The shorter one looked up from the blood pressure monitor he had just applied to Julia's arm.

"Actually, I think we're okay, mate. It's nowhere near as bad as it looks. We've yet to find a puncture wound, and I'm confident our friend here will make a full and speedy recovery. But probably best to get some of your lot here anyway to take statements, as it sounds as if there's been some hanky-panky going on."

As the police car sped off towards Slate Green, a sudden instinct made me dip the tip of my finger in the little red pool beside the phone box door. Gingerly I held it up to my nose, then gasped.

"We should have told the police to bring some white spirit too." I turned my red-tipped finger towards the others. "You see, the red isn't blood. It's paint."

That announcement perked Julia up.

"Who on earth has been painting it?" she cried. "Why didn't they put up a sign? I could have got it all over my clothes. Oh—!" She clapped a hand to her mouth. "As, I suppose, did Trixie Drake. And there was me thinking that was blood on her hands when she opened the door behind me." She broke off, paling as she began to recall what had actually happened. "She had me cornered, you know. After all, in a phone box, there's nowhere to hide." Her eyes widened. "You should have seen her expression! I knew we weren't exactly best friends, but I didn't know she hated me that much. I certainly never dreamed she'd pull a knife on me."

Perhaps it wasn't the sight of blood that had made her faint, but the fear of being stabbed. Or had the shock caused her to have a heart attack? I was glad the paramedics were on hand to check that nothing physical was amiss.

Julia swooned slightly as they helped her into the folding wheelchair they'd produced from the back of the ambulance. They began to check her vital signs. Carol, meanwhile, was crossing back from her shop with a mug of tea and a plate of biscuits for Julia when a familiar cry came from down the lane.

"*Now* you bring out the tea!" cried Billy. "When I've just bin all the way home to get one for meself. I've bin working just as hard as these lads here, you know! And what else have you been up to while I've been gone?" He waved a hand at the array of red footprints on the pavement. "Holding a dance?"

"A sign saying 'wet paint' might have been a good idea, Bill," said Hector. "Sorry, easy to be wise after the event, I know."

Billy shrugged. "You never normally see anyone go near

this old phone box from one week to the next. Now look at it! Some great charlie has put their hands right in the wet bit here."

I looked at Hector. "Well, that accounts for Trixie Drake's bloody handprints."

He chuckled. "Language, Sophie."

Billy carried on as if we hadn't spoken. "I was only tarting it up to make it look nice for you – covering up the odd patch of rust rather than doing an all-over paint job. I just wanted to make Wendlebury's phone box library look better than that mad biddy's old rabbit hutch in Boxford that I've been hearing about." He folded his arms across his chest. "How was I to know people would suddenly be coming at it from all directions, like it's the hog roast at the Village Show? Just be grateful I thought to stow the paint pot and brush behind the phone box when I went for my tea break, so's that young rascal Tommy didn't go getting no ideas about having a go at it himself in my absence." He fetched his can of paint out from its hiding place to show us. "Now, if you'll all clear off out of my way, perhaps a body can get on with his work here."

∽

ONLY AFTER THE paramedics had gone and two more police officers had arrived and taken our statements were Hector and I able to return to the bookshop. Mrs Wetherley, with the help of Tommy, now restored to his usual bouncy self, had held the fort for us.

For the rest of the day the bookshop was far busier than

usual, because word had spread around the village that Hector and I had been witnesses to some outrageous crime at the phone box, and people wanted to find out the facts for themselves. The grapevine was as inaccurate as ever. By nightfall, rumour had it that Billy had thwarted a would-be assassin brandishing only a paintbrush, and that the driver of the Slate Green bus had run them both over to stop them getting away. People also came to leave bags of second-hand books for Julia to add to the phone box library, once she'd recovered from her wounds – reports of which described them as everything from a broken nose to a severed artery. In the unlikely event that it had been Julia who had ransacked Trixie's book box – we never did get to the bottom of that mystery – she wouldn't have needed to resort to such tactics again. Within a few days, we had enough donations to fill the phone box library several times over. Julia, meanwhile, lay resting at home, trying to recover from her shock by escaping into a good book.

It was only after the shop had closed, ten minutes late because it took forever to persuade the last well-wishers to leave, that I had a sudden thought.

"Do you think Trixie Drake thought the stage dagger was real? Do you think she seriously intended to stab Julia in revenge for creating a better community library than her own? Or was she just trying to frighten her off the project? She doesn't strike me as a practical joker – and as a practical joke, it would have been in very poor taste."

Hector leaned back on his stool. "I don't know. Perhaps it was a passing act of madness, the culmination of decades of festering envy, undertaken on a whim when she spotted the discarded dagger in the old props box outside the village shop." He clasped his hands behind his head. "If Julia presses charges, it'll be for the judge to decide. I'm just glad I'd temporarily mislaid my letter-opener, or she might have seized that instead, and the outcome could have been tragic."

"Oh, I found your letter-opener, by the way." I crossed to the tea-room counter and fished it out from under one of the glass cake domes. "Mrs Wetherley had mistaken it for a fancy cake knife and had been using it to slice her strawberry gateau."

I held it up to show him the blade, now encrusted with thick, dark red jam. Then I washed it and dried it on a tea towel before returning it to its usual place on the trade counter. Hector picked it up and pressed the point of it to his fingertip, drawing the tiniest bead of blood. Then he thrust it into the drawer beneath his desk.

"I think that had better be its new home from now on. Out of sight, out of mind."

∽

A FEW MONTHS LATER, Hector set the local paper down on the tea-room table for Billy to read with his elevenses. The story of Trixie's attack on Julia filled the front page. Julia had indeed pressed charges, realising how much more serious the attack could have been if Trixie had chosen a more effective weapon. She was also angry that Trixie had fled the scene, leaving her in a state of collapse. At her trial, Trixie had been let off lightly on the grounds of the minimal impact on Julia's physical well-being and a flurry of character references from various charities for whom Trixie had raised funds over the years. She did not receive a custodial sentence, but a community service order, to be spent teaching prison inmates to read.

Local news coverage created a tourist attraction out of the Wendlebury Phone Box Library, which quickly morphed into a specialist library of murder mystery stories. Eager readers made special trips from neighbouring villages and hamlets to borrow books, and to pose for selfies with their feet in the "bloody" footprints.

Billy glanced at the front page and tutted. "I always knew reading was a dangerous hobby."

"That's why I never do it," said Tommy, enjoying a hot chocolate as his reward for helping Billy clean the shop windows.

"Ha! You think?" said Hector.

"I don't think, I knows," returned Billy. "Didn't I ever tell you about my old Uncle Amos, what used to work as a stevedore down Avonmouth Docks? That was back in the days before containers got invented, and dockers would load and unload all the cargo with their own bare hands."

Hector shook his head, eyes narrowed as he braced himself for one of Billy's tall tales.

"One day, he was unloading a great crateload of encyclopaedias, when the line from the crane snapped, and the whole thing fell on his head. Flat as a piece of paper, he was. You could have used him as a bookmark."

There was a moment's shocked silence, before Billy let out a great bark of laughter, and the rest of us gave a collective sigh of relief.

"I nearly had you there, boy!" yelped Billy, slapping his thighs.

But Hector and I had the last laugh when we noticed, as Billy and Tommy left the shop, that in Tommy's back pocket, the one that wasn't occupied by his phone, there was a battered Agatha Christie paperback. A sticker on its cover identified it as a loan from the Wendlebury Phone Box Library.

ABOUT DEBBIE YOUNG

Debbie Young writes two popular cozy mystery series featuring Sophie Sayers, set in a Cotswold village, and Gemma Lamb, set at a girls' boarding school. One book in each series was shortlisted for the Bookbrunch Selfies Awards for the best independently-published fiction in the UK. She is founder of the Hawkesbury Upton Literature Festival, UK Ambassador for the Alliance of Independent Authors, and a course tutor for Jericho Writers. She writes in the Plotting Shed at the bottom of her cottage garden. Her novels are now published by Boldwood Books and she is represented by the Ethan Ellenberg Literary Agency.

15

MURDER IN THE BOOKSHOP

RACHEL MCLEAN

Freya Garside knew full well that when at a book reading, or at any event for that matter, the best place to sit was in the centre.

At the front, you ran the risk of being singled out. Mocked, if you were unlucky enough to be at the pantomime. Maybe even – shudder – asked to take part in the reading, at an event like this one. At the sides you'd be subject to the jostling and shoving of the idiots who turned up late and wanted to squeeze past you. And at the back – well, Freya wouldn't admit it to anyone, not even her oldest friend, but her hearing wasn't what it had been.

This evening she was in The Heath bookshop, at a reading of Nocturnes by Gareth Smallwood. A pretentious little book, but one rumoured to contain the occasional flash of brilliance. The man had grown up in Birmingham – in Kings Heath, as had Freya. They'd even attended the same primary school in the 1950s. But he'd long since moved away to London. Of course.

And now here he was, gracing the humble residents of Kings Heath with his exalted presence.

Sitting on Freya's right, shifting anxiously in her too-warm pink overcoat, was the woman Freya supposed she would describe as her oldest friend. Doris Jacobsen. Beyond Freya, almost at the end of the row and sitting next to an empty chair, was Munch. Freya still didn't know why he insisted on calling himself that, but the lad seemed harmless enough, and had latched onto her after his parents had moved in next door in the summer. He'd been leaving his parent's house as she'd headed out for the evening, and on learning where she was going, had decided to tag along.

Doris, on the other hand, almost hadn't come. She'd been keen enough when Freya had bought the tickets – two pounds, refunded if you bought a book, as if Freya was going to do that when there was a perfectly good library on the High Street – but tonight she'd been reluctant. It had taken all of Freya's considerable powers of persuasion to convince Doris that she didn't really have a cold, she wasn't contagious and she was certainly not about to precipitate the next global pandemic by turning up to her local bookshop for an evening of prose and cake.

Freya had to admit that the cake had been the main draw. The remains of it – chocolate, her favourite – were sitting on the shop counter behind the rows of assembled book lovers and even more rows of empty chairs. It seemed that on a drizzly Wednesday evening in late March, literary fiction wasn't much of a draw.

But Freya was a pensioner. She certainly wasn't about to venture into the town centre for an evening's entertainment, and she was intrigued by this man who'd grown up around the corner from her before moving on to bigger and better things.

Or so his Wikipedia entry said. Looking at his shabby suit and the spectacles that had been sellotaped at the side, Freya wasn't so sure. Literary fiction, it seemed, wasn't a money spinner.

Smallwood launched into his second reading of the night, causing the assembled fans to shift in their seats and a man immediately behind her to cough surreptitiously. Freya wrinkled her nose, resisted the urge to turn and shush him, and diverted her energy to paying attention.

The author drew himself up to his full height, which was not inconsiderable, and took a deep breath. The room hushed as he began.

"Rufus was a man who'd reached a certain stage in life, one in which he found himself unable to contemplate existence without ruminating on its excesses and exigences, and wondering if he had indeed taken the correct path according to where his heart and the girding of his loins truly wanted to direct him."

Dear God. What was this nonsense?

If this was what he wrote, Freya wasn't surprised the man didn't earn enough to keep him in functioning spectacles.

Maybe she could have a quiet word with the nice ladies who ran the shop, see if she could offset the two pounds against the cost of something a little more... coherent.

There was another cough behind her. Freya straightened

in her chair, her hands tensing in her lap. If people couldn't keep quiet, then they shouldn't be here.

Take Doris, for example. Earlier this evening Doris had complained of a stinking cold, insisting she needed to take to her bed with a box of tissues and a packet of Lemsip. But now here she was, chipper and doughty as she'd always been, and managing to keep herself quiet while their former neighbour bored them all to death with his words. She'd even stopped fidgeting.

"Arriving at the bookkeepers, Rufus lowered the brim of his hat and adopted the manner of all middle-class men on entering such a base establishment, which was to attempt to appear as if he was not, indeed, present in the establishment at all but in reality somewhere else, somewhere more appropriate to Rufus's station in life."

Freya put her hand over her mouth to stifle a yawn. How did this stuff get published?

Her right hand reached for the watch on her left wrist, as if she might be able to determine how long she had to sit through this by touch alone. Freya would never be so impolite as to check the time while another person was speaking.

But then, this wasn't speaking. It was torture by words.

More shuffling behind her. She shifted in her seat – her back was giving her jip again, why didn't they have more comfortable chairs at these things? – but didn't turn to glare or even give a sidelong glance. She'd quickly reached the point where she fully sympathised with her restless comrades, for comrades in misery they all were.

Doris, on the other hand, sat perfectly still. Slumped in her seat, hands loose in her lap, she was clearly rapt.

Either that or she'd done the sensible thing and decided to take a nap.

Freya pushed down a chuckle. What would Gareth Smallwood say if he knew his former classmate had fallen asleep during the reading of his so-called seminal work?

Freya shifted her gaze from the author to the woman at his side, the bookshop owner. She'd introduced her guest as a 'local boy made good', prompting an eye roll from Freya and a grin from Doris. Now she was looking as if she might drop off herself.

Freya turned back to the author, whose words she was allowing to wash over her. She leaned back, trying to get comfortable. Wriggling, she cursed her damn back. A man behind her tutted.

Tut away, she thought. You have no idea.

Movement in the corner of her eye drew her attention back to the bookshop owner. She'd taken a step forward, looking into the audience.

Automatically, Freya's hand went to her chest.

Me?

But the woman wasn't looking at her.

The bookseller took another step forward. She turned to Smallwood and made a gesture: a knife across her throat.

Freya allowed herself a wince. Smallwood was bad, but cutting him short like that...

The bookseller looked across the crowd towards the back of the room. She mouthed something.

Freya looked over her shoulder to see the woman's colleague hurrying forward.

Smallwood stood in his spot, book open, glasses falling down his nose, eyeing the two women as if waiting for his cue.

What was going on?

The bookseller waded into the assembled chairs. The rows at the front were empty, of course, meaning Freya and Doris had only three people in front of them.

"Madam? Are you alright?" The woman leaned over the two men in front of Freya, peering at Doris.

Freya took a tight breath and turned to her friend.

Her heart skipped.

Doris was still slumped in her chair. She was paying no attention to the bookshop owner.

"Madam?"

Freya put a hand on Doris's arm.

"Dor? Doris, wake up."

Munch stood up. He leaned over Doris. "Mrs Jacobsen?"

Sit down, Freya thought. People were watching.

Oh, the humiliation. Falling asleep at a book reading and then being singled out and told to wake up in front of everyone.

But Doris wasn't waking up.

Freya tightened her grip. She gave Doris's arm a shake.

Nothing.

Freya felt the hairs on the back of her neck prickle.

"Doris," she muttered, her lips close to her friend's ear. "Doris. Wake up."

The bookseller pushed the empty chair in front of Doris

to one side, sending it clattering to the floor. She grabbed Doris's wrist and pulled it to her face, making Doris shift in her chair.

Doris didn't open her eyes.

"Doris?" Freya whispered, her voice thin.

The woman dropped Doris's hand. She looked over Freya's head, at her colleague.

"Call an ambulance."

⁓

Freya clutched Doris's vile pink overcoat to her chest as she watched the paramedics bundle her friend into an ambulance. They'd pulled it off her when they'd arrived, easing her to the floor so they could perform CPR.

"Are you alright? Do you want to come back inside?" It was the bookshop owner, the one who'd spotted Doris's collapse.

How had Freya not noticed that her friend wasn't asleep, but unconscious?

"Did they tell you anything?" Freya asked. "Is she going to be alright?"

The woman shrugged. "Do you want to speak to them? Are you her partner?"

Freya gave the woman a frown. "I'm her friend." She hesitated. "Her oldest friend." Which was true. And not just because the two of them were in their eighties.

"You might want to talk to them. I think they're taking her to the QE."

The Queen Elizabeth hospital, named after the late

Queen, God rest her soul. Freya hated the place; a carbuncle on the horizon for miles around and impossible to navigate once you were inside.

She nodded and stepped forward. A female paramedic was closing the back door to the ambulance, hurrying around it to the front.

She needed to be quick.

She was about to speak to the woman when someone stepped in front of her.

"Is there anything I can do? Will she be alright?"

The paramedic smiled at the man.

Gareth Smallwood. He'd butted in, assuming he was the most important person in the room, and was now acting as if it were he who was Doris's oldest friend, and not Freya.

"She'll be at A and E at the QE," replied the paramedic. "Hopefully we won't have to sit outside too long."

The author nodded. "I'll follow on. I have a car."

Freya stepped forward. "I'm her friend. She came with me." She gave the author a stern look then turned to the paramedic. "Please, tell me where I can visit her."

The paramedic gave her a look. "They don't have visitors in A and E."

"Well, which ward will she be taken to?"

"Damned if I know. Are you her next of kin?"

Freya stiffened. Bernard.

In all the to-do, she'd clean forgotten about Doris's poor husband.

"No," she said. "Her husband, Bernard. I'll telephone him."

The paramedic gave her a sympathetic smile. "You do

that. I've no idea where she'll be taken, and it could be a while before she gets anywhere, but if he calls the main switchboard, that's the best way to find out."

Freya nodded.

"Poor Doris," said Smallwood.

Freya narrowed her eyes at him. Poor Doris, indeed. The man hadn't clapped eyes on either of them for decades, and hadn't recognised them when they'd arrived at the reading either. And now he was behaving as if he had some kind of connection to her friend.

The paramedic was gone. The ambulance moved off and Freya stood back.

"Were you her friend?" Smallwood asked.

"I am," Freya replied. "Her oldest friend." She turned away from him, bringing up Bernard's mobile number in her phone contacts. It was past the time when the man went up to bed, but hopefully he'd have his phone with him.

∼

THE WIND SWIRLED around the ugly modern building of Lodge Hill crematorium, causing Freya's black woollen coat to whip up around her shins. She pulled her handbag higher up her shoulder and shrugged, wishing she could get herself warm. Further down the hill, the hearse made its slow journey through the graveyard, bringing poor Doris's body up to be cremated.

She pushed out a shaky breath, watching it progress up the hill. A car followed, containing Doris's husband – widower, she reminded herself – and son, Noah. Freya had known Noah when he was a small boy, running through Doris's house when Freya popped round for tea and causing his mother no end of anxiety as he stormed through the teenage years. Now he was a grown man with a wife of his own, and a house just outside Stratford-upon-Avon. Freya tried to remember the last time Doris had mentioned him visiting. Not recently enough, for a son who lived only twenty miles away.

The hearse reached the covered area at the front of the crematorium and slowed to a halt. Freya pulled back along with the other mourners, her head bowed and her body language subdued.

She recognised three of the other mourners. Doris's next-door neighbour, Mrs Akhtar. Kind of her to come, given that this would be a Christian ceremony. A daughter-in-law whose name Freya couldn't remember as she'd only met the woman once. And Gareth Smallwood.

Freya eyed the author, wondering why he was still here. The book reading had been over a week ago. The man should have been back in London by now. But he'd accosted her as she'd arrived and told her all about how he'd stayed in a budget hotel for the intervening week, unable to bring himself to leave before Doris's body was put to rest.

Freya sniffed. She couldn't see why a man who hadn't clapped eyes on her dear friend since before the advent of decimal currency needed to hang around for her funeral.

The funeral car pulled up behind the hearse and Bernard climbed out, his movements slow and jerky. Bernard was short and stocky, always had been, but today he seemed even smaller.

Freya wanted to step forward and take him by the arm, but Bernard was a proud man and she knew he wouldn't want that kind of fuss. Besides, he had his son, a tall dark-haired man who was emerging from the car's other rear door. He glanced across at his father then locked eyes with his wife. She gave him a tight smile but didn't approach, instead glancing over at Smallwood.

Smallwood had stepped back and was hovering at the back of the paltry group of mourners. He kept shooting wary looks at Bernard, then glancing at Noah before quickly looking away.

Freya narrowed her eyes. He didn't belong here. He wasn't a friend of the family, he certainly hadn't been a friend to Doris, and he should be back in London.

Or was he hoping his attendance here would be made public? Perhaps it would bolster his image, make him look like the sort of man who cared enough to attend the funeral of an old acquaintance – or maybe even a fan, heaven forbid – who'd died at his book reading.

Freya snorted. Gareth Smallwood had been an arrogant boy, the kind who believed himself to be more intelligent than everyone around him. And judging by his performance at the book reading, he hadn't changed.

"Miss Garside."

Freya turned to see the shorter of the two women who owned the bookshop.

"Oh. Hello."

The woman smiled at her. "I'm so sorry about your friend. Did you know her well?"

Freya nodded, suddenly lost for words. "She was…"

The bookseller touched her arm. "It's OK. You don't have to say anything."

Freya blinked. She wasn't the kind of woman who allowed the death of an octogenarian friend who hadn't been in the best of health to floor her. "I'm fine," she said, her voice not as strong as she would have liked.

The woman smiled. "They're going in."

Freya turned to see people moving towards the entrance. Bernard stood to one side, his gaze steady on Doris's coffin.

Freya blinked. Poor man. Bernard was the kind of man who'd never once in his life cooked his own dinner or ironed his own shirts. How would he cope?

She turned towards the door, and noticed that Smallwood had left the crowd and was close to the hearse. Freya frowned and looked over her shoulder, watching him. He was approaching Noah.

The author spoke, his lips barely moving, and Noah turned to him. As Freya entered the darkness of the crematorium, she noticed Noah's eyes widening.

Damn man. Why did he insist on interfering?

∽

DORIS HAD LIVED in a squat 1930s semi on Dad's Lane. Her widower, or possibly the son and daughter-in-law, had laid out a buffet of limp cheese sandwiches and supermarket sausage rolls. Freya surveyed it, her appetite suddenly gone.

She picked up a small triangle of sandwich and a slice of the coffee cake lurking at the back of the table and moved towards the living room, where she hoped to get a seat.

Two generous but threadbare armchairs and a sofa filled the space. All were taken.

A thin woman around Freya's age looked up from her spot on the sofa. She smiled at Freya.

"Here, there's plenty of space." She nudged the elderly man next to her. "George, budge up."

"It's fine," Freya said. "I don't want to impose."

The woman shook her head. "You're not imposing. George. I said budge up."

She shoved George along the sofa and moved up so she was in the middle. Freya took the vacated space at the end, careful not to let her food spill as the sofa dipped under the weight of all three of them. George was not a small man.

The woman turned to Freya and cocked her head in an expression of sympathy. "I'm Sheila. I knew Doris from Lewis's."

"She worked at John Lewis?"

"Not John Lewis. Lewis's. On Corporation Street. She and I worked there until it closed down in 1991."

Freya nodded. "I'm Freya." She wondered why Doris had never mentioned this woman. "You kept in touch, all this time?"

"Not as well as we should have. George and I moved away, to Tewkesbury. It's lovely there." She frowned. "Not as dirty as the city. But we exchanged Christmas cards, birthday gifts for the children sometimes. That kind of thing."

"It's good of you to come." Freya picked up her triangle of sandwich and surveyed it. She took a nibble.

"It's the least I could do," Sheila said, "after such a shock as this."

Freya nodded. It had been a shock. She'd lain awake all night after the book reading, worrying about her friend. And then when the call had come in the morning informing her of Doris's death, she'd been...

Had she been surprised? Doris was elderly, after all. And she seemed to spend half her life asleep.

"I suppose she was getting on," Freya said. "We're slowly popping off. Not that big a surprise."

The woman frowned at her. "But it was the way she died."

Freya shifted her weight, trying to get some space. The two armchairs held a vicar, who someone had evidently invited back from the ceremony, and a younger man she didn't recognise.

"A heart attack, they said," Sheila told her, her voice low.

Freya wanted to close down this conversation and move on. Gossip. She hated it.

Maybe it was time to go home. She needed a decent cup of tea, in the peace and quiet of her own kitchen.

"Caused by anaphylaxis, I've no doubt," Sheila added.

"That's not what they told me."

Sheila sniffed. "Well, it would make sense. And have you seen that Bernard has put peanuts out on the buffet table? Poor Doris isn't even cold in her grave."

Urn, thought Freya, but she knew what the woman meant. She'd spotted the peanuts too, and it had brought her up short. Doris's first attack had taken place when the two of them had gone to a pub in 1956 and Doris, unaware of her allergy, had eaten a single peanut from Freya's bag.

Freya had frozen as she'd watched Doris's body go limp. Thank goodness for the quick-thinking landlord, calling an ambulance while muttering about young women unaccompanied in pubs.

She had a thought.

The book reading. The chocolate cake.

She'd heard Doris asking the bookshop owner about it. The woman had shown her the box the cake came in – shop-bought, to Freya's surprise.

But maybe something had gone wrong. The labelling? Contamination? It seemed everything had a warning on it these days: made in a factory that also works with nuts.

Had Doris been the victim of a simple ingredient mix-up, an inadvertent error? Or something worse?

Should Freya speak to someone at the bookshop?

She looked up to see a man enter the room: the author, Gareth Smallwood.

What was he doing here?

He gave her a small smile accompanied by a raise of the eyebrows. Doris's son, Noah, followed him. His body language was nervous. He kept looking at the author, his gaze wary.

A contamination. An accident.

Or was there more to Doris's death? Was it possible this hadn't been an accident at all?

"I DON'T MEAN to cast aspersions on you or your shop," Freya said, "but it would help to know."

She was in the Heath bookshop again. Today there were no rows of chairs arranged across the room; instead, shoppers perused the shelves. She wondered how many of them would buy, and how many would make note of titles to order online later.

The bookshop owner – the tall one, not the one who'd noticed Doris's collapse – gave her a nervous look.

"We did check," she said. "The coroner's office called, I suppose they were wondering if it might be suspicious. But we still had the packaging. And we gave what was left of the cake to the coroner. They told us it was safe. No nuts at all."

Freya's shoulders dropped. She'd been so convinced that the cake had been responsible for her friend's death.

"Well, that's good news, I suppose." She smiled at the woman. "Thank you."

Munch, beside her, was flicking through his phone screen. Freya gave him a nudge.

"Wha? Oh, yeah. I need to pay for this, please." He pushed a book across the counter. Poetry. Freya hadn't realised Munch was into poetry. But then, the man was an aspiring comedian. Perhaps it gave him inspiration.

"Thanks." The bookseller rang the purchase up and put Munch's book in a bag. "And I'm so sorry for your friend's death, again. We feel somehow responsible."

Freya pulled herself straight. "Clearly, you aren't."

The woman said nothing.

Munch grabbed his bag and Freya tugged his elbow. "Come with me."

Five minutes later, they were sat in a coffee shop on the opposite side of the High Street. Freya wasn't normally a fan of coffee shops: she couldn't see the point of paying for overpriced coffee when she had a perfectly good jar of

Nescafé at home. But today she wanted to ask Munch something. And besides, she'd opted for a pot of tea. Not much they could do to spoil that.

Munch sat down with his chai latte. It smelled of cinnamon and flowers, making Freya's nose wrinkle.

"You were there at the book reading," she said to him. "Did you notice anything strange?"

"What kind of strange?"

"I don't know." If Freya knew what it was she was looking for, she'd have said so. "Anything that was off." She considered. "At the beginning, when I had to go out, what were you and Doris doing?"

She'd had to step across the road into a nearby pub, to use the facilities. She'd been horrified that the bookshop didn't have them, and slipped out without anyone noticing.

"That was before the reading started," Munch said.

"Yes." If the event had already begun, Freya would have crossed her legs instead.

Munch screwed up his face. It wasn't a look that suited him. Freya had recently learned that Munch had been given his nickname by his mum, who said when he was little he was so cute she wanted to munch him. At the age of twenty-five, he still had his moments, but not right now.

"She was talking to the writer."

Freya stopped mid-sip of tea. "She was?"

She'd expected Doris to go straight to her seat, perhaps after picking up a piece of the definitely-not-poisonous chocolate cake, and sit quietly. But hobnobbing with the esteemed author, that was a surprise.

"What did she talk to him about?" Freya tried to

remember if Doris and Smallwood had had much to do with each other at school. She remembered the author appearing at her friend's funeral. What had he been talking to Noah about?

Munch shrugged. "Not sure. I was talking to their social media manager. She told me Mo Pikett had been in the week before."

Mo Pikett was Kings Heath's most famous son. Munch hero-worshipped him.

"Oh, you and Mo Pikett," Freya said. "Stalking him isn't going to help you land that stand-up career, you know."

Munch's face fell. "I'm not stalking him. I just want to meet him."

"Hmm. So did you happen to hear anything of their discussion?"

"No. He did cut her a slice of cake, though. It was good, that cake. Tons of chocolate."

Freya put her cup down. "He cut her cake?"

A shrug. "Yeah. He was handing it out to a few people. Using it as a way to break the ice, I guess. I'll have to try that." He grinned. "When I'm a famous comedian."

"Oh, you'll be much more famous than Gareth Smallwood, Munch. Don't you worry."

He pulled his phone out. "Here. I was taking photos. I tagged this one on Insta, see. Mentioned that Mo had been there too."

Freya leaned over and peered at Munch's phone. She didn't have a smart phone herself, didn't need one. Munch referred to her phone as her 'burner phone'. But it did the job.

Onscreen was an image of half a dozen biddies, all crowding round the author, eyeing him as if he were some sort of pop star. Freya rolled her eyes.

He's just a man. When he was eight, he vomited all over his school desk. He's nothing special.

In the centre of the photo was Doris, smiling up at Gareth. He had one hand on a plate full of chocolate cake, which she was reaching for.

Freya zoomed in and moved down, to the author's other hand.

It looked like he was slipping something into his pocket.

"What's that?" She pointed at the object and looked at Munch.

He cocked his head. "Not sure. A bottle?"

"Small one if it is. Do you have any more photos of the two of them?"

He pulled his phone back and scrolled through it. "Sorry."

"It's alright." Freya stood up. "I need to talk to someone."

~

FREYA CLOSED the door to her house and paused to breathe in the familiar scent. She loved her little terrace on Avenue Road. The fact that once she put something somewhere, no one would move it, that it always smelled of the fresh flowers she bought from the florist on Waterloo Road. And the fact that it gave her a birds-eye view of Kings Heath Park, providing hours of entertainment without the need to switch on her thirty-year-old telly.

The phone was ringing. Halfway through slipping her shoes off, Freya hobbled into the kitchen wearing one shoe, and picked it up.

"Kings Heath 3458, can I help you?"

"Freya, it's Bernard. Bernard Jacobsen."

Freya slid into the chair at her kitchen table. "Bernard. How are you?"

A pause. "I'm not so bad, thank you. All things considering."

"The funeral was lovely. Very fitting."

"Thank you." His voice was quiet. "I... I have some news for you."

Freya clutched the phone tighter. Had Bernard discovered something about Doris's death?

"Yes?" she said. Barely breathing.

"It's Doris's will. She left you something."

Freya felt herself relax. "That's very kind of her. But she didn't need to."

"You were her oldest friend. She used to tell me about the first time you met."

"Miss Durham sat us next to each other to draw a picture of a dog."

"In 1947."

Freya didn't like to be reminded how long she'd known Doris. It made her feel old. "Yes."

Freya wasn't about to be so vulgar as to ask what Doris had left her. An ornament, or some sort of knick-knack. Maybe something from when she and Doris were young. She waited.

"You'll want to know what she left you," Bernard said.

"Well…"

"Her tulip vase," he continued. "The one she barely used. I think you admired it."

"I did. That's so kind of her. It will get good use, I promise you."

"And some cash."

Cash?

"Oh. I'm not sure how I…"

"Two thousand pounds, to be precise."

"Two thousand pounds? How did she—?"

"She had considerable savings. She'd been squirrelling money away since the mid seventies."

"And she didn't leave it to you or your son?"

"Oh, we got most of it. But it seems she wanted to give something to her old school friends."

"School friends?" Freya went through them in her mind. Muriel had died two years earlier. Lizzie had moved to London after her third marriage, and they'd all lost touch. Veronica and Doris had had a falling out. Neither Lizzie nor Veronica had been at the funeral.

"Which school friends?" she asked.

"Well, you. And Gareth Smallwood. The writer. She left him five thousand pounds."

"Five thousand pounds?"

"That's what the solicitor told me. They read the will yesterday. I wasn't there, didn't see the need."

"Why?" she asked.

"Sorry?"

"I mean, why would she leave Gareth Smallwood five

thousand pounds?" Freya resisted the urge to compare the sum to the two thousand she'd been left.

"I'm not sure. It was nice of her, though. Kind. Don't you think?"

"Oh. Yes, I suppose so."

"Anyway, you'll be getting a cheque from the solicitor, once it's all sorted out. I thought you'd want to know."

"Oh. Yes, thank you. Please do let me know if there's anything I can do to help, Bernard."

"I will. I'm sorry, I have to go. That's a neighbour at the door." He hung up.

Freya put down the phone. She still had a single shoe on.

Five thousand pounds, to Gareth Smallwood? Why?

She went into the hall, her mind racing. Slipping off her shoe, she caught sight of Doris's coat hanging on the peg, below where she normally placed her own.

She'd been given it by the paramedic when Doris had collapsed at the book shop. She should return it to Bernard.

Poor Bernard. What must he be thinking, about Gareth Smallwood?

What was she thinking?

Freya took the coat off the peg and flinched as something fell out of its pocket.

She looked down. A folded-up piece of paper.

Swallowing, Freya picked it up and put it back in the pocket. It was roughly folded, some of the text visible.

She caught two words: Yours, Gareth.

What had the author been doing, writing to Doris?

Put it back, Freya. Forget about it. It was none of her business.

But Doris had been her friend. And she'd given a large sum of money to the man. If he'd somehow coerced it out of her...

She opened the letter.

∼

THE POLICEWOMAN WAS A RIDICULOUSLY young black woman with a kind smile and a cheap suit. Freya wondered how much police detectives were paid these days: not enough to buy decent clothes, it seemed.

"Mrs Garside, my name's DC Connie Williams," she said, standing on the doorstep.

"Miss," Freya corrected her. "Miss Garside."

The young detective smiled. "Miss Garside, I'm sorry. Can I come in?"

Freya stood back and let the woman pass, closing the door after taking a brief glance up and down Avenue Road. She wondered whether her neighbours had spotted her young visitor. Perhaps they were wondering what was going on.

"Where would you like me?" the detective asked.

Freya gestured towards the living room.

The young woman walked through and hesitated before taking a seat on the sofa. Freya thought of the last time she'd had the police in here. That tall redheaded Detective Inspector had come round, after poor Mr North five doors down had died.

"Thank you for coming," she said. "I know Doris's death was recorded as natural causes."

The detective nodded, pulling out a notepad. Freya could see the young woman's eyes darting around the room, attempting to take note of anything unusual without her host noticing, and failing.

Freya walked to the side table in the window, where she kept her book next to her favourite chair. She lifted the book and picked up the folded note. For a moment, she'd been worried it might not be there.

Silly old woman, she told herself. It wasn't as if anyone had been in the house to move it.

She handed it to the detective and sat in her chair, smoothing her skirt over her thighs.

The detective put her notebook down on the sofa beside her and unfolded the note. Her eyes widened as she read.

"Where did you find this?" She held the note by its edges, her fingertips barely making contact.

"In Doris's coat pocket. The paramedics gave the coat to me after they arrived at the bookshop."

"The bookshop?"

"We were at a reading. Gareth Smallwood."

"The same Gareth who wrote this note, you think?"

"It would make sense."

Freya thought back to the evening of Doris's death. The chocolate cake. The photo on Munch's phone.

"I think that if you can, you should try to check the chocolate cake," she said. "I think he laced Doris's slice with something containing nuts."

The detective placed the note on the sofa. She pulled a slim plastic bag from her own bag and slid the note into it.

An evidence bag. Freya felt a frisson of excitement, then berated herself.

Doris is dead, and you're getting excited about being involved in a murder case.

"We'll have to speak to Mr Smallwood," the detective said. "And I very much doubt that the cake is still available. But the pathologist might be able to run some tests."

Freya slumped in her chair. "The bookshop had the cake checked. It was clean. And you can't run tests."

The detective raised an eyebrow. "Sorry?"

Freya felt cold. "Doris was cremated. Just three days ago." She swallowed. Dear God. Was Gareth Smallwood going to get away with murder, all because she'd left Doris's coat sitting on the hook in her hall for too long?

The detective stood up. "I'll speak to my DI, and if we think there's grounds to open an investigation, I'll be in touch. We'll need to take a statement from you."

"Of course. I suggest you speak to Munch too."

"Munch?"

Freya smiled. "Mark Isleworth. His friends call him Munch. He lives three doors along, towards Vicarage Road."

"Why should I speak to him?"

"He was there. He took photos." *And he has a young mind, he might have noticed something I didn't.*

Not that Freya was about to admit that.

"Thanks for bringing this to our attention. Miss Garside. I'll contact you if we need to take a statement."

∼

FREYA ENTERED the bookshop to see Bernard standing at the till. The two shop owners were talking to him, expressions of concern on their faces.

She approached and gave him the lightest of touches on the arm. "Bernard. How are you?"

He turned. His face was pale. "Freya. How nice to see you. I was just telling these ladies how much Doris enjoyed browsing books here, before... well, you know."

Freya glanced from him to the booksellers. "That's very kind of you, Bernard."

Surely he had more important things to worry about? She took a breath and lowered her voice. "Have the police been in touch with you?"

He dropped his gaze to the floor. "The detective, DC Williams, she told me you'd alerted them to a note."

Freya bent her head to get closer to him. Bernard was the same height as she was, she realised. And Noah, his son, was so tall.

"Can I get the two of you a cup of tea?" the shorter bookseller asked. "We're quiet this morning, you can sit down."

"Oh..." Freya replied. She hadn't intended to stay out for a cup of tea.

"It's on the house," the woman added. "Least we can do."

"Thank you," said Bernard. "Freya, if you don't mind?"

"Of course." Freya followed him to two easy chairs beside a bookcase in the corner of the room. One of them was probably the very same chair Gareth Smallwood had occupied before he'd stood to give his reading.

She shuddered.

Bernard took the chair furthest from the door, and Freya took the other. The bookshop owner brought a pot of tea and two cups and Freya gave her a grateful smile.

"I'm so sorry about all this," she said to Bernard. "It can't be easy."

He poured milk into his cup, not meeting her eye. "It's a shock." He looked up, his gaze suddenly sharp on her. "Did you know?"

Freya drew back. "About her death, or about…"

"About Noah."

She looked down at her own cup. She felt sick. "I didn't, Bernard. I'm so sorry."

"How could I not have realised? I mean, just look at the boy. Man. He's tall, willowy. I'm short and dumpy. And Doris was the same. Now I know where he got it from."

"Have the police been able to tell you anything more? Have they shown you the note?"

"They have. The bastard was blackmailing her."

Freya nodded. From the contents of the letter, it had been clear that Doris had agreed to leave Gareth money in her will, as long as he left her alone while she was alive.

"There's another letter," Bernard said. "To Noah."

"Oh." Freya touched her cup, then drew back.

"Doris left it with the solicitor. He won't talk to me about it, but suffice to say he now knows who his real father is."

Freya bent her head. The two booksellers were at the other end of the space, pretending to chat between themselves. There were no other customers in, thankfully.

"You're his real father, Bernard. You brought him up. That's what a father does."

"It doesn't feel like that right now." He looked at her, his eyes red-rimmed. "I've lost her, and now I'm going to lose him. What do I do?"

She shook her head. "Did the police say anything about the cake at the book reading? There's a photo…"

He nodded. "Samples were taken from Doris, before she was cremated." He closed his eyes. "At the time I thought it was a violation. I'm glad they did it now."

"What did those samples tell them?"

He gulped down his tea. "There were cupin proteins in her system. That's what causes the allergic reaction, apparently. They went to – they went to that man's house and they found a vial of liquid with enough of them in to…"

"He didn't try to hide it? Or throw it away?"

"It was in his wheelie bin."

Freya nodded. "I hope they throw the book at him."

Her phone rang: DC Williams. She showed it to Bernard. "Do you mind if I take this?"

He blinked a few times, then nodded.

Slowly, she pressed the answer button.

"Freya Garside speaking."

"Miss Garside, it's DC Williams. We spoke the other day."

"I remember you. I'm with Bernard Jacobsen right now."

"How is he?"

Freya looked at her friend's widow. "Not good."

"I can imagine. Please, give him my best wishes."

"I will. What were you calling about?"

"We'll need to take a formal statement from you. We've found forensic evidence and made an arrest, but witness statements will be helpful."

"Of course. Who have you arrested?"

"I'm not supposed to tell you that."

"Is it Gareth Smallwood?"

Beside her, Bernard flinched. Freya put a hand on his arm.

"Please, Miss Garside," the detective said. "We'd be grateful if you could come in. Unless you'd like me to come to you again."

"I'll come to you." She'd always wanted to venture inside a police station. "Does this afternoon work for you?"

"Of course. Thank you."

The detective hung up. Freya looked at her tea, untouched, and stood up.

"Come on, Bernard. Let's get you home. You look like you need a hot meal."

ABOUT RACHEL MCLEAN

Rachel McLean is an award-winning crime author who writes UK-based police procedurals. She is best known for the Dorset Crime series and the DI Zoe Finch series set in her home city of Birmingham. Book 1 in the Dorset Crime series, *The Corfe Castle Murders*, won the Kindle Storyteller Award 2021. Her new McBride and Tanner series is set around Loch Lomond in Scotland.

Printed in Great Britain
by Amazon